Eggshells

Caitriona Lally

Eggshells

A NOVEL

MELVILLE HOUSE
BROOKLYN • LONDON

Eggshells

First published in 2015 by Liberties Press
Copyright © by Caitriona Lally, 2015
First Melville House Printing: February 2017

Melville House Publishing   8 Blackstock Mews
46 John Street and Islington
Brooklyn, NY 11201   London N4 2BT

mhpbooks.com   facebook.com/mhpbooks   @melvillehouse

Library of Congress Cataloging-in-Publication Data
Names: Lally, Caitriona, author.
Title: Eggshells : a novel / Caitriona Lally.
Description: First edition. | Brooklyn : Melville House, [2017] |
"First published in 2015 by Liberties Press."
Identifiers: LCCN 2016024545 (print) | LCCN 2016031930
(ebook) | ISBN 9781612195971 (paperback) | ISBN
9781612195988 (ebook)
Classification: LCC PR6112.A485 E38 2017 (print) | LCC
PR6112.A485 (ebook) | DDC 823/.92—dc23
LC record available at https://lccn.loc.gov/2016024545

Book design by Fritz Metsch

Printed in the United States of America
3 5 7 9 10 8 6 4 2

Sometimes the fairies fancy mortals, and carry them away into their own country, leaving instead some sickly fairy child . . . Most commonly they steal children. If you "over look a child," that is look on it with envy, the fairies have it in their power. Many things can be done to find out if a child's a changeling, but there is one infallible thing—lay it on the fire . . . Then if it be a changeling it will rush up the chimney with a cry . . .

—W. B. YEATS

Eggshells

W HEN I RETURN to my great-aunt's house with her
ashes, the air feels uncertain, as if it doesn't know how
to deal with me. My great-aunt died three weeks ago, but there
is still a faint waft of her in every room—of lavender cologne
mixed with soiled underthings. I close the front door and look
around the house with fresh eyes, the eyes of a new owner. My
great-aunt kept chairs the way some people keep cats. There
are chairs in every room, in the hall, on the wide step at the
bottom of the stairs and on the landing. The four chairs on the
landing are lined up like chairs in a waiting room. I sometimes
sit on one and imagine that I'm waiting for an appointment
with the doctor, or confession with the priest. Then I nod to
the chair beside me and say, "He's in there a long time, must
have an awful lot of diseases or sins, hah." Some of the chairs
are tatty and crusty, with springs poking through the fabric.
Others are amputees. There are chairs in every colour and pattern and style and fabric—except leather, which my great-aunt
said was the hide of the Devil himself. I go into the living room
and sit in a brown armchair and examine the urn. It's shaped

like a coffin on a plinth—I chose it because death in a wooden box is more real than death in a jar. I shake it close to my ear, but I can't hear a thing, not even a cindery whisper. I prise open the lid. The scratch of wood on wood is like a cackle through the ashes, the last laugh of a woman whose mouth never moved beyond a quarter-smile. I've seen people on television scattering ashes in significant places, but the only significant places in my great-aunt's life were her chair and her bed, and if I scatter them there, I'd be sneezing Great-Aunt Maud for years to come.

I take the address book from the shelf and sift through it. There are a few *A*'s and *C*'s, a couple of *G*'s, an *H* and some *M*'s, but my great-aunt seems to have stopped making friends when she hit *N*. I take some envelopes out of the desk drawer and write the addresses on the envelopes: twenty-two in all. Twenty-six would be a symmetrical person-per-alphabet letter ratio, so I take the telephone directory from the shelf and flick through from the end of the alphabet. The pages are Bible-thin, and my fingers show up as ghostly grease-prints. I decide on Mr. Woodlock, Mrs. Xu, Mr. Yeomans and Miss Zacchaeus.

In school we sang about the tax collector who cheated people out of money. "Zacchaeus, Zacchaeus, Nobody liked Zacchaeus," I sing, or I think I sing, but I don't know what other ears can hear from my mouth. I open my laptop and type:

Hello,
*   You knew my Great-Aunt Maud. Here are some*
of her ashes.

*   Yours Sincerely,*
*   Vivian*

I print twenty-two copies of the letter, but it looks bare and mean, so I draw a pencil outline of the coffin-shaped urn in the blank space at the bottom. Now I type a different letter to the four strangers.

> *Hello,*
>> *You didn't know my Great-Aunt Maud. You probably wouldn't have liked her, unless you're very tolerant or your ears are clogged with wax.*
>>> *Yours Sincerely,*
>>> *Vivian*

I print four copies of this letter and fold all the letters into envelopes. I add a good pinch of ashes to each envelope and lick them all shut, my tongue tasting the bitter end of gluey. The pile of envelopes looks so smug and complete, I feel like I'm part of a grand business venture. Now I peer into the urn. The small heap of ashes, probably an elbow's worth, looks like a tired old sandpit after the children have gone home for tea. I close the lid, put the urn on the bookshelf between two books, and sit down. I look around the room. The idea of owning something so unownable is strange: owning a house-sized quantity of air is like owning a patch of the sky. I laugh, but the sound is mean and tinny, so I take in a lung of air and laugh again—this one is bigger, but too baggy. I'll save my laughs until I have worked on them in private. If anyone asks, I'll tell them that I'm between laughs.

My glance keeps returning to the urn; I'm expecting the lid to open and the burnt eye of my great-aunt to peek out. When they were deciding how to bury her, I said she had always wanted to be cremated. It was a lie the size of a graveyard, but I wanted to make sure she was well and truly dead. I spot a thin slip of a book on the middle shelf and pull it out, wondering how a book could be made from so few words, but it's a street map of Dublin, its edges bitten away by mice or silverfish. I unfold the map, spread it on a patch of carpet and write in my notebook the names of places that contain fairytales and magic and portals to another world, a world my parents believed I came from and tried to send me back to, a world they never found but I will:

"Scribblestown, Poppintree, Trimbleston, Dolphin's Barn, Dispensary Lane, Middle Third, Duke Street, Lemon Street, Windmill Lane, Yellow Road, Dame Street, Pig's Lane, Tucketts Lane, Copper Alley, Poddle Park, Stocking Lane, Weavers' Square, Tranquility Grove, The Turrets, Cuckoo Lane, Thundercut Alley, Curved Street, The Thatch Road, Cow Parlour, Cowbooter Lane, Limekiln Lane, Lockkeepers Walk, Prince's Street, Queen Street, Laundry Lane, Joy Street, Hope Avenue, Harmony Row, Fox's Lane, Emerald Cottages, Swan's Nest, Ferrymans Crossing, Bellmans Walk, The Belfry, Tranquility Grove, Misery Hill, Ravens' Court, Obelisk Walk, Bird Avenue, All Hallows Lane, Arbutus Place."

I close my eyes, circle my finger around the map and pick a point. When I open my eyes, I see that my finger has landed nearest to Thundercut Alley. If a thunderclap or lightning flash can transport characters in films and fairytales to other worlds, visiting Thundercut Alley might scoop me up and beam me off to where I belong, or cleave the ground in two and send me shooting down to another world. When my parents were alive, they tried to exchange me for their rightful daughter, but they must not have gone to the right places or asked the right questions. I crouch at the front door in the hallway and listen; I can't hear my neighbours, so it's safe to go out. I walk to the bus stop and stand beside a man wearing a grey jacket with a hood, holding a bottle of cola. He nods at me.

"Baltic, isn't it?"

"Yes."

I give an exaggerated shiver, because one word seems a fairly meagre response. I think about the seas of the world.

"It's really more Arctic than Baltic," I say. "Surely the Arctic is the colder sea."

"Yeah, yeah love."

He unscrews the cap from the bottle, pours some on the ground in a brown hissing puddle and balances the open bottle on a wall. Then he takes a brown paper bag containing a rectangular glass bottle from inside his jacket, pours the clear liquid from the glass bottle into the cola bottle, and puts it back inside his jacket. When he takes a sup from the cola bottle, he smiles like he has solved the whole world.

The bus arrives. I get off on O'Connell Street and walk in the direction of the river, passing the bank on the left, which has a carved stone skull of a cow over each side window. A blue-and-white football is wedged beside one window, as if the dead cows had a kick around in the dark of night. I cross the street near a building with the look of a fairytale, and a sign that reads "E Confectioners Hal." It's a shoe shop now, but maybe they sell shoe measures of jam or sweets, and the people with the biggest feet have the rottenest teeth. I cross Bachelors Walk to the boardwalk, and head west. The river and the traffic flow east on either side of me, which makes me feel the wrong way around. I stop and sit on the wooden bench and look at the other side of the river. From this angle, the buildings on the south quays look like they were dropped from a height and shoved together, with the Central Bank sticking up behind, like a Lego brick they forgot to paint. When the boardwalk ends, I cross the street and pass solicitors' offices, bargain furniture shops and dark pubs, until I reach the museum in Collins Barracks. I come here when I need to look at furniture and containers; I'd rather look at the things that hold other things than at the things themselves. I take out my notebook and walk through the museum, collecting names: "Posset Bowl, Mether, Pitcher, Tankard, Water Bottle, Sweetmeat Box, Chalice, Salt Cellar, Monstrance, Sugar Bowl, Goblet, Vase, Trinket Box, Ewer, Jug, Inkstand, Flagon, Hot Water Urn, Decanter, Snuff Box, Patch Box, Cruet Stand & Bottles, Finger Bowl, Carafe, Pickle Jar, Sweetmeat Cup, Chocolate Pot, Coffee Pot, Teapot, Kettle, Cream Ewer, Strawberry Dish, Sugar Basket, Egg Cup, Butter Dish, Tea Caddy, Salver, Cigar Box, Needlework Box, Correspondence Box, Bridal Coffer, Blanket Chest, Calling-Card Box, Travelling Box, Writing Cabinet, Log Carrier, Coal Scuttle, Double-Compartmented Meal Bin."

Every item in the glass case is labelled with its function. It knows what it's supposed to hold; its task has been assigned. It is clear and ordered and contained. I peer closely at the snuff boxes. If I tried some snuff, I'd probably sneeze ferociously, but they would be pleasant-smelling sneezes. The ornate chests and trunks are behind glass. The caption says that the bridal coffer is decorated with mother-of-pearl and gilt inlays, brass escutcheons and lacquer. I would like to be decorated with escutcheons, but I probably should find out what they are first. My gravestone could read: "Here lies Vivian Lawlor: She wasn't Quite the Thing, but She was Decorated with Escutcheons."

In the Irish furniture section, shelves of chairs face me expectantly, waiting for me to perform; I disappoint. The museum has not half so large a collection of chairs as my great-aunt has, but these ones have names and written histories: "Súgán, Carpenter's Chair, High Comb-Back Chair, Spindle-Back Chair, Comb-Back Hedge Chair."

I can't match my great-aunt's chairs exactly to any of these, she seems to have discovered some odd shapes and sizes that fit under no labels.

I walk back to the quays, turn up Queen Street, and approach Thundercut Alley from the back, not from the Smithfield side, because I want to take it by surprise. It's a curve of an alley, all draught and shade, lined by new buildings that don't speak of magic. I stand in the middle with my eyes shut and wait for thunder. I open my eyes: nothing has changed. I need to rouse a thunderstorm, so I shout "Boom!" and flash the light on my phone: "*boom*"—flash—"*boom*"—flash—"*boom*." I open my eyes but I'm still standing in the alley, un-thundered and un-spirited away. This is clearly not the right opening, so I start walking home through Stoneybatter. Some of the white letters on the street signs have been coloured blue to match the blue background: Manor Street reads "MAI_O_ STR_ _T." "Maiostrt" sounds like a combination of mustard and mayonnaise that would taste good on ham sandwiches. I pass boarded-up houses with small trees growing out of their chimneys, and a supermarket that sells used cars. At "Prussia Street," the "P" on the street sign has been blue-ed out to read "_RUSSIA

STREET." I picture a band of Smurfs combing the city in the black of night with tins of blue paint, daubing over the street letters that offend them. For the higher-up signs they step on each other's shoulders to form a pyramid, placing the most agile Smurf with the best blue head for heights at the top.

When I walk by the greengrocer, my eyes are pulled to a pile of lemons on display outside the shop. I bundle them all into my arms—I need this exact quantity to replicate this intensity of colour—and go into the shop to pay. I walk back to my great-aunt's house, which I have to start calling home. When I enter the house I catch the beginning of my smell, an earthy tang that I plan to grow into. There won't be many visitors to dilute my smell. My sister called over in January but she didn't stay long—I think I was her New Year's resolution. She bothers me to clean the house and get rid of chairs and find a job. Her world is full of children and doings and action verbs, but I'm uncomfortable with verbs; they expect too much. Since our great-aunt's death, we have nothing to talk about, and our conversation is jerky with silences the size of golf balls. I check the answering machine for messages, the numbers on the screen are "oo." They are accusatory; I wish they would act more like their round cuddly shape. I put the lemons in a glass bowl, then I take one out and pull the nubs at either end, imagining that my hands are the hands of two different people playing a peculiarly zesty kind of tug of war. I unfurl the Dublin map onto the kitchen table, and draw black blobs with a marker along the route that I walked today. Then I take out a roll of greaseproof paper, tear off a piece, place it over the map and trace my route with a pencil. I hold the paper up to the world map on the wall: today I covered the shape of an up-side-down and back-to-front Chad.

I put the greaseproof map in the top-left corner of the kitchen table and sit in the rocking chair, hurling to and fro, to and fro. The chair clacks against the wall on the "fro" movement, and this is good: I am causing effect, I am cause and effect.

2

I WANT A friend called Penelope. When I know her well enough, I'll ask her why she doesn't rhyme with *antelope*. I would also like a friend called Amber, but only if she was riddled with jaundice. I take down the phone directory from the shelf and look through it, but there's no easy way to hunt for a first name. After too many Phylises, Patricias and Paulas, I concede paper defeat and go to my laptop. I type "Penelope Dublin" into the search box and an image of a girl appears, but she's wearing only her underwear and she wants to be my date. I close the lid of the laptop. I need to turn the search farther afield—or farther astreet, seeing as I'm in a city. I will search for a Penelope-friend the old-fashioned way. I take a black marker and a sheet of paper from the desk, and write:

WANTED: Friend Called Penelope.
Must Enjoy Talking Because I Don't Have Much to Say.
Good Sense of Humour Not Required
Because My Laugh Is a Work in Progress.
Must Answer to Penelope: Pennies Need Not Apply.
Phone Vivian.

I choose the plural "Pennies" instead of "Pennys," because the "nys" looks like a misspelt boy band, and "ies" is like a lipsmack of strawberries and cream. I put the poster in a see-through plastic pouch, then I stick pieces of Sellotape around the edges. I leave the house but I forget to check for the neighbours, and Bernie sticks her head around the front door as I pass her house.

"What's that you've got there?"

"Just a poster."

"Show me."

She grabs it out of my hands.

"Mind the Sellotape," I say.

She holds it an arm's length away from herself and squints, muttering the words aloud. They sound different in her voice, different like I never wrote them, different like they came from another language. I snatch the poster from her hands.

"Why do you want a friend called Penelope?"

She stares at me, her face contorted. Even her nose frowns at me. I don't know how to respond. I never know how to respond to people who want small complete sentences with one tidy meaning, I can't explain myself to people who peer out windows and think they know the world.

"I just do," I say.

I turn onto the North Circular Road holding my head high because that sounds dignified, but I trip on a bump in the footpath, so I lower my head. The first tree I pass looks unfriendly so I walk to the next one, which has kinder branches. I mash the poster hard against the bark and stand back. It looks a bit bare without a photo of a missing pet, but I can't add a photo of Penelope until I know what she looks like. Two men walk by speaking in a foreign tongue. Their consonants come from the backs of their throats, and their words run headlong into one another like boisterous children. I try repeating their words aloud, and think how I would like to learn a language that almost no one else speaks, especially if the few who do speak it are old or almost dead. I start walking home, but home feels empty without Penelope and I'm distracted by the neon sign of my local fish bar. I'm not sure that I can call it my local anything if I've never gone into it, so I press my middle fingers alternately against the heels of my hands and whisper "safe safe safe" and walk inside. It smells bright, it smells hot, it smells good. A man with a shiny forehead looks up.

"What can I get you?"

I look at the menu on the wall behind the man, but there are too many choices and the words blur into one.

"Do you have chips?"

"Just put on a fresh batch—five minutes."

I would like to drop pronouns and verbs as readily as this man, he seems so comfortable with his language.

"I'd like two bags please. Himself is hungry."

I throw my eyes up to heaven and give a little snort, the way I've seen women do when they talk about their boyfriends and husbands. I won't have the belly space for two bags of chips, but the man will think I have a "himself," and I can reheat the leftovers tomorrow. I walk to one side and read the posters on the wall. There's an ad for discounted meals, a programme for a local festival and a notice about a fundraiser for a smiling woman called Marie. More people come in and I sneak peeps at them to see how they're dealing with this wait. One leans against the counter and two lean against the window; they look as if they were born to stand in fish bars. I try leaning against the wall, but I haven't moved my feet and the top part of my body strains at an uncomfortable angle from my hips. A couple of the men are looking at their phones, so I reach into my pocket and pull out mine. I open my inbox, it contains one old message. I read it again.

> *Vivian,*
> *Maud is getting worse, come to the hospital*
> *quickly.*
>
> *Vivian.*

This is the only unprompted message my sister has ever sent me, so I can't delete it; it's like a line from a family poem. My sister and I have the same name. She was born first and has more rights to the name; I whisper mine in apology. I would like a nickname, but nicknames must be given, not taken. I hear the soft thud of chips on paper.

"Salt and vinegar?"

"Yes, please."

He hands me the bags and I pay. I clasp them tight, one in each hand, and walk home like I have won a grand potato prize. Next morning I wake to the voices of my neighbours, Mary and Bernie, talking outside. I get out of bed and open the curtains a jot, then I stand behind the curtain and watch. Mary and Bernie live on either side of me, like a sandwich. They are white sliced pan because they know everything, and I am mild cheddar.

"Lauren's communion is on the twenty-first, I'm putting a bit by every week," Bernie says.

She has the most great-grandchildren so she is superior.

"I'm looking forward to Shannon's christening," Mary shouts over her.

"They've booked the Skylon, should be a lovely day out—"

"—then Ryan's wedding is on the twenty-eighth," Bernie says.

"I've the dress got and all."

They each talk as if the other wasn't there. They would shove their words into the ears of a cockroach if they thought it would listen.

"Any word from herself?"

Mary nods in the direction of my house.

"Last I heard she's advertising for a friend," Bernie says.

"Jaysus."

They shake their heads. At least they listen to each other when they're talking about me. I stay as still as I can, still as a wall, still as a girl in a painting. I used to win musical statues in school, but here the prize is to be not-noticed. When Mary and Bernie have gone into their houses I watch the daytime people pass: elderly people in beige, women with prams, men in tracksuits. There's a sudden smack of blue and the postman comes out of a house further down the terrace. He's moving in and out of houses like a needle stitching a hem. He stops at my gate, looks at his bundle of letters and walks to the front door. I listen for the clatter of the letter box, then I run downstairs and look at the hall floor.

There are two envelopes: a large white one and a smaller brown one. My name is handwritten in looped, slanted letters on the brown envelope: "*Vivian Lawlor.*" It could be the name of a film star or a businesswoman in a suit or an Olympic gymnast—it could be anyone but me. I open it. A man called David from the Social Welfare office will pay me a visit on Wednesday. I put it down and pick up the second envelope and sniff, it doesn't smell of people at all. I open it and stop reading after "To the House-holder." Even though I don't like the dead hope the envelope gives me, I like the fact that circulars are delivered to a street off the North Circular Road. I'd like to use this topic of conversation at the bus stop, but I can't find a way to introduce it casually. I would need to get to a second conversation before I could announce those kinds of things.

I go into the kitchen and take a red bowl from the cupboard, because I need some red in my day. Then I take the least battered-looking spoon from the drawer—I want to wear out the cutlery evenly. Next I take out the box of cornflakes, scoop up a fistful and scrunch hard. I bring my fist to the bowl and open it, watching the orange silt form a small heap. I repeat the process three times then I pour in a good dash of milk until the corn dust is sodden, and eat. After breakfast, I go up to my bedroom and climb inside the wardrobe. I tap the wood at the back, but the door to Narnia hasn't opened today so I close my eyes, feel around for a jumper and pair of jeans and climb out. I get dressed without adding water to my body or looking in a mirror. I want to grow into my smell. I want to grow out of my appearance. I want a smell-presence and a sight-absence. The mirrors were covered with sheets when my great-aunt died, and I haven't uncovered them since. I pick up my bag, go downstairs and stand in the hall, listening. I time my comings and goings around my neighbours' Mass trips, pension collections and shopping expeditions; I time my life around theirs. I can't hear anything, so I let myself out and pull the door quietly behind me. I repeat *safe safe safe* in my mind, and it seems safe safe safe until Bernie's head pops up—she'd been kneeling down, weeding the garden.

"Ah, Vivian, there you are!"

I think, *Where else would I be?* And I stand still and clenched, waiting to soak up her paragraphs. She speaks whole troughs of words, words about the priest who upped and died in the middle of his sermon and the neighbour who had a stroke and the other neighbour who's been diagnosed with cancer and the jobs that aren't there and the foreigners that are taking the jobs that are there and the social welfare benefits the foreigners are getting and the benefits the likes of me and you aren't getting. Her sentences leave no gaps for me to fill, so I take advantage of the word-torrent and start to creep further and further away until she is shouting louder words about the government cutting her pension and my feet are walking down the street away away away and I am free. "Poor Vivian," I've heard her call me, but she is the poor one, with her rage and conniptions.

I walk through Phibsborough and head down towards Constitution Hill, passing King's Inns Court. Some letters have been blue-ed out so that it reads "K_N_ _ _O_RT." "Knort," I say aloud—a lovely word, but only if the "K" is silent and reassuring. One arm of the "T" has been blue-ed out—it looks like an upside-down and back-to-front "L"—so I try saying it some place between a "T" and an "L." I turn left onto Western Way, and then right onto Dominick Street. I don't go into the church today, because I'm too unsettled from Bernie's ravings to enjoy the silence. I have no religion, but I like big silent echoey buildings with seats all facing one thing. I would like to believe in that thing they are facing. I would like to believe in something so much that I would turn myself inside out for it. I wave at the carved stone heads staring down from the church spires. Some of them look quite serious, as if they don't approve of my doings, but one of them looks like she's on my side. I call her Caroline, a nice open name with a gaping "C," like a gum-filled toothless grin. I cross Parnell Street and head onto O'Connell Street. The statues this end of the street have outstretched arms—Parnell, Larkin, Jesus at the taxi rank—all have arms agape in half a hug. I walk down the middle island of O'Connell Street, by a group of taxi drivers chatting at the rank. When the first driver on my left gets into his car and drives around the island, the other drivers go to their cars, open the drivers' doors, grip the insides of the cars and push them forward to close the gap. They might be birthing calves or playing tug of war or straining against the weight of an automated world.

I cross at the Spire onto North Earl Street, passing the statue of James Joyce with his legs crossed. He looks easy to topple and, if I had to read *Finnegans Wake*, I'd probably try to topple him. I skip the bustling café on the corner—it's all show-face and windows—and go into the long narrow café a few doors down. I order coffee and a chocolate eclair. The staff here know me and are kind; they greet me with short sentences that end in "love." I like living in a city where I am mostly unknown, and going into small places where I am known. There are metal knives and forks in the cutlery holder but only plastic teaspoons, probably to deter the masked spoon thief who steals spoons from the city's cafés to build a gigantic spoon tower. I sit at the table nearest to the toilets, at the back, and take out my notebook, which has kind blank pages that don't scream at me to stay within the lines. I make a List of Things That I Like: "Conkers, Sherbert, Gold Ingots, The Smell of Petrol, Dessert Trolleys, Graveyards, Sneezes, Terrapins, Scars that Tell Stories, The Number 49, The Smell of Pencil Parings."

Now I imagine I can smell pencil parings, so I sniff deeply. The man at a nearby table turns to look at me. He has three mobile phones laid out like playing cards on the table in front of him. One of them rings and he turns back to answer it. I continue with my list: "Donkey's Tufty Heads, Marshmallowed Silences, Butter Lumps, Elephants, Zoos in Winter, Pencils that Write Sootily, The Name Aloysius, Anything Egg-Shaped, Moths that Think They Are Butterflies, Hospital Noises, Liquorice Sweets in the Shape of Pink Toilet Rolls, The Smell of Garden Sheds, Damp Canteen Trays, Marbles with Coloured Swirls."

I've smeared some chocolate from the eclair onto the page, so I include "Chocolate Eclair," with an arrow to explain the stain. The man in front of me is still talking on his phone. I take out mine and put it on the table. There's a greyish tint to the screen: I have a message! I open the message and an unfamiliar number appears. It reads: "Hello, Vivian, I am Penelope. Can you meet me in the tearooms beside the hardware tomorrow at eleven?"

As I re-read the message, my belly feels like a pot boiling over. I have a new friend called Penelope who spells out her numbers; it just can't get much better than this. Now I decide to make a List of Words That I Like. I start off with "Propane and Butane." I want to go on a camping trip just so I can use these words. I don't know exactly what they are, but I imagine myself saying to the person in the next tent, "My propane's running low, mind if I borrow some?" Or I could show off my camping experience with an abbreviation, "I'm all out of bute, have you any to spare?" I've written down "Propane and Butane" because they go together, but now it looks like "and" is one of my favourite words, which would be like saying that flour is my favourite food. I scratch out "and" and write: "Propane, Butane, Smear, Pufferfish, Trodden, Eiderdown, Plethora (but only the way I pronounce it, pleh-THOWE-ra), Beachcomber, Mischief, Bumble Bee."

I like the words "Bumble Bee" so much that I once said them over and over until they stopped making sense as words, and became meaningless babble. I drain the last of my coffee—I love meals that are all puff and froth and little else besides—and walk up North Frederick Street, my knees crunching like overcooked biscuits. If I have biscuit knees, maybe I have chocolate blood and a blancmange brain, a Hansel and Gretel house of a body. When I get home, I trace my route. Today I walked the shape of a head with a hollow scooped out of the back, and a quiff of hair blown flat to the front. I place it on the kitchen table, next to yesterday's route.

To celebrate my success in finding a Penelope, I pour a dash of my great-aunt's wine into a mug. It tastes sweet and sneezy but it isn't cold. There's no ice in the freezer so I drop some frozen peas into mug; now it looks like a diseased pond. I sit on the blue velvet armchair, the kind of chair an off-duty policeman might sit in, and drink with my lips pursed to keep the peas out. After some large gulps, I feel garrulous and wine-smug. I don't want to waste this fruity connected feeling, so I call my sister.

"Hello?" She whispers the word, as if the phone has threatened to bite her ear.

"Vivian? Hi, it's Vivian," I giggle.

Never has this sentence sounded funnier.

"Vivian? Is everything alright?"

"Everything is better than alright," I say. "I tried to make thunder, and I advertised for a friend."

My sister sighs, a sigh so long that I snatch it up in my mouth and spit it right out again.

"What are you doing?"

"I'm cancelling out your sigh."

"Oh, Vivian."

Her voice sounds like it's coming from another century.

"How are Lucy and Oisín?"

"Oh, they're great. Lucy is . . . Oisín is . . ."

Her voice has plumped up again, and she sends a clatter of words down the line. In between sups of wine, I say words like, "wow, ooh, mm, really, oh, aren't they great, ah that's nice." The small words seem to be the most important, but I'm not sure if they count as actual words.

"I'd better go, there's something in the oven," I say, when I have run out of new words to use.

"This late?"

"I'm making midnight cake."

"Oh?"

She has managed to make a full question out of a two-letter word.

"Good night," I say and hang up.

I write "Call my sister" on a blank sheet of paper, and put a line through it with a pencil. A pen is too neat; a smudged grey line is more like my relationship with my sister. I check the oven, hoping that a cake has magically appeared from my lie, but there are only crumbs and stalactites of old cheese that could feed a family of three gerbils for a week.

3

I WAKE EARLY and it's cold, so I decide to keep my night clothes on under my day clothes like stealth pyjamas. I get up, open my wardrobe, close my eyes and feel around for enough clothes to cover all parts of my body. I go into the hoard-room and take a fresh notebook from the pile. My great-aunt allowed me to keep all my treasures in the small box room, which I call the hoard-room. No dragon guards my hoard because there isn't a nugget of gold within it. I collect: stationery, sweet wrappers (only the jewel-coloured ones), old milk bottle tops, newspaper photographs of animals, bows, ribbons, wrapping paper, stamps, bus tickets with symmetrical dates on them, maps, old Irish punt currency, jigsaws, dolls, teddy bears, toys, games, knick-knacks and everything anyone has ever given me.

I'm missing a dice from Snakes and Ladders, the candle-stick from Cluedo and an "H" and a "V" from Scrabble. If I replaced the pieces, though, the newer ones would be too clean and unused and might be mocked by the older pieces, so I do without. My hoard is made up of things from my childhood and early teens, with a big gap from my adulthood that I am trying to fill. I don't like to separate it into containers, so it piles up in two large mounds with a Vivian-wide path running through the middle. I see a small cloth foot sticking out from the left mound and pull out my sister's old doll. She has dangly limbs filled with sawdust, a happy face on one side and a sad face on the other. I put her on a chair in the landing and sit on another chair facing her. I suck my pencil and try to remember what people on buses and in cafés talk about. I write:

1. *Weather*
2. *Transport*

I could say "Traffic was a NIGHTMARE." People always speak in capital letters when they talk about traffic, but I'll be walking to the café. I'll say that I noticed from the footpath that traffic on the road was terrible. I continue:

3. *Favourite Colour*
4. *Favourite Sweet Food*
5. *Favourite Salty Food*
6. *Favourite Zoo Animal*
7. *Favourite Farm Animal*

I need to practise using my voice aloud because sometimes it squeaks and gets pulled back into my throat if it's been out of use for a while.

"Hi, Penelope," I say, holding out my hand and shaking a small sawdust hand. "Lovely day, isn't it?"

I lean forward and look out the bedroom window. The coat of a passer-by is flapping and an empty crisp packet is a salty whirligig around his feet. I turn back to the doll and start again.

"Hi, Penelope, bit windy, isn't it?"

The doll just smiles.

"No sign of spring yet."

I turn the doll around, and her crying eyes face me. This is my cue to stop the conversation. I go into the bathroom and wash my hands with a fresh bar of soap in preparation for a handshake with Penelope. I feel like saying some kind of prayer or performing a ritual dance—the occasion feels *this* big—so I stand in the living room and roar "Gaaaaaaaaah!" from the bottoms of my lungs, and slap each hand in turn across my chest. I put my notebook in my bag, leave the house, sprint past Bernie's and then turn the sprint into a calm walk. I huddle and tighten myself against the wind, and think up ways to describe it to Penelope. Is "a rape of a wind" too strong for the first sentence of a first meeting? I push the door of the café and the bell jangles. There are men in navy overalls eating fried breakfasts and elderly people sitting alone or in pairs. I walk up to the counter and order coffee and a coffee slice.

"Normally I wouldn't double up," I say to the lady in the white uniform with the white cap, who looks like a medieval wench. She stares at me.

"Double up how?"

"A coffee drink and coffee-flavoured bun might seem excessive, but today's a special day."

"Yeah, okay, love," she says. "I'll bring them down to you, have a seat."

I have wasted this topic on someone who doesn't like it, but no matter, I can reuse it on Penelope. I sit in the corner table facing the window. The lady brings my coffee and cake, and I squash the coffee slice flat so that the cream oozes out the sides. Then I scoop it up and add it to my coffee. A couple of pastry flakes poke out of the cream, like planks of wood in a miniature snow scene. I look out the window. Potted plants and huge tubs of paint and garden ornaments are laid out on the footpath in front of the hardware next door. A woman comes up to the café window, a thin woman who should be fat, with the kind of face that looks like an empty sack when it's not smiling. Her clothes are red and yellow and screaming. This must be Penelope: only people with three "E"s in their names could dress so loud. I wave. She smiles, the kind of smile that could reheat cold coffee, with yellow gappy teeth in need of a power hose. She bustles into the café, sweeping in leaves with her long skirt. A net bag swings from the crook of her elbow, and she is carrying a melon. In two giant steps, her feet eat up the floor and reach me.

"You must be Vivian, I'm Penelope."

She grabs my hand and thrusts the melon into my chest, as if playing some kind of new fruit sport.

"Hold this, I'm going to get some tea. You're alright for everything?"

I open my mouth to speak but she is gone, and I'm left holding the melon. It's yellow, the kind of yellow that seas should be made of, or swimming pools at least. I sit down and put the melon on Penelope's chair. She scuttles back in a breeze, squeezing between tables and knocking a salt cellar off a table: *smash!* Penelope doesn't look surprised; smashes must soundtrack her every move. I take a breath to warn her about the melon, but she sits straight down on the yellow hump and doesn't seem to notice.

"So, Vivian, what possessed you to go on a Penelope hunt?"

She guffaws and her breath hits me, a stench so powerful it could fell trees. It's too soon for this question. I hadn't prepared for it, so I stick to my original conversation plan.

"Bit of a nip in the air, isn't there?"

Penelope's forehead bunches and warps, and she squints at me. "I wanted to know why Penelope doesn't rhyme with antelope."

"Right."

She stares somewhere above my right eyebrows and nods. Then she shifts in her chair, raises one haunch and pulls out the melon as if she has just birthed it. She takes the little packets of sugar out of the bowl on the table and balances the melon on top of it, like a golden fairytale egg in an ordinary egg cup. She looks like she does this kind of thing every day.

"What's your favourite colour?" I ask.

"Red."

The lady brings Penelope's tea. She looks at the melon, but says nothing.

"Favourite animal?"

"Cat."

I feel a twinge of unease, as if a cat has slunk between my ankles and curled its tail around my leg.

"I don't like cats," I say.

"Oh, you're one of *those*." She narrows her eyes and spits out "those."

"Those what?"

"Cat bigots. Catists. Member of the anti-cat brigade."

I start to sweat. We haven't spoken many sentences to each other and an argument is already forming. I jerk my arm and knock over the remains of my coffee. A grease-bubbled liquid flows across the table; Penelope grabs a napkin and wipes the stream. The cat conversation has vanished.

"Do you work?" I ask.

"Not a suit-and-desk job," she says. "I paint."

"What do you paint?"

"Cats, mainly."

She grins at me, and my eyes are drawn to her tooth gaps. A piece of corn is wedged between two particularly wonky teeth.

"Did you have corn on the cob for breakfast?"

"I had it for dinner yesterday."

"It's in your teeth."

"Oh."

She digs it out and puts it on her saucer.

"Sometimes I forget to wash my teeth. I believe hygiene is overrated."

The way she drawls her "L"s rips through my ears, but I allow her this fright of a vowel, because we have found common ground.

"I agree," I say.

I look at the piece of corn—it's yellow and inscrutable.

"Do you think it's lonesome without the rest of the cob?" I ask.

"Probably. It's like separating thousand-tuplets."

"Are frogspawn called million-tuplets?"

"I don't see why not."

This is the kind of conversation that I've been dreaming of, or half-dreaming of, in that part of my brain that conjures up the nicest most suitable things, things that never enter my mouth or my waking brain, things that I feel for a few seconds somewhere on the edge of my eyeballs, on the edge of my waking.

"What do you do, Vivian?"

I haven't prepared this question and I start to feel sticky.

"I had a job once but the company put me out of my desk."

"I'm sorry. The job hunt can be a bit grim."

"I used to hunt," I say, "but I've had hundreds of silences from employers, so now I regard my job seeking as more of a hobby, rather than an action that could produce results."

Penelope laughs, the sort of laugh that makes me think of wolf cubs being reunited with their mothers: it's the tail end of despairing. I think about how to end our meeting and my heart thunks faster. I hate arriving, but I hate leaving even more. Penelope gulps down the rest of her tea and claps her hands.

"Must rush, Vivian, I've to bring one of the cats to the vet. Come over to my place next week?"

"Yes, please."

She says her address and I say mine and she says, "It's in the computer," which must mean her brain because she taps her temple with her finger. We say goodbye and her body seems to be shaping up for a hug, so I move backwards and wave. I walk home and close the front door behind me.

"It's in the computer," I say, in what I think is a light-hearted tone, and then I tap my left temple, but the two need to be done together so I try again.

"It's in the computer."

I'm so happy about how my Penelope meeting went that I consider burning down the house with me in it, so good things can't unravel. My legs are too excited to sit down and the day hasn't yet been emptied of light, so I decide to visit my thin places—places in which non-humans might live, potential gateways to the world I came from. My parents used force to try and shunt me back to this Otherworld; I will use willing.

After the Phibsborough crossroads, I walk down the steps into Broadstone Park. A sign tells users not to drink alcohol or cycle and to keep dogs on leashes; in this part of the park alone, people are disobeying all of these rules. At the end of the park, I close my eyes and pass through a black door in a wall into Blessington Basin. Doors in outdoor walls remind me of the magic door of a red-haired puppet in a children's television programme that I used to watch as a child. No magic world opens for me now. I emerge facing the basin and walk to a bench to sit for a while and watch the birds. I like pigeons; I like their greed and their laziness and their determination to avoid flying if at all possible. A sign says: DON'T FEED THE PIGEONS, which seems unfair. I don't understand how people are supposed to feed the swans and ducks without feeding the pigeons. I watch a thin pigeon eating a chunk of bread. A fat pigeon comes along and pecks him until he drops the bread. I wave my arms to shoo away the fat pigeon, but both fly off and I'm left with a half-pecked chunk of bread. When a woman in a fluorescent yellow vest passes, I stop her.

"What's your policy on bird bullying?"

She looks at me like I'm Christmas in July.

"Sorry, what's that?"

"I'm just wondering how you deal with the issue of big pigeons bullying smaller ones."

The woman checks her walkie-talkie.

"I'll have to get back to you on that, excuse me."

And before I can ask about the possibility of kitting out Thin Pigeon with a helmet and wing pads, she quickly walks away. The gate leading onto Blessington Street isn't as good as a door in a wall, but I make a wish as I pass through, just in case. I walk straight down North Frederick Street and stop by the Gate Theatre, in front of a small grey metal box that could be a small hut (or hutlet) for elves. It's rectangular, with a slanted metal roof and two metal doors, the perfect size for a shin-high elf couple. I picture rocking chairs on either side of a stove, and a spiral staircase leading to a four-poster bed covered with a patchwork quilt. I stop and crouch down on my hunkers, pretending to fix my shoe and peek in, but I don't look too closely in case I see wires and circuit boards and no elves. My elves wear tracksuits and play Scrabble when they're tired, or Twister when they're full of energy. I whisper goodbye, straighten up and head south to D'Olier Street. I cross at the lights, follow the curve of the college around to College Green and stop outside an ivy-covered house at the edge of the college, facing the hotel that used to be a bank. I imagine a kind of everyday Santa Claus and his wife living in this house, plotting ways to rid the world of its problems. The ground floor is a control room, with lots of maps and gadgets and wires and devices all connected to enormous screens. Everyday Santa and Everyday Mrs. Claus wear headsets and hold remote controls and joysticks to give the superheroes the coordinates of their missions: "Delta Spiderman, bike thief on the quays, Roger that" or "Oscar Superman, girl weeping in front of Central Bank, bring tissues, stat."

I leave before I catch any detail that would sully my imaginings, and walk up Grafton Street, turning right onto South King Street and into Zara. I take the escalator up to the first floor and walk to the left, to the opposite wall. I pick up a shirt from the rail and drop it like a hot mistake. Then I kneel down to pick it up and catch sight of the small door in the wall. I saw a shop assistant step out of that door some years ago, and I've kept it on my list of thin places ever since. Inside that door I picture a kind of candy-laden paradise, a combination of the Hansel and Gretel house made of sweets, the mountain the Pied Piper led the children into and the chocolate factory that Charlie visits. I put the shirt back on the rail and leave before I can be disenchanted by a glimpse of a non-chocolate reality.

I head west along St. Stephen's Green and down Kildare Street, passing Leinster House and a small band of protesters outside carrying posters of foetuses or foxes. A man wearing a cycle helmet walks up and down holding a small black-and-white sign on a stick, a paper lollipop that says "Close Sellafield."

I go into the library, leave my bag and coat in the locker, and climb the stairs to the reading room with my pencil and notebook. At the bottom of every recessed bookshelf lining the room is a small wooden door coated in mesh. I pretend to look at a Welsh dictionary and bend down and peek through the mesh. Behind these doors I picture a maze of tunnels that house living examples of creatures believed to be extinct. There's a dodo, of course, and an auk and an Irish elk, along with others I have written in my notebook: "Pygmy Mammoth, Stilt-legged Llama, Shrub-Ox, Pocket Gophers, Dwarf Elephant, Cave Bear, Spectacled Cormorant, Heath Hen, Golden Toad, Cebu Warty Pig, Caspian Tiger, Gastric Brooding Frog, Sharp-Snouted Day Frog, Pig-Footed Bandicoot, Toolache Wallaby, Laughing Owl, Narrow-Bodied Skink, Big-Eared Hopping Mouse, Indefatigable Galapagos Mouse, Chadwick Beach

Cotton Mouse, Christmas Island Pipistrelle, Scimitar-Toothed Cat, Giant Aye-Aye, Quagga."

They have duped the human race into believing they're extinct, so that they can live un-pestered by zoos and breeding programmes, animal versions of death-faking tricksters.

I sit down and open my notebook on a fresh page. I read somewhere that the words "month," "silver" and "purple" cannot be rhymed with. I stare hard at my silver pencil and try to come up with rhymes, but I can only invent words:

Pilver: To quietly steal from one's wealthy hostess.

Bilver: A dry retch at the end of a vomiting bout.

I try "month." The problem with "month" is that I pronounce it "munth," so my definitions are:

Bunth: A collective noun for a group of flags.

Thunth: The noise a jaw makes on contact with the bottom step of the stairs.

They don't quite reach the essence of the thing, so I have a go at "purple":

Gurple: The sound of a baby post-feed when it's full of wind and joy.

Vurple: The chief of a fox clan with jaunty taste in clothes.

I could keep inventing words, but that is not my place. I stare at the backs of the other library users. They seem to know what they're doing and are getting on with doing it, instead of making up words that will never be used. I stare up at the domed ceiling. The coloured ceiling panels run from white through peppermint to old-library green, like a swatch of paint-colour charts.

When my stomach rumbles, I gather my belongings and head downstairs to the café. I sit at the table nearest to the cash register, from where I can see the inner workings of the café. I see the waitresses spill milk when they pour it into the coffee machine, and I see their faces get red and tense when lines of lunchers form, demanding all manner of breads I have never heard of. Where do they hear about such breads, and why does it matter so much? Bread is beige or white fluff that will be swallowed in as much time as it takes them to complain. I like seeing the mismatched delph scattered about the perfectly matched Tupperware tubs of dry foodstuffs: a tinge of disorder in an ordered system. I don't want to seem nosy so I act as if I'm staring thoughtfully into the middle distance, then I scribble some words in my notebook. But the words I write are just "mischief mischief mischief," over and over again; "mischief" should always be spelt with a lower case "m"—it seems more mischievous than its sensible big sister, upper case "M." And "mumps" should never be capitalised, but "Measles," its spottier cousin, should. "Rubella" works either way. We should be allowed to choose when to use lower and upper case letters; having to use a capital letter at the start of a sentence is like saying the firstborn son gets all the money, no matter how vile he is. Some words should be spelt entirely in capital letters: TORRENTIAL, BELLOWS, RIPPED, FLED, GLEEFUL. And if letters have capitals, why don't numbers? I could invent capital numbers, but schoolchildren would hate me for increasing their learning-load and they would throw eggs at my face. My brain has got carried away with crossover branches and twigs, all grabbing and twisting and outgrowing each other, and my hand can't keep up with writing these knotted thoughts, so I finish my food and leave the café. I'd like to be the type of person that calls a cheery farewell to the café staff, but I settle instead for a skulk.

I make for the Liffey. As I wait to cross O'Connell Bridge, I see a sign at the bottom of a tall red-brick building with a curly roof on O'Connell Street saying: "Witches' Attic." I look up and see a man wearing jeans and a grey T-shirt in the attic window, near the weather vane. I wish he was wearing a cape and a pointy hat, but maybe the modern warlock needs to go under-cover. When I enter my house, the waft of myself hits me. I sniff around me, turning my nose to different pockets of air. The smell from upstairs is strongest, because I haven't changed my sheets for a long time. I like them to smell properly of me, and I like to find papery shards of foot skin and debris from my body in the bed-nest. I heard on the radio that the rise in asthma is caused by an increase in the use of cleaning products, and I don't want to get asthma. If I have to get a disease, I want one that contains multiple syllables and a range of vowels. I tuck my nose into my jumper and sniff. A pleasant sort of lived-in smell comes from my body, of meat and sweat and damp newspaper. I sit at the kitchen table and map my route and trace it onto greaseproof paper. Today I walked a slice of batch loaf with an aerial poking out.

4

I LOOK OUT the kitchen window at the giant pear tree in the back garden. I don't like pears, so when the fruit falls in autumn it rots, and the garden is full of wasps and squelches. Now that the tree is bare, it's as if pears don't exist and autumn never happens. I open the back door and go outside to look at the treetop. I once read a children's book about the magical lands at the top of a tree in an enchanted wood. I swing one leg onto a low branch and hoist my other leg up. I climb up a few branches, but there are no signs of elves or fairies or the little man wearing saucepans who appeared in that book. In Bernie's garden I can see gnomes and ceramic swans, and a small concrete boy who used to piss into a concrete basin. Mary's back door suddenly opens. I try to hide, but the branches are wintry-bare.

"Jaysus, Vivian, what are you doing up there? Are you stuck?"

"No, I'm fine, thanks. Lovely day, isn't it?"

These are the wrong weather words, no sooner are they out of my mouth than I feel the damp chill of the air.

"Ah, Vivian, would you look at yourself, a grown woman up a tree on a day like today."

Even if it wasn't a day like today—if it was a day like yesterday or tomorrow—I don't think she would have liked to see me up a tree.

"I'm looking for the lands at the top," I say.

"The what?" She says "what" like it hurts her teeth.

"In the book *The Magic Faraway Tree*, the Land of Spells and the Land of Dreams and the Land of Topsy-Turvy appeared on the treetop. I'm trying to find those lands, you see."

Mary doesn't see, and she doesn't really hear either. From this angle she looks neckless, like an up-tilted face mashed onto a body. Her mouth hangs open, and while she's stuck in the gap between questions I climb back down and escape into the house. I look around the living room to decide which chair I will sit in today. The one with the plastic cover is quite scratchy so I say "No" to that one. I don't want to hurt its feelings so I stroke its plastic back six times. I have to comfort the chairs in strokes of three, but three itself is uneven and unsatisfactory so I double it and stroke in sixes. Some of the chairs give off a homely smell, of boiled cabbage and unwashed great-aunt. I choose the dark green armchair. It's ripped and the stuffing peeks through and there's a great-aunt-sized dent in it, but it's comfortable. Today I will search for jobs, but first I need to conjure up some company in the room. I turn on the television with the sound down. If I squint and stare at the laptop, the people on the television look like small live people on the other side of the room, a silent gathering which I am sitting apart from. The soap operas are best because the characters spend lots of time in kitchens and on living room sofas, but they argue a lot and even though the sound is down, it causes tension in my living room.

I open the laptop. If I'm in a serious mood, I type "Assistant" into the search box of the job website. I have no particular skills or experience, so I can't be in charge of anything or anybody, but maybe I can assist with something. Today, however, I am looking for dream jobs. I type "Bubble-blower" into the search box. The computer doesn't even pretend to search, which is a bit rude. A blank screen appears almost instantly saying:

"The search for 'Bubble-blower' in Dublin did not match any jobs."

The bold type is mocking me, and the language is harsh. It advises me to "Sign up for email updates on the latest Bubble-blower jobs in Dublin." I try "Walker" next because I'm good at walking, and two jobs appear: a vacancy for a "Dog Walker" in Lucan (I have enough bother controlling my own limbs when I walk, never mind an additional four) and a "Commercial Analyst and Management Accountant" for Walkers Crisps. I'd best not apply for jobs whose titles I can't understand. Next, I type "Changeling" into the search box. A vacancy for "Graphic Design Print Manager" comes up. It's suitable for someone who wants "Changeling Roles," so I scour the print for a description of me. The applicant must have a: "Personality for Sales and Upselling to Clients. Great Personality with Energy. Excellent Communication and Interpersonal Skills."

None of those things sounds like me. It must be a different kind of changeling they are looking for. I close the lid of the laptop; I never switch it off because that seems so final, like writing a will.

It's between mealtimes, so I will cook a fry. Somebody has decided that breakfast + lunch = brunch, but I think lunkfast suits this meat-heavy meal better. I melt butter in the pan and cook sausages, rashers and black pudding. The sausages hiss and I'm glad. I like food that sounds like itself. I don't know when the black pudding is starting to burn because black can't get any blacker. When the skin of the pudding has hardened, I heap the fry between two slices of white bread. The bread turns soggy with grease—a damp towel of a sandwich—but sog is good in food. I think of other black foods: *burnt anything, liquorice, black pepper, half a bullseye boiled sweet.* Then I go through other coloured foods in my head until I'm struck with a plan: I will eat only blue foods for the rest of the day. I search the kitchen cupboards but they are bare of blue, so I put on my coat. It's a heavy coat, packed with wool, and it feels like I'm putting on summer. I put my keys and some money in my bag, but it still seems empty, and I'm not quite sure what else to put in. I've seen women carry such big bags—what big lives they must have!—so I take two books from the shelf and put them in my bag. Now I'm someone who could pile six planets on her shoulders and carry them off.

I bang the front door loudly when I leave the house, to rouse the neighbours. I want to tell them about my plan, but no heads pop up from flower beds or peer out from behind doors. I walk to the supermarket, take a basket and move slowly up and down each aisle. I feel like I've won a competition where the prize is blue food. I find: blueberries, which are more of a nunnish navy; blue cheese, which smells of socks and tastes of wet dust; blue freeze-pops in mouth-ripping plastic tubes; and a blue sports drink the colour of an ambulance siren. I also pick up several multipacks of Smarties and M&Ms, so that I can sift out only the blues. At the till, a heap of giddy rises up my throat. The shop assistant starts scanning my food.

"Do you notice anything about my items?" I ask.

40

She looks like she doesn't want to play my game, so I make it easy for her.

"They're all blue!"

"Oh yeah, why?"

"I'm having a blue party!"

The snarl on her face melts a little.

"Is it his favourite colour?" she asks.

"Whose favourite colour?"

She looks confused.

"Your little boy, are these not for his birthday party?"

I think for a moment.

"Yes, they are. And I'm making a Smurf cake!"

The woman behind me in the queue pokes her head into the conversation.

"Ah, that's lovely, what age is he?"

"They're six, I have boy twins."

The words glide out of my mouth like a silk thread.

"You must have your hands full with them," the woman behind me says, but the shop assistant only stares.

"How come you never have them in here with you?"

"Oh . . ."

I think for a minute.

"They're in wheelchairs."

"Ah, God, that's terrible, terrible!"

"Who minds them?" asks the shop assistant. Her face is squeezed into strange shapes.

"What?"

"When you come in here to do your shopping, who minds them?"

"Oh, they're fine on their own."

"You leave them alone?"

Her voice sounds like a cup shattered on a tile.

I look from one angry face to the other.

"They can't get out of the wheelchairs, they're fine."

They look at each other the way that girls in school used to look at each other: an eye-lock that doesn't include me. Then they look at me with a purity of hate that stiffens me. I pack my blue items into my bag—I wish I'd remembered to bring a blue plastic bag—and pay. The woman behind me is muttering to the woman behind her, and I catch the words ". . . social services . . . shouldn't be let have kids . . . something wrong with her . . ." I take my change and hurry off with great big gulps of marbles in my throat. When I reach the house I rush in, close the door and bolt it. If social services come, they might be angrier that I'm not neglecting children I don't have than if I was neglecting children I did have. I feel sadder than I've ever felt before, sad like the end of the world has come and gone without me.

I crawl under the kitchen table with my bag, and crouch among the chair legs. This is the perfect picnic spot with no chance of rain, and it isn't too uncomfortable if I lean forward. I lay out my blue feast on the black tiles, empty out the M&Ms and Smarties, pick out the blue ones and put the rest away. I start off with the sweet food then I eat some blue cheese—a horror of a food, so I stuff spongy blueberry muffin into my mouth to cancel out the stinking taste. This feels like cheating, because the muffin is mostly beige with only an inky blue stain. It seems right that on the day of my blue feast I'm feeling blue myself. My belly feels bruised inside, as if all the blue foods were having a fist fight among themselves. The underside of the table reminds me of the inside of a coffin lid, so I decide to practise being buried alive. I crawl out from under the table, take the thickest cushions from the sofa and lay them out under the table. I pile them on top of one another until they nearly reach the top, then I squeeze between the cushions and the table and lie down, with my nose tip touching the wood. I lie staring at the table-ceiling, in the muffled peace of the cushions. I don't know why people talk of the terror of being buried alive—surely the terror is in being alive.

When my mind has settled, I get out and look up world news on the Internet. The news is: "Possibility of war," "Terror Threats," "Elections," "Bomb Blasts," "Nuclear Threats," "Global Downturn," "Anti-Government Protests," "School Shooting," "Potential Chemical Weapons Attacks," "Alleged Murder," "Suspected Abuse." My neighbours like to speak of these potentials and possiblys as definitelys and certainlys. Next I look up national news. A politician is calling on another politician to do something. I would like to call on someone to do something, but I don't know if anyone would listen. A dossier has been compiled about an organisation. I wonder if there's a dossier about me somewhere. I close the laptop. The news stories are bouncing off each other in my head and words are producing more words and I picture reams of paper hurtling out of printers, filled with unspaced, unparagraphed, unchaptered words. I switch on the radio and turn the dial to the static between stations, but this isn't enough to fetch me out of a jangle: I must walk. I put on my coat and pick up my bag. I need some gold in my life because blue has not served me well; I will buy a goldfish. I put on my great-aunt's double-glazed spectacles as a disguise, in case I bump into anyone from the supermarket, and leave the house. I don't bump into anyone from the supermarket, but I do bump into the garden gate and the kerb, my eyes watery and blind behind the thick glass. I walk through Phibsborough with my arms outstretched in front of me, feeling for obstacles, then I take off the glasses when I turn onto Western Way. This street makes me think of the lifestyle choices of country singers. I head down Dominick Street and swing left onto Parnell Street. A burly man stands at the door of the taxi company smoking.

"Taxi, love?"

"No, goldfish."

I go into the pet shop and head for the fish tanks. The man behind the counter comes over with a net.

"Looking for a goldfish?"

"Yes," I say.

"Right so."

He lifts the lid off the tank and dips in the net.

"Wait!" I say.

"For what?"

"I haven't decided which one I want yet. I need to see their personalities."

The man's top lip curls up.

"You want one with a good sense of humour?"

I laugh to show that I have a good sense of humour, even though I don't think his joke is very funny. I lean over the tank. The fish are all swimming in the same direction, except for a slightly slower fish drifting at the bottom. He's more yellow than orange, and some of his scales are missing. I turn to the man.

"I'll take the yellow one, please."

"Are you sure?"

"Yes."

The man scoops out my Lemonfish and puts him in a plastic bag of water, then ties the top of the bag in a knot. I buy
some goldfish food, pay the man and put the plastic bag in my
handbag. Lemonfish will be happier in the dark of my bag
than in a moving house with a see-through floor and a knotted
roof. I walk back home, putting my great-aunt's glasses loosely
on my nose so that I can see out from over them. Then I let
myself into the house, add water to the bowl containing the
lemons I bought yesterday and pour in Lemonfish. At first he
keeps crashing into lemons, but soon he swims around cau-
tiously and noses the fruit. Maybe he thinks they're obese, bit-
ter-smelling new friends. I sit at the table and trace the route I
just walked onto greaseproof paper: it's shaped like a fishing
rod that has caught another fishing rod.

I DECIDE TO sleep on chairs in the living room tonight. They
will be kinder to me than the bed, which creaks and hisses when
I can't sleep. Tea is a comfort but it keeps me awake, so I boil
the kettle and make tea in my hot water bottle. The smell of tea
and rubber is a good solid combination, like grandmothers and
classrooms. I go upstairs and swallow a blue pill from the bath-

room cabinet, one for coughs and colds that makes me drowsy. This will be the last of the day's blue party. I go downstairs and arrange two soft chairs in front of the red chair in the living room. This way, I get to use three chairs and hurt fewer chairs' feelings. I take up the spongy cushion from the red chair, and put the hot tea bottle on the chair top. Then I lie face down on the chair, pull the cushion over my head and press it down over my ears. The inside of the chair is musty and my nose is tickled by dust-clumps and crumbs, but it smells of something close to home. I count "One-two-three-four-five-six, one-two-three-four-five-six" until I fall asleep, a sleep so delicious that it has the quality of toasted peaches.

5

I WAKE TO the sound of me grinding my teeth. I should probably sleep with cotton wool or marshmallow in my mouth to soften the attack. David from the Social Welfare office is visiting today but I don't want to think about that just yet, so I lie in bed snatching at my dream-thoughts before they vanish through my eyelids: I am in a tunnel that's split in two, each side rising up to the roof in turn, crushing anything on it. I have to keep jumping from the rising part to the falling part until that too starts to rise. No wonder I feel tired, I saved my own life in my sleep. My throat feels scratched where the scream clogged, I only wake from a nightmare if the scream scrapes through. I wish it were a song and not a scream. Or a laugh. My sister laughs in her sleep. When I used to share her room I would wake in the night to hear her laughing, eyes shut tight, at something that didn't seem funny in the morning.

I get up and root through the wardrobe for a pair of khaki combats that will show David I am a serious job hunter. Then I take a dark-green jumper from the shelf. I bring my clothes into the bathroom, put the plug in the bath and run the taps. I duck my head under my pyjama top and breathe in my smell for the last time—even when I leave it another while to wash, the smell will not be this exact combination of sweat and food emissions. I pick up a bottle of pink bubble bath that my great-aunt left behind. The bottle is heart-shaped and ugly, like two inward-facing question marks with no interest in the world. I tip the bottle into the bath. It pours like a thick gluey syrup, turning the bathwater pink and adding white bubbles on top: beer for little girls. Then I hold the bottle over my head and thrust it onto the floor with all my might. The bottle has been transformed into dozens of shards and pieces. I examine them for a while, then step into the bath, squat on my hunkers and lower myself into the water. I stretch out my legs and raise them out of the water, but they haven't turned into a tail and my skin hasn't turned into scales and I haven't turned into a mermaid. I lie back, the bubbles *scrinch scrinching*, and try to form an expression of extreme calm on my face like the women in television ads, but I'm so hot my heart is rattling in my chest and my toes feel like they belong to somebody else and I can't relax when I smell like strawberry bubblegum and feel like dirty dishes. I'm not sure how long I have to stay in the bath to be clean, so I swirl the water around and sluice it over my face. Then I lie back with my head facing the ceiling to wash my hair. The water fills my ears and muffles my world; this must be what Lemonfish's world sounds like. I pull the plug and sit in the bath while it drains. It feels like I should be dying, like my internal organs are being slowly sucked out of my body and down the plughole. I get out, crouch under a towel and tug my clothes on. Then I blast my head with the hairdryer, breathing in the smell of hot burning dust. I eat breakfast and bring Lemonfish's bowl to the sink. I slowly pour some water out, trying not to lose fish or lemons. Then I turn on the tap and add some fresh water. I've just changed Lemonfish's liquid nappy. I brush my teeth at the kitchen sink and imagine a tooth-brush so small that it could brush each tooth individually. If only there was an elf section in the supermarket.

David has the name of a king, so I will clean the house and make it fit for a king-guest. I bring the hoover upstairs and open the door to the hoard-room. A huge toy gun, the kind that stretches across the body and makes a *ratatatatatatat* noise when you pull the trigger, catches my eye from the childhood-toys pile. It could be useful for a job-hunter so I bring it downstairs. I hoover the landing, then I hoover the stairs, which is like trying to slide down a fireman's pole in stops and starts, then I hoover the hall and, finally, I bash the hoover in between the chair legs in the living room. I wish I'd made a list of chores so I could put a thick pencil mark through "Hoover House." Or, to get more pencil strikes, I might divide the chores into:

1. *Hoover Landing*
2. *Hoover Stairs*
3. *Hoover Hall*
4. *Hoover Living Room*

When the doorbell rings, I'm standing in the hall sniffing my strawberry hands, which smell unfamiliar and hateful. I open the door.

"Hello, David," I say.

His face doesn't match his name, David is a gentle name, with soft indecisive "D"s and an open "V," but this David is pursed and definite.

"Good morning, Vivian," he says, and shakes my hand—a crisp formality of a handshake.

"Come on through," I say, because that's what people in soap operas on television say to visitors, but the words come out in a Manchester accent. He sits at the kitchen table, and Lemonfish swims bowl-side to look out.

"You're his first visitor, so you must excuse him if he's shy," I say.

David half-laughs, a cautious kind of sound without much bark in it.

"Would you like some tea?"

"Please, a drop of milk, two sugars."

He speaks with an admirable abruptness, but his sentences don't provide enough information.

"A big drop or a small drop—like a thundershower or a drizzle?"

His face puckers and narrows, as if something under the skin is pulling it back.

"A big drop."

"Right. Heaped or level?"

"Sorry?"

"Your sugars. Heaped or level teaspoons?"

"Either."

David waves his hand as if swatting away my question, pulls out a grey folder from his briefcase, lays it on the table and opens it. I fill the kettle and whisper, "Take your time, boil slowly." I should have added ice to the kettle to slow it down. David clears his throat.

"So you've been out of work since when?"

I don't like being asked questions that are already answered in grey folders.

"Since somewhere between Grand Stretch in the Evening and We Won't Feel it Now Till Christmas," I say.

"I'm sorry?"

David is a lot of sorry it seems.

"September."

"Okay."

He writes something on a page. David seems like the kind of man who likes neat black words to fit into neat white boxes. I look at his black biro and try to imagine all the other unworkers it has written about. I wonder if he ever writes things like, "Her house smells of boiled mutton" or "His ears stick out strangely." The roar from the kettle becomes a gurgle and then a click. I pull the lid off the teapot and—*oh no!*—there is mouldy fur inside. I scoop it out and secretly sniff it—it smells like soil multiplied. When the tea has brewed, I bring the mugs to the table.

"What kind of jobs have you been applying for, Vivian?"

"I'll show you."

I go into the living room to get my list. The toy gun is sitting on the red chair like a gift for a king—now is a good time for my trick. I run back into the kitchen pointing the gun at David and holding down the trigger: *ratatatatatatatatatat!* David jumps at the noise; he turns to face me and squeals when he sees the gun pointed at him. Then he scrapes back his chair and dives under the table, his papers scattering around him. I stop to admire the arrangement of white paper on black tiles, it looks like the kitchen has been paper-bombed. David's face peeks out from under the table—his eyes bulge, he looks like fear has taken him over.

"It's nice under there, isn't it?" I say. "That's where I had my blue feast."

"Jesus Christ, woman, what the fuck are you playing at?"

I didn't think officials were allowed to curse.

"I'm playing at Job-hunters, that's why I'm dressed in khaki. I thought you'd join in the game."

He gets up from the floor with a creak, his black trouser-knees covered in grey dust and cornflake silt. He sits in the chair, but he doesn't sit up quite so straight. Then he leans his elbows on the table and puts his head in his hands. When he takes a sup of tea, the mug shakes and spills. I put the gun on the floor and gather up his papers. The top page reads, in squat handwriting:

"Client appears to have inappropriate—"

I put the pages on the table and look away. David is breathing in short gasps that don't seem to take in much air. I sit opposite him and stare, in silence, until he gives his head a small toss, like a pony or a snooty child, and straightens his papers.

"Right, where were we?" he asks.

"Well, you were on the chair, until I started shooting, so you moved to the floor—"

He waves his hand in the air like a conductor, so I shriek "Lalalalalalala" as loud as I can. He cowers under his papers and hisses,

"Christ, what are you at now?"

"You were conducting, it'd be rude not to make some kind of music in return."

I like singing—the breath and effort of it—even though I can't tell from my own ears if I'm in tune. I was told to whisper in my school choir, but maybe I've grown in tune since then. I start singing "Doe a Deer," but I sing quietly so that I don't scare David. He looks at me like I have bled the last drop of milk from the carton and left none for him, so I drop my tune.

"What kinds of jobs have you been applying for?"

I push my list across the table. He reads aloud:

"Dog walker, bubble-blower, changeling, assistant."

He turns the page over but that's all there is. He looks at the list again and seems to wilt.

"Assistant what?"

He has barely enough up-breath to form a question mark.

"Assistant anything, I won't know until I see the job description."

"I see."

His tongue doesn't quite reach the roof of his mouth, so it sounds more like "I hee." He picks up the list with his fingertips as if it's a paper disease, takes a sip of tea and coughs.

"Excuse me."

"That's okay, I put half a cough and a quarter of a hiccup in the teapot."

David closes his eyes and, I think if he had glue, he would have stuck his lids shut. When he opens them again, his eyes seem to have sunk further back into their sockets, as if he's showcasing his corpse look.

"Have you ever pretended to be dead?" I ask.

His face doesn't move and his voice, when it comes, is sealed good and tight.

"Have you considered other areas—administration jobs, for instance?"

I prefer an example to an instance, but David won't understand this.

"I don't like telephones, and there are lots of them in offices."

His face twists into a tormented expression, the kind of expression I've seen on the faces of war victims on news reports.

"*Indeed*" is all he says, but he says it like it's the last word before the end of the world. He rustles through his papers as if he's looking for an official response, then he straightens up and makes a small speech about benefits and credits and signing on and job seeking and computer courses and upskilling and qualifications in pharmaceuticals or marketing or industries where they are hiring. I nod my head and say "hmm yes" and "oh I hadn't thought of that," but I know this is all a cod. Employers won't hire me to work in their offices when they can hire a shiny woman who speaks in exclamation marks.

"It's important to keep an open mind," he says.

"I am open-minded," I say. "Sometimes I wear my slippers on the opposite feet to change my worldview, even though it makes me hobble."

David takes a deep breath. He looks like a faded mural in a children's ward.

"Right, I think we're all done here," he says on a new gust of breath, and he bundles his papers and stuffs them into his briefcase. He says half a goodbye and leaves in a great hurry, such a great hurry that it makes me think there's a fire, so I follow him outside and look up at the house. There are no flames, but the house seems more menacing now that David's been in it. The smell will be all wrong: the smell of fake strawberry and David and fresh paper. I regret my bath—David didn't even ask to smell me. I tuck my nose into my jumper and sniff. I still smell strawberry-sweet, but there is also the start of a sweaty tang. I go back inside and walk through the house, closing every blind and every curtain and every door. I crouch in the bathroom, pick up a piece of the smashed bottle and stare into it. I will check every shard, surely in one of them there'll be a glimpse of where I'm supposed to be.

6

I WAKE ON a damp pillow; my dreams must have leaked. I put my head under the blankets and sniff: it smells aged. I creep out of bed, pull on some clothes from the floor and go downstairs to look at Lemonfish's bowl. The water is a little cloudy and smells of lemons. I take the lemons out, before he gets too attached to them and knows enough to miss them. He looks at my fingers and the fruit and doesn't seem to care, but I'm not sure how I'd know if a goldfish cared. I put a pinch of goldfish food in the bowl. I eat a pinch myself—it looks like Brunch ice cream, but it tastes bland and pointless. I eat my mashed cornflakes breakfast and wipe the lemons dry. I'll bring them to their home in Lemon Street.

I leave the house at a run, calling "Bye" to Lemonfish. The lemons take up most of my bag space. I look busy with life plans. I walk to the bus stop and wait. Two old ladies with tartan shopping trolleys are chatting. A woman is making big exaggerated faces at her child. I wish the bus would come, because the wind is skinning. It's the kind of vicious easterly wind that makes my eyes water and my nose drip, the kind of cold that makes me hate. I bounce at the bus stop to stay not warm but as not-cold as possible. A man jogs by in shorts and a T-shirt; just watching him makes my eyes cold. When the bus comes we rush the door, and the old ladies use their trolleys as moving barricades to get on first. I sit near the back, beside a man who is on the phone.

"NO!" he shouts. "I had the score and I was outside the off-license an' it blew out of me hand an' I went down to pick it up, but some prick got there ahead of me, an' when I said that's *my* money he said he had a knife and if I didn't fuck off he'd bleedin' knife me, I'm *tellin'* yeh that's what happened."

He talks like he's being chased by words, swallowed up by sentences. Other people in the bus are giving little secret glances over their shoulders at him.

"For fuck's sake, yeh can go and shite," he shouts, and hangs up. I root around in my bag to look busy in case he wants to tell me his problems but his phone rings again, a blast of shouty music that makes me jump.

"Hello!" he shouts as if there is a bad connection.

There's shouting on the other end, and he shouts back: what a feast of shouting.

"I *told* ya, I was walkin' to the off-license and some prick held a knife to me throat and said he'd fuckin' kill me if I didn't give him a score, that's what happened, I swear on me daughter's life."

The rest of the passengers are silently listening, and I feel proud to have picked the best seat on the bus; some of this man's fame has trickled onto me.

"Listen, I have to go, me battery's dyin', I'll give yeh a buzz later, alright?"

From the shouting on the other end of the line it isn't alright, but he hangs up.

"Fuckin' prick?" he says, and I wonder if I'm supposed to answer. He turns to me.

"Here, you wouldn't have the lend of a twenty, would yeh? I got mugged, right, by this fucker with a gun, and I owe me friend a score, an' if he doesn't get it there'll be killings."

"I'll see what I have," I say, and I open my bag and pull out two damp lemons.

"You can have these."

I hold out the lemons. He looks at my hand and then at my face, his mouth hanging open.

"What the fuck am I supposed to do with lemons?"

He says "lemons" like it has two "L"s.

"They're two for a euro, so if you give him two lemons, you only owe him €19."

"Are you fuckin' mental or wha'?"

He puts two syllables into "you"—maybe it's an honour to get double-syllabled—but he isn't looking at me in a pleasant way and other passengers have turned around to watch.

"I don't know," I say. "All I know is that I have twelve lemons and no money to give you."

He shakes his head and mutters "fuck's sake," but it's a despairing "fuck's sake," not an angry one. He sits silently beside me, shaking his head and giving off alcohol and anger fumes until he gets out at O'Connell Street. As I'm waiting to get off at Nassau Street, the driver looks at me in the mirror.

"He wasn't bothering you, love, was he?"

"No, he just didn't think much of my lemons."

"Ah, I see."

I get off the bus and cross the street. I walk up Dawson Street and turn into the little arch with shops that sell Celtic jewellery and paintings of horses and chocolates without wrappers. It's windy in here; there's a picnic bench in the middle of the plaza, but only a polar bear would enjoy a picnic there today. I walk through to Lemon Street, check that there's no one behind me, and drop a piece of fruit every couple of steps. When my bag is empty, I look back. The street looks like it has been lemon-bombed. I come out onto Grafton Street, opposite the red-and-white awning of Bewley's Café. I go inside and sit near the fireplace. It's cosy here, with red velvet seats and an orange fire and blue stained glass windows. I order black coffee. I prefer milky coffee, but I've heard things on the radio about lactose intolerance and I sometimes think that if I stopped drinking milk my life would be a different thing. When I leave the café I take Grafton Street at a saunter, and head east along Stephen's Green. I make for the Natural History Museum. Students walk by in groups, laughing and in no hurry. It must be a weekday— weekdays churn out people in suits and students with large bags. Weekends have wardrobes full of suits on hangers and school uniforms on floors and children moving about in large doses. I prefer weekdays to weekends; there are fewer people around and expectations are lower.

I walk into the museum. It smells of something old and musty, furniture polish or mothballs. There are glass cases of birds and fish and animals, most of them some shade of beige or brown, with typewritten descriptions on faded, tea-coloured paper. I'm looking for new names of things, a list of new words in a particular order that could form a pattern and give me a clue as to how to find my way back. I take out my notebook and write out the names of interesting-sounding birds: "Chats, Warblers, Wrynecks, Choughs, Buntings, Pipits."

My list is short: too many names are ordinary and not worth writing down. In the fish section, an enormous goldfish from Mrs. McComas in County Dublin looks healthier than Lemonfish, even though it's almost a hundred years dead. There are strange specimens in glass coffins and long cylindrical jars, like kitchen jars for foodstuffs. I write the interesting-sounding names: "Natterjack Toad, Butterfish, Butterfly Blenny, Tompot Blenny, Spotted Dragonet, Atlantic Football Fish, Barrelfish, Porcupine Bight, Crystal Goby, Bogue, Poor Cod, Purple Sunstar, Cuckoo Wrasse, Lumpsucker, Boarfish, Comber, Pouting, Beadlet Anemone, Snakelocks Anemone, Dead Men's Fingers, Sea Pen, Boring Sponge, Smelt, Stone Loach, Shad, Porbeagle Shark, Gudgeon, Darkie Charlie, Leafscale Gulper Shark, Spurdog. Bluntsnout Smooth-Head." "Bluntsnout Smooth-Head" is like giving an insult and then softening it with a compliment.

Next I head for the cases of butterflies and moths, and pull back the red leather covers. I write nearly all these names in my notebook; they're like patches of words from a beautiful poem: "Purple Hairstreak, Red Admiral, Heath Fritallary, Painted Lady, Pearl-bordered Fritallary, Small Tortoiseshell, Speckled Wood, Pale Clouded Yellow, Brimstone, Brown Hairstreak, Peacock, Silver-Washed Fritallary, Marsh Fritallary, Ringlet, Bath White, Cinnabar, Grayling, Small Copper, Meadow Brown, Gatekeeper, The Wall."

The people who name butterflies must be more imaginative than those who name birds—naming a bird Great Finch or Little Owl is like naming a street New Street or Main Street. If I could name things, I'd squeeze chains of consonants together mercilessly without a vowel for breathing room, I'd shove letters together that should never sit side by side in the English language. I'd add numbers and symbols and insist that they be pronounced. I move onto the moths and write: "Ruby Tiger, Puss, Elephant Hawk-Moth, Hummingbird Hawk-Moth, Oleander Hawk-Moth, Bedstraw Hawk-Moth, Eyed Hawk-Moth, Convolvulus Hawk-Moth, Coxcomb Prominent, Sallow Kitten, White Ermine, Pebble Prominent, Buff-Tip, Buff Ermine, Purple-Bordered Gold, Mottled Umber, Scalloped Oak, Early Thorn, Chimney Sweeper, Purple Bar, Magpie Moth, Speckled Yellow, Red Sword-Grass, The Shears, Grey Dagger, The Ear Moth, Burnished Brass, Heart and Dart, Silver Y, Middle-Barred Minor, Flounced Rustic, The Grey Pug, Latticed Heath, Satyr Pug, The Tissue, Plume Moth, The Drinker, Large Emerald, Lunar Hornet Moth, Goat Moth, Vapourer, Red-Necked Footman (which has disappeared and left just a beige stain, probably in a sulk over its name), Northern Eggar, Ghost Moth, Fox Moth, Emperor Moth, Lobster Moth, Figure of Eight Moth, Mouse Moth, Satellite, Garden Carpet Moth, Belled Beauty, Grass Emerald Moth, Straw Belle, Brindled Beauty and The November Moth," which I imagine is prone to fits of melancholy.

I look through my lists for a pattern or code, but all I find are the names of creatures that include the names of creatures of a different species: "Elephant Hawk-Moth, Mouse Moth, Hummingbird Hawk-Moth, Fox Moth, Lobster Moth, Sallow Kitten Moth, Spider Crab, Goat Moth, Cuckoo Wrasse, Butterfly Blenny, Cuckoo Ray, Nursehound Shark, Sea Horse."

The moth-namer seems to be overly dependent on his animal- and fish-namer colleagues; he needs to be jolted into originality. I leave the museum and walk down Merrion Street, past the bookshop on Lincoln Place that used to be a chemist and that sells lemon soap regardless of what else it sells. Either James Joyce or Leopold Bloom or Stephen Daedalus (or maybe all three) bought soap there, so it attracts citrus-seeking literary tourists. I walk down Westland Row to Pearse Street—the clock on the tower of the red-brick fire station tells the wrong time—and cross at the garda station. This would be the worst stretch of street for a botched self-immolation; after the firemen quenched the fire, the guards would arrest you for public disorder. I walk by The Steine which, I have read, is also called Ivar the Boneless' Pillar, after a ninth-century Viking ruler. Two faces are carved into opposite sides of the base of the pillar: those of Ivar, a berserker, and Mary de Hogges. I like that I don't have to name these faces—I don't think I could top Mary de Hogges for originality—and I like that Ivar was a berserker; I think I could go berserk myself if certain things happened to me in a certain order without my consent. I catch the number 4 bus heading north. I wonder if the drivers with the fewest accidents and the cleanest buses are rewarded with the single-digit routes, or the routes with a mixture of numbers and letters, or the even-numbered routes, or if it matters at all.

7

I CAN'T SLEEP, in a night-before-Christmas or night-before-funeral kind of way; tomorrow I will visit Penelope's house. I watch the red numbers on the clock radio turn 4:44. The 4s look like three unstable chairs. I get up and stalk the rooms, trying out different beds and chairs, like Goldilocks. The house feels fraught in the small hours, like it has a secret it won't divulge. I turn on all the lights, I need to know that my hands and face are real and connected to me, that I'm not about to dissolve. I go back to bed and watch a patch of the wardrobe by the window turn green, amber, red from the traffic lights up the road. I have to watch closely for the amber-red changeover. I watch 4:58 turn into 4:59; it seems important that I do. I stare at the time for so long that I can't figure out how the numbers on the clock radio relate to me. Their shapes look familiar and I know their sequence, but I don't understand what they signify. Two 0os look smug, like they know everything there is to know about ovals. The 2 seems confident, assured. The 3 is living in the past. The 9 just looks surprised.

I wake in a fug, with excitement peeking through my tiredness. This is my first invitation anywhere in a good many years.

I wish Penelope had put it in writing, so that I could prove I was asked to come. I go downstairs and feed Lemonfish and eat breakfast—a small breakfast because I want to keep stomach room for a feed of sweet things. When the clock says a quarter to eleven, I get up and put on my coat. I take my bag with a notebook and pencil, in case Penelope says anything noteworthy or I need to draw a map of her flat. I put some stride in my walk and put a smile on my face—this is how an invited person would look—and I set off. I walk past the pub on the corner with the man selling newspapers from the windowsill. There is a large stone on the papers to stop them escaping. A garda car passes, pulling a horsebox; the garda horse must be starting his shift soon. I wonder if it gets the same pay and conditions the guards get and if it can work overtime for extra hay. I turn onto Penelope's street and ring her doorbell. I feel like I should fix my hair or straighten my tie like people do in films, but Penelope would not notice such things. A noise like galloping hooves comes from the flat, the door is whooshed open, and Penelope's face appears. She's wearing red lipstick but it has escaped her lips. There is less face and more mouth than I remember.

"Hello, Penelope, thank you for having me."

"You're very welcome, Vivian, come on in."

I step into the hall and sniff the air. It smells earthy like the zoo, a smell I shouldn't like but I do. Downstairs, there are two closed doors at right angles to each other and a flight of stairs. I follow Penelope up the wooden stairs. My feet clack, Penelope's shuffle in thick woolen socks. She leads me into a large bright living room at the top of the stairs. It has white walls and a door leading out to a balcony, but the carpet, oh the carpet! It's purple with huge red and green and pink flowers; it's a rage of a carpet. My eyes are drawn to it, even though it hurts to look. There are four cats sitting on two sofas. The kitchen is part of the living room, with open shelves displaying Penelope's food; I feel like I'm snooping around her digestive system.

"Sit down, Vivian, and make yourself comfortable. I'll put the kettle on."

I don't sit because the cats are taking up all the sofa space, they are staring at me with deep nothing in their eyes. I look at the books on the shelves. There are books on cats and angels and druids and fairies and darker-coloured books on the occult. In the corner of one shelf is a stack of hardbound marbled note-books. I pick up one, open it, and see "January 1st" written at the top. The handwriting is smudged and bouncy, like it was writ-ten in fountain pen with ink made from frogs. I close the diary.

"I see you've discovered my secrets," Penelope says with a laugh.

I wish she wouldn't laugh when things aren't funny, laughs should be dealt out sparingly.

"I didn't look," I say, "I mean I looked but when I saw it was a diary I stopped—"

"Vivian, it's fine. Do you keep a diary?"

"I used to," I say, "but it took too long to write everything I thought or saw or did. I couldn't go anywhere without my diary, and my sister got annoyed when I wrote down every-thing she said. But if I didn't do that, it wasn't a true diary."

"It's all or nothing with you, isn't it, Vivian?"

I sense she's going to laugh again, so I speak hastily.

"There are boxes of my old diaries in the attic, but they're so tiring to read. It's like reliving a whole part of my old life while living in my current life. And I've forgotten most of what's written, so what's the point of living these details in the first place if I'm not going to remember them?"

I take a big gasp of air because this is the most I have spoken out loud in a long while.

"I understand," Penelope says, nodding.

I'm glad she doesn't laugh this time. She clears the cats off one sofa with a sweep of her arm, and I sit down. Then she brings two white mugs of tea over to the table. The mugs are chipped with old tea stains, I can tell I'll feel at home here. She brings over a tray of biscuits. The tray is wooden and round, the size of six of my heads. I have never seen so many biscuits in one place. I take my notebook from my bag.

"Can I write the names of all those biscuits?" I ask.

"Of course," she says.

I write: "Jam Rings, Custard Creams, Lemon Puffs, Raspberry Creams, Nice Biscuits, Coconut Creams, Milk Chocolate Digestives, Dark Chocolate Digestives, Caramel Digestives, Plain Digestives, Rich Teas, Mariettas, Bourbon Creams, Pink Wafers, Chocolate Wafers, Fig Rolls, Fruit Shorties, Shortcakes, Orange Creams, Jersey Creams."

The biscuits are scattered and heaped and bunched like so many mute-coloured dead things. I start with a plain digestive, the calm before the chocolate storm.

"Where do you keep the biscuits?" I ask.

"In a huge tin, but I should probably separate them to stop the flavours mixing."

She's right; the digestive tastes of raspberry, but if I choose the strongest-tasting biscuits, they will surely defy contamination.

"So, Vivian, what's your story?"

I don't have a once-upon-a-time fairytale of a life, so I tell

Penelope about my search for a portal and my blue party and Lemonfish. She says her cats would make short work of Lemonfish and I tell her that Lemonfish could take on a hundred cats, but only if he was in a large body of water and the cats stayed around the edge.

"What kind of edges?"

"Door frames mostly. That's where I'd stand if the world ended. Cliffs and piers and shelf edges, where the dust gathers. And the lip of Lemonfish's bowl, where the water meets the air, the gap between the carpet and skirting board. I like the place where one thing meets another—that's where magic gets in."

I snatch a gulp of air. I must learn to breathe as I talk.

"The middle is the scary part," I say.

Penelope nods.

"I'm more of a middle person myself," she says, and she is. She is sprawled in the middle of one sofa with two cats on one side, one cat on the other, and one asleep behind her. I'm perched on the left side of the other sofa, with a world's worth of space to my right. It is a waste of a sofa; I should take up more space.

"I'm going to become more middle," I say.

I would like to proclaim it, but I don't quite know how. I lean back and throw out my right arm to use up the seat beside me. This feels awkward. There is a vast chunk of space between my body and the back of the sofa and I can't reach my mug or the biscuits. I want to move but the effort has been made. I slide further back into the sofa and I spread my body wider without tossing out my limbs.

"What's your story?" I ask Penelope so I can get stuck into the biscuits and keep my mouth full and my head nodding. She talks about her art and her cats and I stop listening when she mentions her angel guides and her spiritual paths. When I've had enough biscuits, and while the angels are still flying around the conversation, I ask to see some of her work. She leads me through a door into a small bright room off the living room. There are white walls and wooden easels with canvases on them. Every canvas has a cat on it: close-ups of cats' faces; cats' bodies and faces; ocean scenes with cats swimming and sunning themselves; cats dressed as clowns, farmers, Sherlock Holmes, ghosts, witches, even a cat dressed as a communist leader with ecstatic peasants saluting it.

"Told you I liked drawing cats," she says with a grin.

I don't know where to look. Communist Cat is staring at me, examining my face for signs of dissent.

"They're very original," I say, "what a unique perspective."

My mind whirrs for more adjectives, and I fear my silence is degrees from rude so I let out a *Raaaaar!* Penelope's shoulders scoot up to her ears and she jumps and squeals. The movements are so connected, they're somewhere between comical and graceful. The subject has been changed.

"What's wrong, Vivian?"

"I thought I saw a ghost, but it's just the ghost-cat in the painting."

"Right, let's go back inside."

We sit down again, I widen myself and take up a fair amount of space.

"So, Vivian, where did you grow up?"

"Dublin."

"Whereabouts?"

"Not far from here."

Sweat begins to trickle down my lower back, and I press my vest against the skin to mop it up.

"Do your family live nearby?"

"My sister lives on the other side of the city, my parents are dead."

"Oh, I'm sorry."

"Don't be sorry, I was sorry when they were alive."

I've said a good ways too much. Penelope looks quickly at me and then at the cat on her lap and starts talking about her childhood. It was unhappy, by the sounds, so I put a glass wall over my ears and let Penelope's words thunk against the glass and slide down to my shoulders. I can't bear tales of abuse and neglect and unwashed corduroy trousers so I replace her words with candyfloss and sherbet fountains and cake with buttercream so smooth it glides down the throat like a greasy angel.

"You're a very good listener, Vivian, most people keep interrupting when I talk about this."

"Mmm," I say.

I've learned to crinkle my forehead like an accordion and draw in my lips like I'm sucking on a straw when people tell me sad things. Then my mind can climb up the Magic Faraway Tree or fly away on the Magic Wishing Chair. Penelope's eyes are plump and wet, I should do something. I've read about patting unhappy people's knees reassuringly but I'm not quite sure how. I cup her kneecap with my right hand a few times. She is weeping loudly now.

"There there," I say, but I'm thinking, *Where where?* And does cupping a kneecap ever bring them there, wherever there is? When my hand gets stiff from cupping, I flatten it to a gentle slapping gesture. Penelope's body heaves with great big sniffs that seem to go all the way up to her brain.

"Thank you," she says, "it's good to talk about these things you know."

I don't know because I don't know what she was talking about and I don't know why she would want to talk about things that make her do such ugly sobs. I want to take my hand off her knee and reach for another biscuit, but it might be too soon, so I reach my left hand under my right arm and strain for the table. Penelope snorts a laugh and I scoot away before I am covered in snot or tears or needless sorrow. I move onto the fruit course of biscuits and stuff anything with pink or orange or yellow cream into my mouth. Penelope's voice fattens and rises, she mentions angels setting her on the right path, the sixth sense of her cats and art as a form of therapy. These words should be spoken to a person with wider, more welcoming ears than me but I'm the only one here, apart from the pointy-eared cats. When I have sucked the last drop of tea from the mug and eaten all the biscuits my stomach will allow, I decide to leave.

"Right," I say.

"Right?"

"I must go," I say. "Please visit me at the same time next week."

I get up and dust biscuit crumbs off my lap. I don't know any suitable departing sentences so I think about how characters in Coronation Street leave.

"Ta-ra chuck," I say, but it comes out flat and wrong, it lacks accent and punctuation and a Manchester upbringing.

"Bye, Vivian."

We walk down the stairs and I jump out the door and wave before Penelope decides a hug after a weep would be a good idea.

8

I WAKE IN a hurry, as if I've been blown out of sleep by a
giant puff of wind. I get dressed, making sure that every
piece of clothing is the right way around; today is not a day
for being inside out or back to front. I go downstairs to the
kitchen, put on the kettle, and toast some bread. When the
toast pops, it's burnt black. I take the slices to the bin with a
knife and scrape a map of Dublin onto the first slice, and the
letter "V" onto the second. The kettle boils and clicks off. Most
of my meals involve waiting for pops and clicks and beeps.
Someday I would like to get a stove with real fire and toast
bread on a fork through the slats, and put a pyramid-shaped
kettle on the hob and wait for it to whistle. I spread butter
on my toast from the butter dish, trying not to transfer the
burnt specks from the toast onto the dish, and make tea with
one heaped spoon of tea leaves, stirring until it's a deep red-
brown. I don't really like tea that strong, but I like the phrase
"heaped teaspoon" and I can't use it if I don't heap the spoon.
The colour is spoiled when I add milk; milky tea is so sad and
lonely and grey. I take David's chair from the kitchen table
and return it to the living room, then I sit down on the only

chair and eat. My ears have been saturated with other people's words recently; today I will hear only my own.

When I've finished eating, I take the blue folder from the drawer of the desk in the living room. There is no chair decision to make when I sit here, because only one chair fits into the desk. It has a round wooden seat and round wooden arms, which enclose me like a wrist in a cuff. I sit down and open the folder containing my Last Words Project, which I would like to abbreviate to LWP, but that sounds like a political organisation whose members all believe the same thing. My project involves trawling through all my great-aunt's books, and writing out the last word from each one. When I'm finished, I will examine them to find some kind of pattern. I expect this word-pattern to be a code or a message or a map, leading me to my rightful world. Last week I finished "G," today I will work through H. I go to the bookshelves and take down as many "H" books as will fit in my arms, carry them to the desk and arrange them into two jagged piles. Then I sit down again and peel back the cover of *King Solomon's Mines*. The last words is "else" and I write it in the notebook under "Last Words: H." Next comes "existence," from Radclyffe Hall's *The Well of Loneliness*, "cambo" from L. P. Hartley's *The Shrimp and the Anemone* and "Spain," "now," "things," "pain," "on," "accordingly," "known" and "boterel," from the Thomas Hardy books. From Nathaniel Hawthorne's *The Scarlet Letter* comes "Gules." My favourites so far are "Cambo," "Boterel" and "Gules." I don't know what these words signify—they sound like a company of solicitors—but I feel certain that they hold meaning for me. From Ernest Hemingway's books come "forest," "stream," "lions" and "go"; from Thomas Hughes's *Tom Brown's Schooldays* I get "fulness" and from Victor Hugo's *The Hunchback of Notre Dame* comes "dust." I look at my list of "H" words and let them swirl around my eyes, but seeking meaning in small clumps of words could weaken the final pattern. I close the notebook and put it in the folder, then I put the books back on the shelves. I swipe the palm of one hand against the palm of the other, then I repeat the gesture in the opposite direction. This means I have completed something; it feels clean and good.

Now I look through the shelves for books that I have no intention of reading, and pick out three. Inside the cover of the first book I write:

> *Zolanda,*
>> *The sardines have eluded us yet again.*
>> *Someday, Zolanda; some day.*

The second book is called The Girl You Left Behind. Inside its cover I write:

> *To The One Who Was Replaced By Me,*
>> *Show me the way back, and I will give you the*
>> *keys to Great-Aunt Maud's house.*
>>> *Expectantly Yours,*
>>> *Vivian.*

The third book is about horoscopes. Inside it I write:

> *Gobnait,*
>> *The heart of a maiden runs deeper than her*
>> *monthly forecast.*

Godspeed, young Gobnait, Godspeed.

Your Godsib Ethel.

I don't know who Zolanda, Gobnait or Ethel are, but I imagine that Ethel is a wise older lady who will guide Gobnait through this world and beyond. Maybe I should advertise for an Ethel-friend next. I take a plastic bag from the wad in the cupboard under the kitchen sink, and put the three books in the bag. Then I put on my coat and walk to the charity shop near the post office. I give the bag to the woman behind the counter and leave before she talks to me. If I see "Wanted" posters tacked to local trees looking for Zolanda or Gobnait or Ethel, I will answer them and be that friend. I walk down Phibsborough Road into town feeling giddy with success, but it's a success that I don't know how to measure; I may never know the consequences of that book drop.

I walk down Constitution Hill and veer left, onto Coleraine Street. Men in fluorescent vests are laying fresh tarmac on the street. It smells like chemical heaven. I walk slowly and inhale deeply, then I bend down and pretend to tie my shoelace so that I can sniff closer to the source. I cross North King Street and head for Cuckoo Lane. The "CUCK" has been blacked out so that it reads "_ _ _ _ OO LANE," which sounds like the chorus to a new song. I come out onto Mary's Lane facing the redbrick fruit markets, which have the look of a court or a temple. The whole street sign has been blue-ed out: I have walked off-map onto a street that doesn't exist, not in this world, at least. Vans and trucks and forklifts scud about through arched doorways, emitting a constant low-grade *beeeeeeeep*. Fruit-sellers and drivers call to one another inside the market buildings, their voices echoing in these great caverns with their wrought-iron doors. Boxes of fruit and vegetables are piled high on wooden pallets outside the shops facing the market—their smell is of the world being born. I wonder whether vegetables get jealous that they smell so silently, with fruit getting all the glory. I walk by the shops staring at the produce, my feet skidding on squashed fruit. There is something so appealing about seeing so much of every grown thing heaped together in one place. There are cabbages, turnips, mushrooms, lettuces, tomatoes, swedes, carrots, onions, tomatoes, cherries, strawberries, apples, oranges, nectarines, peaches, clementines, melons, watermelons, raspberries, blueberries, bananas and grapes, all so fat and full and squelching with life.

I picture the inside of the market as a gigantic barrel filled with a huge fruit salad. I don't want to be rid of this image, so I circle the outside of the building, taking care not to peer too closely inside. There are stone clumps of fruit and vegetables and fish carved into the wall, and white stone faces above the doors. The faces look stoical and wise, but silently judging. Statues of two ancient Greek goddesses stand on the roof next to the city crest—they might be fruit muses who inspire the invention of new fruit and, from that height, they could point out the thinnest boundary between worlds if they felt so inclined. When I look up to wave to them, I bump into a man in a fluorescent vest ("Mind your step, love") and am forced to jump out of the path of a forklift truck (Beeeeeeeeeep). I leave the markets to avoid a fruit incident, and head for the quays. On a building on the north quays, the words "I like scaldy mots" are scrawled in black. "I like scaldy mots," I say aloud, and it sounds like I know what I'm talking about. Near this is written: "The army are coming." But it doesn't state which country's army is coming, what they plan on doing when they get here and whether the army is in any way connected to the scaldy mots. Further along the quays, on the front wall of the abandoned whitewashed hotel, the words "Not Me" are written. I would like to meet the writer of those words: I'm not me either, and there's a possibility we could be each other, or we could be friends at least. I'd also like to ask if I could borrow those words for my epitaph ("Here Lies Vivian Lawlor: Not Me"). I cross the Ha'penny Bridge. The words "Troll Below?" are stencilled on the tarmac, which reminds me of the troll underneath the bridge in the "Three Billy Goats Gruff" fairy-tale, and makes me want to point to the fattest person and say, "There's more eating in him, don't bother with me." The question mark suggests uncertainty, and I'm glad of it: there's another person who doesn't have the world and its underneath figured out. I stop and read the messages on the love locks tied to the railings of the bridge. Someone loves someone and someone else loves their mama and someone else says "Fuck love." The man begging on the bridge says to a passer-by, "Any spare change, bud? I like your haircut." The man thanks him and walks on, the compliment unpaid for. I pass underneath Merchant's Arch and close my eyes, hoping for a transforma-tion—an arch is surely as good a portal as any—but the smell of stale piss doesn't fade to flowers, and the noise of the traffic doesn't change to fairy bells. I open my eyes and walk back through the arch. The sign for Fownes Street Lower has been blue-ed out to read "_ _ _I_S_STRE[_OWER." The middle prong of the second "E" in "street" has been blue-ed out, leav-ing a symbol that looks like a square bracket, which could be a letter in an alphabet from another world. I write "Isstre[ower" in my notebook. I will keep it safe, until I find someone who can tell me what [means. I head for College Green. The fountain by the statue of the four skinny angels is spewing out multiplications of bubbles—someone must have put washing-up liquid in the water. I walk to the statue and pick up handfuls of suds. It always surprises me that bubbles are wet; from their whiteness, I expect dry fluff. I put some in my mouth, but they taste sharp and clean when I expected soft and sweet. I take the bus home from Dame Street, and buy a carton of milk in the local newsagent. I try to creep past Bernie's house, but she's standing by her open window, smoking.

"Nice drop of milk for the tea, wha," she calls out the window.

I nod, and hurry on. I never know if she is making statements or asking questions. When I enter the house, I sniff the air, then tuck my nose under my jumper and smell my top half. A homely smell comes from my body, somewhere between old milk and red meat on the turn. I sit at the kitchen table and trace my route on greaseproof paper. Today, I walked a staircase dangling on a fishing rod.

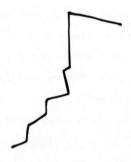

9

I GO INTO the hoard-room to find some things that I can bring as presents to my sister's family—I'm going to surprise them with a visit. There's a small pile of paper crumbs beside the notebook pile, and a scattering of droppings like burnt rice, the aftermath of a paper feast. At least the house mice appreciate quality notepaper. I quite like the idea of sharing my home with small creatures that come alive at night, like toys in a children's story. I go downstairs, open the laptop and look up what diseases mice carry. The web site says: "Leptospirosis, Murine Typhus, Rickettsialpox, Tularamia, Lymphocytic Choriomeningitis and potentially Bubonic Plague."

I like the way it says "potentially" bubonic plague, as if the other diseases were a given. The mice on the Internet look like squirrels with shaved tails. The wiry tails look mean and unfinished, so I'll turn my house mice into squirrels. I take a scissors out of the kitchen drawer, cut two strips of bristles from the sweeping brush and bring them upstairs. I lean one strip against the bottom of the door of the hoardroom, and the other against the jamb. Then I squeeze some glue along the tips of the bristles, and pull the door almost shut. It looks like a car wash for an elf's car. If the bristles successfully squirrelify one mouse, I will make more for his friends. I don't mind mice walking around my house—or maybe they think it's their house but I don't want to catch potential bubonic plague and have my own private Black Death. I will make them a disinfectant footbath. I go down to the kitchen and take a saucer out of the cupboard. I pour in a dash of disinfectant, carry it upstairs and put it outside the hoardroom. When the mice have hospital-clean feet and sweeping-brush tails, they can be my pets. I'll call them Mork and Mindy, after the two friendly aliens in the television show. I write the mouse diseases in my notebook, then I write a List of Old Disease Names That Sound More Like The Thing Than Their Modern Names: "Dropsy, Yellow Jack, Puerperal Exhaustion, Scrofula, Consumption (I especially like Galloping Consumption), Ablepsy, Ague, Biliousness, Boils, Canker, Carbuncle, Cowpox, Pox, French Pox, Great Pox, Grocer's Itch, Milk Leg, Gout, Quinsy, Rag-Picker's Disease, St. Vitus's Dance."

I leave the house, and walk to one of the dark little shops nearby that sells an unpredictable range of goods. A middle-aged man sits smoking behind the till, next to a gas heater that smells of warm evil. He looks annoyed to see a customer.

"I always wanted to smoke," I say.

He puffs out some smoke.

"I tried but I couldn't inhale."

He digs his thumb into his nose and roots around.

"Where are the toys?" I ask.

He points and I follow his finger down to the toys. The shop bulges with goods. The hooks on the walls are crammed, the shelves are bursting, the containers in the middle heave with stuff. Everything is covered with a whisper of dust. There are mouse traps, clothes pegs, glow-in-the-dark Jesuses, bicycle lights, insoles for shoes, cooking utensils, potpourri, picture frames, notebooks, toys, pots, pans, calculators, pens and pencils, bathroom furniture, toiletries.

I try to remember the ages of my niece and nephew, but all I know is that the boy is smaller than the girl. I pick up a net of marbles for him and a plastic cooker for her, bring them to the counter and pay the silent man. He hands me my change.

"Thanks," I say. "I hope you have a merry Christmas and a happy new year."

"It's April," he says, his jaw hanging like a door that won't close.

"I know, but I may not be in here again this year. I rarely visit my sister."

His face has even less welcome in it, so I take the toys and leave the shop. I walk to Phibsborough, and wait for the bus that crosses the city and goes straight to my sister's house. When the bus comes, I sit upstairs and look at the tops of people's heads as they get on. That's the part of their body they forget about, their upper scalps are not as well-tended as their faces. A girl with a wide pretty face gets on and sits beside me. She looks unhappy, which surprises me; if I looked like her, I would be laughing all the way to the mirror. Every time the bus stops, I look out at the passengers getting off and on. I picture plus signs over the heads of the people getting on and minus signs over the heads of the ones getting off. When we reach the city centre, there are so many minuses I fear I'll be the only passenger left, but a swell of pluses immediately gets on. The bus stops at the traffic lights on O'Connell Bridge, next to the statue of Daniel O'Connell surrounded by Winged Victories. One of the Victories holds a snake casually in one hand and an axe in the other. She stares hard at me, her eyes insisting on mine no matter how far back or forward I lean, accusing me of doing too much of something or not enough of something.

"What did I do?" I ask her.

"What?"

I get off the bus on the main road of my sister's suburb. The silence of the place is a shock, all hush and muffle and muted shop lighting. A woman passes by with a face so stuck that I think she's had a stroke. Her hair is yellow, her face is orange, her lips are red. She looks so coloured-in, it's probably plastic surgery. I walk quickly to my sister's house, crunch through the gravel in her driveway and ring the bell. My sister answers the door with a smile like watery sunshine.

"*Surprise!*" I shout.

I hold out the presents. Her eyes move north and her mouth moves south and her face settles into dismay.

"Vivian, what are you doing here?"

"I thought I'd surprise you and the children. I'm using my initiative, like you always told me to."

I try to talk brightly, but I don't know exactly how to inject luminosity into my voice so I just aim for a higher pitch. My sister's whole body seems to turn in on itself. She stands back and I walk into the hall and sniff the air. It smells of soap and dinner. She closes the door and leads me into the kitchen, which is huge, with black surfaces and a white floor. It looks empty.

"Where is everything?" I ask.

"Where's what?"

"Your kitchen stuff—the kettle, microwave, cooker, fridge."

She starts opening the black doors and points to the appliances behind those doors.

"Why are you keeping the kitchen a secret?" I ask. "Are you hiding it from someone?"

My sister starts throwing words at me, whole lists of words, words that she took from her architect or her friends, words that mean nothing, words that say nothing, words from advertisements and brochures and people who sell things for a living: "Rain-sensing . . . utilitarian . . . space . . . ergonomic . . . clean lines . . . neutral . . . timeless . . . transitional . . . accents . . ."

"What accent does this kitchen have?" I ask.

She looks at me through a scrunch of eyelids, her opinion of me seeping through her eyeballs and dripping (*plip*) onto the timeless floor. She starts talking about Angelique's splashbacks and Saoirse's counters. Her friends all sound like bridalwear shops or Gaelic chieftains. Then she points out the window to an L-shaped concrete pond with giant goldfish in it.

"How do you like my new water feature?" she asks.

"Did you overfeed the goldfish?" I ask. "They look mutant."

My sister withers.

"They're *koi*, Vivian. They symbolise strength and perseverance."

I look at the fish. They've certainly persevered at eating if they grew to that size.

"I have a water feature too," I say.

"Oh?"

"An outdoor one, it came with the property."

My great-aunt's house was the first thing I got that my sister didn't get. I call it a property around her to emphasise ownership.

"Don't be silly," she says, "Great-Aunt Maud had no time for such things."

"There's a leaking drainpipe that drips water onto the concrete around the drain," I say. "If I crouch down on my hunkers and close my eyes, I can pretend I'm in the grounds of a miniature palace, surrounded by fountains and elves."

My sister doesn't answer. She copes better with her own words than mine.

"Where are Lucy and Oisin?" I ask. "They're in the living room."

"I want to see them," I say. "I have presents."

My sister grips her clean-lined counter.

"Sure," she says in a sewn-up voice. "They'd love to see you."

She leads the way to the living room, where the children are sitting in front of the television. They look at me, then look back at the television.

"I have *presents* for you!" I shout, because children's presenters on television always shout and children seem to like it, but these children just look frightened. The boy runs to his mother and she nudges him in my direction. I take out the cooker and give it to the girl. She rips the box open and starts to play with it. The boy edges closer to me and I hand him the net of marbles. He takes it, looks at it, then looks at my bag.

"Does he want my bag?" I ask my sister.

The boy's face curls up and he starts to wail "Not fair" and "Lucy got big present!"

"Vivian, get me a weighing scales."

I try to say this with authority.

"Why?"

"David's marbles are heavier than Lucy's cooker. Gram for toy gram, he wins."

"Oh, Vivian."

The world is in the way she says my name, and it's not a good thing. I ask my sister for a glass of water and while she's gone, I say "hugger-mugger" over and over to the children. Their ears sharpen and they look from me to the door.

"Hugger-mugger," I hiss. *"Hugger-mugger hugger-mugger hugger-mugger HUGGER-MUGGER!"*

My sister rushes in.

"Vivian?"

"I'm trying to reintroduce forgotten words back into the system," I say. "Targeting children has a better chance of success."

She claps her hands and says, "Lucy and Oisin, run into the kitchen, we'll have a treat!"

The children barrel past and my sister turns to me.

"You need to go home now. The children have had enough excitement."

I pick up my bag and follow her to the front door. As I move past her, she says, "And Vivian? Maybe you should think about showering once in a while."

I thought I showered twice in a while, but my whiles must be longer than hers. I say goodbye, but my sister's face is already turned back to the kitchen with her children and hidden appliances. The visit has been two-thirds successful because only one child cried and their mother didn't. I walk home, retracing the route the bus took, ignoring the shortcuts. The yellow bus stops mark my progress and, when I get tired, I imagine them clapping invisible hands and cheering me on. If I follow the route exactly, this will cancel out the awkward smudge of the visit. When I let myself in the front door, I find a note from the city council advertising its annual collection of old furniture and junk in a couple of days' time. I note the date; I have nothing to throw out, but I have all to find. I unfurl the map of Dublin and plot my route—just the walking part—and trace it onto greaseproof paper. Today I covered a headless armless man, sliced vertically in two.

10

I WAKE EARLY and listen to the wind in the fireplace in my bedroom. It's loud, and pieces of soot are blowing down the chimney. This is good; I need a big wind that could turn into a cyclone, because today I'm going to visit Yellow Road and Emerald Street. In *The Wonderful Wizard of Oz*, the cyclone carried Dorothy to Oz, and she followed the Yellow Brick Road to the Emerald Palace to find her way home. If I find these coloured roads in Dublin, I might find my way home too. I pull on a jumper and jeans and a pair of my great-aunt's shoes that are one size too big. They are a light grey that could pass for silver. If I had red shoes, I'd have to decide whether to go with the silver-shoed Dorothy in the book or the red-shoed Dorothy in the film. I go to the bathroom and wedge toilet paper in the toes to make them fit better. My silver-shoed walk is more of a clomp, but I plan on being lifted off by a cyclone so I shouldn't have to walk both ways.

I eat breakfast, put a notebook and pen in my bag and set off. I walk to a discount shop in Phibsborough—I can't go back to the one I visited yesterday because I've already wished the man a happy Christmas—and choose a yellow ball, a yellow colouring book and a yellow pen. I also find a plastic bracelet with a shiny green stone that looks like an emerald. I pay for my yellow and emerald goods, then I walk a little further down the road to a shop that sells "Grocery Sweets Ices." I don't know whether ices are ice creams, ice pops or bags of ice, but this is not my concern today. Inside, the shop smells of warm linoleum. Birthday cards are stacked in front of the window, faded into pastels by the sun. Fluorescent cardboard stars hang from shelves, advertising bargains on toilet paper and baked beans and custard. I go to the rack selling pouches of sweets, and find a pouch of Emerald sweets. I don't know how a pouch differs from a bag, but I suspect there are kangaroos involved. At the counter, there are jars of sweets on the shelves and chocolate bars piled on the counter behind a Perspex cover that makes them look like museum exhibits. Looking at them gives me the spits, and I have to close my mouth so that I don't drool aloud. I love sweets. I love sweets out of packets and sweets out of boxes and sweets out of tins and tubs, but, most of all, I love sweets out of jars. When I've paid for my Emeralds, I leave the shop, take my notebook out of my bag, and write a list of my favourite sweets: "Marshmallows, Candy Cigarettes, Sherbet Fountains, Bullseyes, Fried Eggs, Toffees, Apple Drops, Pips, Chocolate Brazil Nuts, Apple Jacks, Sherbet Flying Saucers, Jelly Tots, Popping Candy, Wham Bars, Fizzy Cola Bottles, Dip-dabs, Love Hearts, Chocolate Mice, Jelly Beans, Sherbet Lemons, Sugared Almonds, Butter Candy, Rhubarb-and-Custard Sweets, Candy Floss, Fruit Salads, Marshmallow Snowballs, Chocolate Raisins, Teacakes, Candy Necklaces, Fizzy Soothers, Jelly Babies, Refresher Bars, Drumstick Lollipops, Frosties, Parma Violets, Pear Drops."

Some of the entries on my Sweets List might be better suited to a Buns List (teacakes, for example), but until I make such a list, I will keep them here.

I put my notebook away, head through Phibsborough, and walk higher and higher up Mobhi Road until it turns into Ballymun Road. I like roads with names of whole suburbs in them: it's grand and ambitious and a little bit hopeless. I turn onto Collins Avenue after the yellow church, pass the university and go through the Swords Road junction—another suburb of a road. After a left and a right, I'm on Yellow Road, which, I'm disappointed to see, is grey. I'd expected a yellow surface or yellow walls, or even a yellow cloud dangling over the road, but never mind: I've brought my own yellow. I take out the ball and colouring book and pen and lay them on the street next to the sign. I click my heels together as best I can in these loose shoes, but no sudden gust swoops me to Oz, so I walk back to the main road, find a bus stop and catch the next bus to town. When I get on, the bus is quite full. A steam of heat hits me, along with the mushroomy tang of unwashed underthings that could be bottled as The Smell of Dublin Bus.

I get off the bus on O'Connell Street, and turn left onto the quays. I pass the Custom House, where men with red faces and soiled clothes drink from cans and shout to one another. The stone heads above the windows don't seem to care what I'm doing or where I'm going. The woman's head over the door looks out at me, bald-eyed and unseeing, but the clock tells the right time. Just before the convention centre—that giant tin of beans gone slant—I turn left and head towards Emerald Street. The disused Emerald Dairy on the corner doesn't look like the Emerald Palace; it's shuttered and grey with boarded-up windows, but if I were wearing green-tinted glasses, it might appear green. I listen hard for the clank of the Tin Woodman or the rustle of the Scarecrow's straw or the growl of the Cowardly Lion, but I hear nothing, not even a ghostly *moooooo* from the dairy (which I presume produced green milk). I take out the plastic bracelet and the Emerald sweets, and place them under the street sign, opposite the dairy. A man with a bald head and tattoos covering his arms walks by with a small girl. I peer closely at the man's face.

"What are you looking at?"

He juts out his face. Now I can examine it more closely.

"I'm looking for wrinkles—the wizard had a wrinkled face. Are you old?"

"What the fuck kind of a question is that?"

"I'm looking for a little old man with a wrinkled face," I say. "I know what you're thinking—wizards have long white hair and beards, but this one is a bit of a chancer."

"Are you taking the piss?"

His voice is like the scrape of steel wool across a saucepan. I don't know what to say; there are not enough words for these kinds of explanations. He looks over at the small girl—she has found my emerald pile.

"What's that, Shannon?"

The girl holds up the bracelet and the sweets. The man turns back to me.

"What's the story with them?"

He moves his face closer. His teeth are packed tight, like a story with too many words.

"I'm looking for the Emerald Palace, do you know where it is?"

"Do I know where *what* is?"

The "what" is so complete in itself, it could be framed.

"The Emerald Palace from *The Wizard of Oz*—it's made of green glass and emeralds. But we might need green-tinted glasses to see it—you know, the ones that Dorothy wore."

"Are you touched in the head or what?"

"I don't know," I say, "but I was hoping you could tell me how to get back. To where I come from."

"Are you a foreigner?"

"I'm not sure."

My voice comes out sideways. I need to get away from this man and his menace of questions, I'm not a person with answers. I turn my body around—this will surely put my voice to rights—and walk as quickly as my baggy silver shoes will take me, towards the quays. Near O'Connell Bridge, a sign reads: "Taxis to Airport €19." I walk up the rank and get into the first taxi.

"Airport, please," I say, "and *step* on it."

This is what busy people in films say. The driver takes off at a roar and looks at me in the rear-view mirror.

"Late for your flight, love?"

"No, I'm not taking a flight."

"Ah, picking someone up?"

"No."

"Why are you going to the airport, then?"

"I'm looking for something."

"You're a copper?"

"No."

I'm out of answers, so I stare out the window. The radio is squeezing out big deep notes, notes that make me want to dance even though I don't quite know how. We've left the city by now and we're in the port tunnel. A loud *whoosh*, with an undernote of engine thrum, makes me think that if death is to happen, it must surely happen here. The driver is a motorised Pied Piper, leading me inside a mountain. But there's no magic here, only harsh lighting that reminds me of a mortuary.

"Mortuary," I say.

The driver looks at me in the mirror.

"You want to go to the airport mortuary?"

"No, thanks," I say. "Which word do you prefer: 'mortuary' or 'morgue'?"

"Couldn't tell you, love."

"I prefer 'morgue' because it's softer, but the G doesn't smack of slabs and gurneys and fluorescent lighting the way that the harsh 'T' in 'mortuary' does."

"I'll take your word for it," he says.

When we come out of the tunnel, I look at the cars around us.

"Do you ever wonder where these cars are going?" I ask.

"Some of them to the airport, I reckon."

"And then where?"

"On their holidays, I suppose."

"But where on their holidays, and why?"

"Couldn't tell you, why don't you ask them?"

He looks at me in the mirror.

"You sure you're not a detective?"

"I'm sure."

I would like to be Miss Marple or Poirot or Columbo, because even though they seem to dither, they are quietly certain. The driver turns off the motorway.

"Terminal one or two?"

"There are two?"

He looks at me in the mirror, his eyes narrowing.

"The nearest one," I say quickly.

He drives up to a huge silver building with two short legs, like the silver shorts of a sleeping giant. I want to go under the gusset, but he parks under an enclosed footbridge that's the giant's intestines, spurting out indigestible people. I pay and get out. Everyone else stepping out of cars and taxis is carrying huge quantities of luggage; I feel bald and empty with only my handbag. I walk into the building and head for the newsagent, to buy bags of popcorn and crisps. When I put them in my bag it swells, and no longer looks inferior to the massive suitcases.

I watch what passengers do when they enter the airport. They go straight to the departure board and then move off purposefully. I walk over to the board and look at it. There are flights to places that exist, even though I've never heard of them. The flight codes start with letters and end with numbers. I look down the list of letters and spell them out. They don't make any word that I know, but maybe it's an anagram. I take out my notebook and write the codes down. I try jumbling the letters, but I can't make English words. A man in a suit walks quickly to the screen, looks at it, extends his arm in an air-punch and reads his watch. He tuts and sighs, and walks away. I should do something airport-appropriate like this, so I go back to the newsagent and pretend to look at the magazines. A woman is buying a newspaper; I don't understand why she is buying the news of a country she is leaving. I wait until all the people at the departures board have moved off, and a new batch has arrived. Then I walk quickly back, look at the screen for a few seconds, make a *tuh* noise, sigh and walk away. I search for the tutting businessman and find him in the bookshop. He reads the back of a book, and when he brings it to the till, I pick up the book and read the blurb at the back: "body has been discovered . . ." I write the first and last sentence of the blurb in my notebook, but there is no code or anagram, even when I add all the first letters of each word together. I follow the businessman out of the bookshop. I know his taste in books and his walk from behind; we are something close to friends. He walks quickly to the departure gates, which puts a full stop to the trail. Now I walk to a green sign saying: "Meeting Point" and wait under it, but nobody comes. A woman with a hard face and a jagged haircut passes by, wielding a wheelie suitcase like a sword, and I step back to spare my toes. I leave the terminal because it has no centre, and it unmoors me. The airport is for people who are clean and efficient, people who dress like people they are not, people who know where they are going and why.

I walk to the bus stop and get on a meandering bus into town. I sniff the used, lived-in smell of the bus, the smell of warm upholstery and passenger breath, and whisper "safe safe safe." I need to be where buses are, so I decide to go to the bus station. I get off on O'Connell Street, and walk down North Earl Street onto Talbot Street. There's a rattle and a clatter up ahead, the sound of an uneasy ghost clanking his chains. A man with a face so grey it matches the footpath tugs at a bicycle locked to a lamppost. The lock isn't giving up easily, and he yanks it with a force that rattles the earth, his face pure bug-eyed frenzy. A small boy walking in front of me with his father stares at the bike thief.

"Da, the man's trying to rob the bike."

"Don't be looking, son, turn the other way."

"But, Da, he's breaking the lock."

"Lee, don't make me tell you again, turn the other way."

I do as Lee does, and keep walking. I stop at the pub with the carved heads in the brickwork. The stone lady over the door looks serene and welcoming. I call her Anna, because a symmetrical name would go with a calm face. The stone man with the conical hat looks full of mischief, I call him Timmy. (He's Timothy when he's not messing around.) I turn right onto Talbot Place, and walk around to the front of Busáras. It's a merry-go-round of a building with a corrugated wavy roof and circular glass walls, but instead of wooden horses there are metal buses. I step over the bags of a group of men wearing football scarves and jerseys, and go inside to look at the departures board. I'm glad that I've heard mention of all the cities and towns on it. I buy coffee and a muffin from the café, and sit on a wooden slatted seat to eat. The muffin is a regret—it always is. The overhang is appealing, the sense of there being too much, but the consistency is bathroom sponge with an after-cleave to the teeth.

Above me, in a far corner, two men in fluorescent vests sit inside a glass control room, like rare yellow-backed creatures on display. When I see one of the controllers' jackets hanging on a hook, I feel like I've caught a secret glimpse of the inside of the man's wardrobe. A bus pulls up outside one of the gates and people decant onto it from the queue. Beyond the bus stands the green-glass financial centre; it looks like Oz's Emerald Palace, but I don't think I'd find a way home among debits and credits and ledgers. I stretch out my legs. I could belong here, with the dingy off-whiteness of it all, the head-bobbing pigeons wandering around, the piles of oddly shaped bags. There are more edges and corners here; the airport is all middle with no pigeons. I watch the luggage being stowed away in the belly of the bus, and wonder if there are life jackets and whistles on buses that travel by the sea.

After I walk home, I map my route. Today's walks were splintered into fits and starts, the shape confused by doubling back and a taxi ride and a bus ride in the middle. I covered three different shapes: a slightly misshapen floor lamp minus the bulb, a tub with one side bashed inwards and a jagged peak with an oversized footrest at its base. I can't find any connection between the shapes or any way of linking them; it's up to the taxi driver and bus driver to map their own routes.

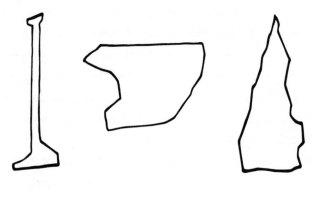

I TURN ON the television to a hidden camera show, in which an actor jumps out at shoppers in a supermarket from under a pile of apples. I find it very soothing to watch people get frights. A documentary comes on next. The presenter is driving a car and talking to the camera. If she had an accident, they could show the crash and make it into a documentary about road safety. The presenter is trying hard to teach me something, something

I will never learn, so I change channels to a film. Two cars are racing through narrow streets lined with stalls. The cars plunge through the stalls, people scatter, tables of fruit and vegetables and meat and fish are knocked and sprawled and squashed and smashed. I want to see the film about the cleanup, the film about the people who are injured by the cars, the film about the people whose livelihoods have been ruined by a man in sunglasses who values his life above all else. I feel like I'm the only person rooting for the fruit seller instead of the hero.

11

I CAN SEE the bus stop from the queue for the ATM. A bus arrives and picks up passengers and leaves (*oh no*), another one comes and goes (*oh no*), and I'm still waiting. When I reach the ATM, I request €20. The machine chugs hard, it might be printing and slicing the notes for all I know, and I take the money and walk to the newsagent.

"Can you give me four €5 notes for €20?" I ask.

The man behind the till shakes his head.

"We don't give change, you have to buy something."

"Okay."

I rummage in my purse for some coins, take a chocolate bar from the pile near the counter, and hand the coins to the man along with the €20. He stares at the money.

"I can't break the €20," I say. "I can't give three people €5 notes, and one person leftover coins."

"Okay, okay."

He takes four notes from the till, and hands them to me with my coin change.

"Thank you," I say, and I wave, but the man doesn't wave back. I get on the next bus into town, and sit midway down. I look out the window. Elderly people huddle in menacing twos or threes outside the church, plotting all manner of I-don't-know-what. Last night, I had an unpleasant dream about losing something I really shouldn't have lost, and it was a relief to be evicted from the dream. The bus takes on more passengers in Phibsborough. Seats fill up around me, and I know the one next to me will be the last one filled, if it is filled at all. I haven't looked at my face in a mirror in a long while—I don't know what other people see that keeps them away. A woman shuffles onto the bus outside the hospital, and sits beside me with a whoosh of coat flaps.

"Cold enough for this time of year, isn't it?"

"It is," I say. "It's so cold that I'm going to buy a hoodie."

"Ah, that's terrible, we were promised a good summer after the bad winter."

She says it like she was personally let down by the weather forecast.

"It is terrible," I say, but there are no more words in me. She starts talking to the woman in the seat across the aisle; it disappoints me that I couldn't maintain the weather conversation, or progress to another topic. I press the bell on O'Connell Street.

"Excuse me," I say to the woman, but the sentence sounds abrupt and unfinished. I don't think I can call her "love," but "missus" sounds rude and "chicken" sounds wrong, when she's more of an old hen. Maybe my voice was built for a different language, one with words for every conversation. I walk down North Earl Street to the discount shop that's bursting with children's clothes and men's workwear and bedding and long pastel-coloured nightwear. The overflow spills from wire baskets out front. I walk up the orange stairs and look through the rails for cardigans with pockets. Then I take four thick, spongy-feeling cardigans into the changing room, a poky cubicle beside the till, and slide a €5 note into the pocket of each cardigan, making sure the money is well hidden. I come out of the changing room, put the cardigans back on the rail at evenly spaced intervals and walk downstairs. I feel anxious until I get out of the shop; it would be hard to explain to the security guard behind the screen at the door that what I was doing was the opposite of stealing, the back-to-front of stealing: "gnilaets," I'll call it. I hope four people without much spare cash for treats find the money and use it to buy cakes or peaches, and not bread or apples.

I walk to Eason's to look at the books. Its clock tells the right time. The new books are too brightly covered, the titles too looped and swirling, so I go downstairs to the books with quiet, straw-coloured covers of people dressed in old-fashioned clothes, and run my hand along the spines. A man with a long ponytail is reading aloud from a classical novel to a woman with short hair. He waves his arms in sweeping circles, like an actor on television pretending to be an actor on stage. His vowels take in entire continents, and his consonants are liquid silk. The girl looks impressed. He passes the book to her and she starts to read aloud. The man corrects her pronunciation of the French words, and she apologises. If only I could impress people, or be so easily impressed by them. I walk the shelves, but no book makes me want to stop and pick it up—they're too new and alphabetically ordered and they smell too clean. I need a chaos of books, so I leave the shop, cross the river and walk along the south quays. I turn onto Parliament Street and go into the second-hand charity bookshop. The books here are different shapes and sizes and feels, they smell of their previous owners in the same way that dogs look like their owners or undertakers look like corpses. I buy a large hardback book with watercolor drawings of birds and a softback book about how to get things done. I would like to get things done and ticked off of lists; some of my projects are endlessly roaming like lemmings without a leader.

On Dame Street I stop to buy a bottle of orange juice and a bar of chocolate, and walk through the front arch of Trinity College, across the slippery cobbles to the benches facing the arts block. The benches are empty because they're wet. I swoosh the rain away with my sleeve, and sit on my bag. I drink the orange juice and eat the chocolate, making sure not to mix the two in my mouth because that would be like eating orange-flavoured chocolate, a scourge of a food. The inscription on the bench reads: "In Memory of Theodora Bevan Née Tichborne 1920."

Theodora should have kept her surname when she married—Theodora Tichborne sounds like a stage actress or a good witch or a fairy godmother in a children's story. I wonder what you have to do to get a bench named after you—either donate pots of money to the college or die young and horribly from a starting point of great beauty. When I've finished eating I head into the arts block to go to the toilet. There are messages written on the door and walls of my cubicle. Next to "Phoebe + Jess" is written: "YOU ARE NOT STUCK." I write that in my notebook, but it seems wrong that I have to write it with hands that are tainted with toilet duties. Underneath that is written: "Exams aren't everything," to which someone else has added: "Exactly! Thousands of children starve to death needlessly every day. Perspective." This is followed by a picture of a smiling face, but thousands of starving children is more of a sulking matter than a smiling one, so I use my pen to turn the basin of a smile into the mound of a pout. On the door is scrawled in marker: "If you have to ask, she is not your friend." I wonder at the certainty of these women: how did they acquire beliefs so definite that they needed to share them with others in print? The message I like best, the message I write hugely over seven pages in my notebook, the message I want to tattoo—no, *etch*, no, *BRAND*—onto my left arm is next to "Louise loves Connor." It says it's a quote by François Rabelais via John Green: "I go to seek a Great Perhaps." I would like to write this quote all over the city myself, but then I would be ripping off Rabelais, Green and the toilet scrawler. I close my notebook and open the cubicle door. I could do worse than live by toilet-door wisdom.

I leave the college through the Nassau Street gate and wait at the traffic lights. A clock on the green dome of the building at the corner tells the right time. A woman across the street with long grey hair eases herself into a sitting position against a bin. She's stiff and stooped and hardly able to walk. She pulls a dirty blanket over her knees and keens a wail of a song, cupping her hands and asking for money. Maybe she's a banshee looking to get back to her world. A garda car turns onto the street and my banshee is suddenly sprightly—she jumps up and scuttles off, clutching her blanket. I cross the road and walk up Dawson Street; it's nice to be on a street that's one letter away from a damson. I cut through Duke Street and onto Grafton Street, walking slowly and looking in the shop windows, which display gleaming jewels on headless necks and glamorous mannequins wearing dresses, but no hoodies. A group of earnest-looking violinists play soaring music from the parts of films in which people die in slow motion; a man manoeuvres a huge sausage-shaped bubble with two sticks as if he's conducting a watery symphony; a group of men painted black all over stand still as statues until somebody puts money in their cup (then they doff their caps); a man puts the finishing touches to a sand dog which I have never seen the start of (how can someone always be finishing and never be starting?).

I don't know how to shop for clothes or where to begin. I would prefer to shop in haberdasheries, drapers, fishmongers, hatters, cobblers, coopers, chandlers, but I would need to wear hats and sew clothes and own barrels and ships. I once had a hoodie, but I threw it out during a long, hot summer that I thought would never turn to winter. The hoodie I buy today must be the zipless kind I can pull over my head, with a pouch to keep sweets in. I walk until I see a shop that I know sells affordable goods. I go inside and find a blue hoodie with white ropes, which I try on over my top. I don't go into changing rooms because there can be mirrors on all sides, and it's impossible to cover them all. A shop assistant walks by with an armful of hangers, she looks like she's about to embark on an intense bout of water divining.

"There's a mirror over there if you need it," she says.

"No, thanks," I say, "I don't like mirrors."

"Ah, we all have days like that," she laughs.

"I have whole years like that," I say, but she's gone in a flurry of plastic and metal. I push out my arms to their full length and the sleeves follow my hands and coat them nicely. The hoodie is so comfortable that I keep it on and bring the hanger to the till.

"Can I pay for this while I'm wearing it?" I ask the assistant.

She looks long and soft at me and says, in the kind of voice that could knit a teddy bear, "Of course you can, love, turn around now."

I turn around so my back is to her and she pulls out the price tag and scans the price.

"Will I take the tag off for you?"

"Yes, please."

There is a *pock* sound like something has come unstuck.

"It suits you," she says. "Blue suits you."

"Thank you," I say, "it's my favourite colour. I don't buy clothes much because I can wear my dead great-aunt's things, but when I do, I buy blue clothes."

She smiles at me, a small sad smile, as if the lights on a Christmas tree have dimmed. I pay and take the receipt.

"Bye," I say, and I wave.

"Bye," she says, "take care now."

I don't know if she means I've to take care of myself or the hoodie, but I suspect it's the hoodie with its white ropes. I leave the shop and walk around Stephen's Green in an outside loop, because I don't have the energy to engage with a park. The sign for Hume Street has been partially blue-ed out; only a quarter of an "H" and the "STREET" remain, so it looks like a dotless "i STREET." I walk up Leeson Street, because I need to see some cheery double "EE"s in a street sign. Pembroke Street has been blue-ed out to read "_ E_BROKE STREET," which sounds like the name of a very cool band whose music I wouldn't like. Groups of students stand outside language schools and secondary schools. I'm amazed by how much smiling is going on—what do they find to smile so hard about? I walk to the bottom of E-Broke Street to the bus stop opposite a hardware shop. The shop looks so domestic and unexpected in a city centre, surrounded by offices and high-volume cafés and efficiency, like a thatched cottage in the middle of an airport. I wait for the bus, feeling shielded in my hoodie, like nothing can hurt me, no rain can wet me or words upset me.

FROM DUSK, THE vans start slowly circling. None of my neighbours have put out their junk, except for two rolls of carpet and a rusted bicycle leaning against Bernie's wall. As soon as there is complete darkness, I creep out of the house and sidle slowly along the walls in the quest for the perfect chair. It must not be too hard or too soft, too big or too small, too wide or too narrow, too long or too short. It must hold the possibility of magic, as well as all of me. I head down the North Circular Road and up through Cabra. Vans pass at walking pace, their diesel-clatter soundtracking this grand streetcombing venture. Two boys dart out from the passenger seat of the van nearest me, grab a couple of children's bicycles, fling them into the back of the van, and hop back into the seat—all in the space of an in-breath. I find a grubby, fawn-coloured armchair with cigarette holes in one arm that seems just the right proportion of dent and comfort, but it's too big to carry home. I decide against an office chair with a broken swivel, and a child's plastic chair that will only accept me sideways. When I come across a folded deckchair with bright flower-spatters on the fabric, I know I have found my chair. I unfold it and sit down, squinting at the yellow streetlights like so many miniature suns. My lower body hangs perilously close to the footpath; perhaps this is a chair for any lighter friends I make. I fold the chair, tuck it under my oxter like a holiday briefcase and walk quickly home.

FOR PENELOPE'S VISIT, I will buy a cake. I would like the icing to read "Welcome Penelope" but I have no time to order such a cake, so I walk to the bakery and choose a Victoria sponge. The middle contains strawberries and whipped cream and the top is sprinkled with icing sugar. I wish Penelope's middle name was Victoria—next time I will put up a notice for a Victoria-friend. When I turn onto my road, I draw back; Bernie and Mary are outside my house talking. It feels like an attack of words that haven't reached me yet.

Their voices float in my direction and I catch "have to say . . . something has to be done . . . it's not right . . . bringing down the look of the place." I walk slowly towards them. By the time I'm near they're in a shouty loop; this must be what high dudgeon sounds like. Bernie jabs a finger at me.

"Here, why don't you do something about your garden? How long has it been since you cut the grass?"

"It's been a year, or a good many months anyway," I say. It feels like confessing to a priest. Mary shakes her head.

"Ah, Vivian, you'll get mice. I'll send Johnno in with the mower."

Johnno is her son who doesn't speak unless he's drunk, and then he shouts.

"No, thanks, I'm doing an experiment," I say. "I want to create a miniature forest and attract lots of wildlife."

Bernie snorts.

"That's what we're trying to tell you, there's mice running about in there and before you know it, they'll be in your house."

"They're already in the house," I say. "We're doing an inter-species house-share."

They stop talking as if they've run out of words, their mouths slackening as if the lower parts of their faces have died abruptly. I take advantage of the word-gap to run into the house. I put the cake on the kitchen table and set out cups and saucers and cake plates, and the good bone-handled cutlery my great-aunt saved for the visitors who never came. Then I bring the sugar bowl to the table and fill the jug with milk.

The doorbell rings or, more, it sings, because it's Penelope and not official David. I open the door and Penelope swoops in. She seems to gather up the outside and bring it in with her. She drips words, pours sentences, gushes paragraphs on me, but the words have increased in cheer from the last visit and I'm glad. I bring her into the kitchen and introduce her to Lemonfish.

"Oh!" she says. "He's yellow."

"Yes, he's golder than most goldfish," I say, "he's the luckiest fish in the world."

I look at Lemonfish and think that might not be true. He's starting to grow a furry beard that gives him a certain fungal dignity, but he's missing patches of scales and looks like an unfinished jigsaw. Penelope taps his bowl.

"Yellow with a white topping," she says. "He's like a swimming lemon meringue pie."

She laughs, but I don't: I watch her in case she tries to eat him.

"Sit down," I say.

I must learn to say it so it doesn't sound like a teacher telling a class of schoolchildren to sit down. I put on the kettle. I don't know where to stand while the water is boiling so I turn to the kettle and watch it. I hear a rustling and a scratching and a general swoosh, and I know that Penelope must have sat down. She scrapes her throat and speaks in a thin voice.

"I feel I must apologise for unloading my past on you, Vivian. We've only known each other a short time, and it's probably too soon to inflict such secrets on you."

"Oh, it's no problem," I say, and I mean it—it's not a problem to not know her secret.

"It's good to let it all out," I add, but if she lets all her words out, her voicebox will collapse with the weight of them.

The kettle has boiled. I pour hot water into the teapot. "Thanks, Vivian, your friendship means a lot."

I almost drop the kettle. I am in a friendship. I am a friend and I have a friend and this friend will come to my funeral. "How old are you, Penelope?" I ask.

Penelope laughs.

"Guess."

"Sixty."

Her cheeks sink and her mouth drops. "Vivian, I'm only forty-nine."

"Oh."

I don't know what to say but I know I shouldn't point out all her wrinkles as my explanation.

"Are you sick at all?" I ask. "Any heart complaints? How's your diet?"

"What is this, Vivian, an inquisition?"

Penelope is older than me and, if she dies before me, she can't come to my funeral; this friendship would be pointless. She reaches for a slice of cake.

"No!" I shout. "Wouldn't you prefer a carrot?"

"No, thanks, the cake looks lovely."

"But think of the years a carrot will add to your life."

"Thank you for your concern, Vivian, but I'll just enjoy the cake if you don't mind."

The words are polite, but they are rimmed with steel. I don't want to risk this new friendship, so I let her have cake. I pour tea and we sit and talk about usual things, and after a while I start to resent Penelope's presence. I feel suffocated and vexed that I can't escape her to sit in my lone, twenty-tog silence. She is touching my things and taking up my time and diluting the house-smell with her own. The mirrors are snarling under their sheet-covers, the chairs are joining leg-forces and preparing for an almighty kicking, the bannister is silently plotting to smack her in the gut. The hands of the kitchen clock might stop time long enough to punch her in the nose. Penelope is my friend, but she holds my great-aunt's cup the wrong way, she sprawls in the chair with no heed for its feelings, she takes up more room in the kitchen than I do. I don't know how to end the visit; I don't know how to say, "Please go, go now, just leave." In films I've seen people yawn widely to hint at guests to go home, so I open my mouth long and wide but the yawn doesn't come.

"Is there something wrong with your jaw, Vivian?"

"No, I'm just seeing how wide it will open."

Penelope opens her mouth as wide as she can: it's a void of a mouth, like a voiceless scream. The teeth are chipped and muddy, and the smell from her mouth is like the smell from a month-old bin. I close my mouth and scrunch up my lips; Penelope does the same. This is better, the stench is contained. I run upstairs and come down with a tube of toothpaste, squeeze some onto my finger and put it in my mouth.

"You want some?"

I'm experimenting with cutting my sentence length and tossing out needless verbs. Penelope shakes her head.

"No, thanks, I like the taste of my mouth."

If she tastes what I smell, how could a mouth be so wrong?

"You have to go because I need to talk to my great-aunt in private," I say.

"I thought she was dead?"

"She is. I need to check which way she went."

Penelope's eyes widen.

"Can you commune with the dead?"

"I don't know, but my great-aunt shouted so much in her lifetime, the echo might still be in her ashes."

Penelope looks like she has unwrapped a train set on Christmas morning.

"I'd love to listen in if I could . . . ?"

"No, my great-aunt didn't like other people much."

Also, Penelope's breath would be enough to wake the dead, and that's the last thing I need. I get up from the chair and rub my temples.

"Ooh, are you starting to feel her presence?"

"Yes, I am," I say, "please hurry—if she senses you're here, she won't come."

Penelope gets up, grabs her coat, and rushes for the door. I follow her to the hall and say goodbye in as otherworldly a voice as I can muster. On the doorstep, she turns to me, her eyes big and curious.

"You will tell me, if you get through to her?"

"If the law of the spirit world permits."

I frown and set my mouth in a solemn grimace, then I close the door slowly. I walk into the living room, pick up the urn and give it a shake. I take a deep breath, and the house breathes out with me; it gives a judder, and shakes off the last of the intruder.

12

I WAKE UP in a frown. Things don't seem right already, and I have barely opened my eyes. It was a struggle of a night, one of those nights when I felt itchy all over: itchy arms, itchy scalp, even itchy breath. I coughed up a tickle all night. I can hear the wind whistling through the gaps where the walls join: the sound that a comb makes when I put a tissue over it and blow. I can't stay in my pyjamas today—they're marshmallow-coloured and would get mucky on the streets—so I peel them off and pull on some clothes from the floor and go downstairs.

"Morning, Lemonfish," I say.

He's looking more ragged by the day, and a dark thread of waste hangs from his underside. Maybe he needs more roughage. I cut up an apple and throw in small pieces, which he ignores. I tap on the bowl and shout: "Drink more water!" at him, but that would be like trying to cure human constipation with gulps of air. I put a pouch of chocolate buttons in my bag, a big pouch to share, along with a Greek drachma coin from my coin collection in the hoardroom, and leave the house. People seem to be crossing my path, and I have to swerve to avoid them. I press the thumb of each hand onto the side of its first finger and whisper "safe safe safe" to get me through the streets. I turn off Berkeley Road onto Eccles Street, because I need to walk on a street that's also a cake. At the junction with Dorset Street, I wait for the lights to turn red. The Eccles Street sign has been entirely blue-ed out, but, higher up on the same wall, the letters of an old green street sign haven't been greened out—either the leprechauns are seriously unmotivated, or their union doesn't allow them to climb ladders.

I need to go to the toilet so I head for Clerys on O'Connell Street. A scrawny grey-faced man is splayed against the home furnishings window, being searched by two guards. The man looks unsurprised, as if this is as normal as window shopping. I walk up the carpeted middle staircase—I might be an elegant rich lady going to a ball or a passenger on the *Titanic* staircase, and I struggle with the urge to wave daintily to my subjects. I join the queue for the toilet, trying to ignore the big mirror to my right. An elderly lady with a fresh hairstyle smiles shyly at herself in the mirror, and cups the bottom of her hair as if she's catching drips of water. When I'm finished, I walk back to North Earl Street and look at the carved stone face of a woman above the café on the corner. I call her Naomi because she looks like she deals mostly in vowels. Today she is calm, which is a good sign. I follow North Earl Street until it turns into Talbot Street, then I cross at Connolly Station and walk up Seville Place. On Seville Place I think of orange marmalade, and on Dawson Street I think of damson jam; maybe the streets should be twinned in a cross-river fruit-preserve initiative.

When I reach the church, I turn left onto Ferryman's Crossing. The houses have pale tops like pebbledash shirts and orange bottoms like brick skirts. I need to find Charon, the ferryman in the Greek myth, who brought dead people across the River Styx to Hades, the Otherworld. I'm not dead, but if I stay very still, I could pass for a corpse. The Liffey is not the Styx, but I don't want to travel to ancient Greece—crossing so many time zones would make for unbearable travel sickness. I walk to the end of the street, looking into the porches of the houses for oars, but the street ends in a wall topped by a railing, the river on the other side. I put the drachma in my mouth: it tastes thinly metallic, like blood when I bite my tongue. I look out over the railings at the tall grey office buildings and wonder if they are in Hades. A man walks by with a dog.

"Are you looking for something, love?"

"I'm looking for Charon."

My words come out thick and spitty with the coin in my mouth.

"Sharon Larkin or Sharon Eliot?"

"A different Charon," I say.

The dog is sticking its nose between my legs quite strenuously, and I push it back.

"He likes you," the man says.

"I'd prefer if he didn't like me so much," I say.

I cover my legs with my hands and the dog starts licking them. I say goodbye to the man, and walk back down Ferrymans Crossing. A taxi is parked outside one of the houses, and a man comes out and walks over to it. Maybe this is a motorised, land-based version of Charon.

"Are you a taxi driver?"

The coin clogs my palate and my tongue stumbles over the "X."

"Yeah, why?"

"Could you drive me over the river?"

"Alright, where to?"

"Just over to the other side. Or maybe over and back a few times."

"Okay," he says. "Different bridges?"

"Yes, there's more chance of it happening then."

The coin clacks against my teeth. I have to clench my jaw to form words, but they come out tight and distorted.

"Of what happening?"

"Of me finding my way back."

"Are you Dorothy or what?"

"Not today," I say. "I tried looking for the Yellow Brick Road, and also Emerald Street and the Emerald Palace, but I had no luck."

The man looks at me as if I'm an interesting disease and shakes his head slowly.

"Right," he says, "hop in."

He sticks his fingers into his belt loops, yanks up his jeans, walks around to the driver's side and opens the door. I stand on one leg and hop the few steps to the car because, if this is Charon, it's important that I follow his instructions exactly.

"Is your leg hurt?"

"No, you said to hop in."

"Jaysus," he says, "I've a right genius here."

I look at the name on his identity card on the dashboard: it's Charlie Larkin. I'm glad he's Charlie and not Charles, because a middle "I" is more friendly than a final "S."

"Do you know Charon?" I ask.

"The missus is called Sharon," he says. "Why?"

He starts the car.

"Wait!" I say. "Does Sharon want to come too?"

Spit wells up in my mouth every time I say Sharon. Charlie turns around in his seat.

"Are you for real?"

"Yes, Sharon can sit with you in the passenger seat and I'll sit back here, and we can all drive over the bridges together."

He looks at me like there's something behind my eyes that I don't know about.

"I'll pay you double fare, for two drivers."

He turns back to the steering wheel and stops the engine. "Wait here."

He gets out of the car and walks back into the house. I'm so excited I could burst out of my face. A woman is standing by the window looking out at me. I wave, but she looks cross and doesn't wave back. I know from watching television with the sound turned down that they're arguing, because her mouth is opening wide and her lips are moving quickly and her face is jutting forward. She disappears from the window, Charlie comes out of the house, and she follows, slamming the front door behind her. Charlie walks around to the driver's seat and she gets in the passenger side. I lean forward between the seats.

"Hello, Sharon, thank you for coming on the journey."

My jaw is not moving as fast as I need it to and the coin goes *clack clack clack* against my teeth. Sharon stares at me with an expression that contains a menace of question marks, and lets out a sigh the length of a caterpillar. Charlie starts the car.

"Alright to start with the Eastlink?"

"Yes, thanks."

Sharon stares out the side window even though the view is

better from the front. She's wasting the front seat but I don't want to make her angrier by asking to swap. I take out the pouch of chocolate buttons, open it, and hold it through the gap in the seats.

"But-tons?"

The coin shifts in my mouth and it comes out like two separate words.

"No, thanks," says Charlie.

Sharon just stares out the window. We turn onto Seville Place and head for the river. I sit back content because I'm going for a spin with two adults in charge and I have chocolate in my hand. I take out the drachma and stuff some buttons into my mouth and chew them quickly before we hit a bridge. Sharon hasn't talked yet but I know how to get her to talk, I've read the covers of women's magazines in the shops.

"What's your favourite hair colour, Sharon?" I ask.

She keeps staring out the window and shakes her head and mutters something short that ends in "*Christ.*"

"I like clothes," I say. "I like jumpers best because they are warmest and cover the most area but cardigans come second."

"Sharon, you like clothes too, don't you," Charlie says, and there's a quiet tightness in his voice. She turns her head slowly to me.

"Yeah, I like clothes."

Her sentence changes the situation to an almost friendship, even though her voice sounds like jagged rocks.

"It's the gaps between the buttons that let in the cold," I say. "That's why cardigans come second to jumpers."

"Got it," she says.

Charlie starts talking about the bridges he can drive over and the ones he can't and the ones he can drive south over but not north and the ones he can drive north over but not south: the Eastlink Toll bridge, Samuel Beckett Bridge, Talbot Memorial Bridge, Butt Bridge, O'Connell Bridge, Grattan Bridge, O'Donovan Rossa Bridge, Father Mathew Bridge, James Joyce Bridge, Rory O'More Bridge, Frank Sherwin Bridge, Islandbridge.

His list spans the city, and I realise I don't know many of the people the bridges are named for. A bridge is currently being built for the tram, and I have half a hope it will be named after me if I do something noble and grand, but I must do it quickly.

When I've swallowed all the chocolate, I put the coin back in my mouth. It's not so bad when it tastes of chocolate.

"Sharon," I say (because she likes clothes), "if I swallowed a whole bag of chocolate buttons, would it be like swallowing one-fifth of a chocolate cardigan?"

Charlie snorts. Sharon turns fully around in her seat to look at me, and this time she is an inch from a smile.

"Are you taking the piss?" she asks, but her voice is not like rocks any more, it's like pebbles, pebbles that have been washed smooth on a lakeshore.

"I don't think so," I say, and now the two of them laugh. We cross the first bridge and I close my eyes, because this is what you do when you make a wish.

"Charlie?"

"Yeah?"

He looks at me in the mirror.

"Which side of the river would you say is earth and which would you say is Hades?"

"Hades?"

"Yeah, Hades, the Underworld."

"Oh, well there's dodgy goings-on both sides of the river, I'd say there's parts of the criminal underworld everywhere."

"Oh, okay."

I look out the window. We're on the south quays about to cross another bridge back to the Northside. It would help if I knew in which direction I should be wishing the hardest. I close my eyes, but when we turn left onto the north quays, I open my eyes and look at my arms and my legs— they haven't changed. We continue over and back across the Liffey, making a shape like a wide-toothed comb. I squeeze my eyes shut for each crossing, but there is no change. When we cross Islandbridge, the final bridge, I feel sad that we haven't found the portal to the Underworld, but happy that we've had a nice trip. I direct Charlie back to my road off the North Circular.

"Ah, the Norrier," he says.

"The what?"

"The North Circular, it's known as The Norrier."

"Oh, does that make me a Norrierer? Maybe an honorary Norrierer if I wasn't born here. 'Honorary Norrierer honorary Norrierer honorary Norrierer,'" I say, until my tongue twists on the coin and there is too much spit to continue. Sharon shakes her head. When he pulls up outside my house, Charlie names the price of the trip. I reach into my bag and pull out my purse but (*oh no*), there are only small coins. I empty them out onto my hand, take the coin out of my mouth, add it to the pile on my palm and push my hand between the seats.

"Would you take this much euro and a wet drachma?"

Charlie and Sharon look at each other. Before they can respond with some words that would ruin our nice afternoon, I say, "Only joking," because that would be a funny joke, then I say, "Please come in and I'll get you the money."

They look at each other again. Sharon bursts open her car door. "Come on, Charlie."

I get out of the car and they follow me into the front garden and I feel so proud that I have visitors, that I'm leading people instead of following so I say very loudly for Mary's and Bernie's ears, "Please follow me. I hope you enjoy your visit."

I open the door and stand back to let them in. They come in slow and hesitant, like they're being pulled from behind by strings.

"Come into the living room."

I sweep my arm forwards but now my arm is sticking straight out from my body and I don't know how to lower it casually, so I keep it stuck out in front of me.

"Do sit down," I say, because I've heard this on *Fawlty Towers* and it sounds welcoming. Charlie and Sharon don't look welcomed, though—they look like they've just found out their child has a disease.

"Do you have any diseased children?" I ask.

People always enquire about the health of other people's children. Charlie makes a noise like a bark and says, "Three children, two grandchildren, no diseases. Now love, have you got the fare?"

"Yes, yes, would you like a cup of tea first?"

"No, thanks, I've got to get back to work. So that's—"

He repeats the amount I owe him. The neighbours won't think it's a proper visit unless I keep them for at least a quarter of an hour, so I say: "You can choose your favourite chair and sit in it, but you might have to squeeze through or climb over other chairs to get to the ones at the back."

Charlie clears his throat and yanks up his jeans again. He looks like he's about to make a funeral speech, so I clear my throat too.

"Could you both turn around and close your eyes?"

"What?"

"I need to go to my secret hiding place and I don't want you to see where it is."

Sharon growls. They have both turned into dogs with their noises.

"For fuck's sake, are you going to get the fuckin money or what?"

They stare at me as if they want to peel off my skin and put it in a scrapbook.

"Alright," Charlie says, with a sigh as long as November. "Come on, Sharon, let's turn around."

"And close your eyes?"

"And close our eyes."

They both turn and, when I'm sure that they're not peeking, I tiptoe to the bookshelf and take down *Grimm's Fairytales*. I open it at the Hansel and Gretel story, on the page where the woodcutter and his wife leave the children in the forest because they can't afford to feed them. I keep money between those pages so that the woodcutter can buy food for his family and Hansel and Gretel will be safe from the witch's oven.

"Okay, you can say 'ready *or not*' now!"

"What?"

"We're playing hide-and-seek and you're both on," I say. "I'm ready to be caught now."

"How about you just give me the fare and we'll head on."

I hand Charlie the money, and they both walk quickly into

the hall. I am considering the best way to say goodbye—whether handshakes would be more appropriate than a wave, whether I should take both of their phone numbers so as not to offend one of them—but Sharon has the door opened and they're wedged together in the doorway in their rush to get out. Once he's outside, Charlie waves and says, "Cheerio, love." I wave and close the door behind them slowly. If they have to leave so quickly, I'm glad it's while calling the name of a cereal. Next time I say goodbye to someone, I will end with a shout of "Cornflakes" or "Rice Krispies"—or "All-Bran"—to a sturdy aunt. I sit down on the dark green patterned armchair and take off my shoes and socks and rub my bare feet against each other; this feels like a ritual performed at the end of a journey. The tops of my feet are butter-soft, but the soles are leathery, like one of those bath sponges with a soft yellow body and a green scouring base. I peel open the map of Dublin and plot today's route, just the part where I walked to Ferryman's Crossing, because Charlie might want to plot the drive on his own map, and it's really not mine to draw. Today I walked the ECG of a patient who flatlined briefly, before rallying into a healthy peak.

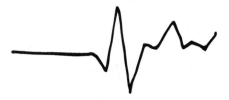

13

ARLY ON MAY Day morning, I take yesterday's clothes off the floor (April's clothes), turn them inside out to appease the fairies and put them on. I'm going to visit the hidden pagan well under the Nassau Street entrance to Trinity College. My heart threatens to rise up my gullet with excitement. The idea of eating a full breakfast is like trying to climb a ladder with missing rungs; instead, I sup milk from the carton and eat three chocolate biscuits. I eat things in threes and sevens because that third biscuit or seventh slice of bread could have transformative powers, even though this sometimes means eating more than I want. I let myself out of the house quietly, tiptoe past Bernie's and sprint for the main road. A woman wearing a yellow raincoat hands out free newspapers at Phibsborough cross-roads. I take one and glance through the pictures as I walk. There are men in football jerseys, women in dark headscarves weeping and holding photos of children, a man with his head facing the ground being led away by policemen, a row of women in what seems to be a smiling competition and a crowd of people with scarves over their mouths being hosed by police. The news is either too good or too bad, so I throw the paper in the bin and walk down the North Circular Road. I pass the hospital on the right and the prison on the left and try to decide which I'd rather be: a patient or a prisoner. If I was either, I would read so many books that my eyeballs would bulge out of my head. Just before the junction with Dorset Street, I pass the cul-de-sac with a grotto of the Virgin Mary. Mary is painted white and blue like a concrete seaside. I give her a wave as I pass—it is one of her feast days after all—but she doesn't wave back. I turn onto Dorset Street and then swing left onto North Frederick Street. People are walking quickly to work, swinging their arms. Some of them clutch coffee cups as if these cups hold their beating hearts, as if their careers depend on how tightly they hold these cups: these cups must contain the secret to the world. As I walk down Westmoreland Street, the tang of coffee seeps from a glass-walled café. I push the door and join the queue. When it's my turn, I say, "Coffee to take away, please."

"Would you like . . ." He lists out coffees that sound like Italian movie stars or cars but they mean nothing to me. I point at the frothy coffee the girl before me is getting.

"Would you like . . ." Now he lists the sizes and I recognise "tall," so I say, "Tall, please." I am sweating Italian vowels now, picturing the kettle at home and the jar of instant coffee and the carton of milk and simplicity.

"What's your name?"

"My name?"

"To put on the cup," he smiles, holding his pen expectantly.

"Cuthbert," I say.

He frowns, but writes the name on the cup anyway. The noise and vibrations from the machine are primal, it feels like my belly has been sliced open and filled with ramming magnets, but other people don't seem to notice. When the man calls, "Cuthbert," I take my coffee and leave, watching how the girl in front of me holds her cup. I'm holding mine outstretched like it's on fire, so I pull it closer and walk towards College Green.

A tall man across the road leans so far into a cash machine to see the screen, he has curled himself into a candy cane. He looks like he's trying to climb into the screen; maybe he's looking for his way back, too. I turn onto Nassau Street and head to the side entrance of the college. I climb onto the step and flatten myself against the railings, then I look down but I can see nothing. If this is my portal, then surely I will be shrunk and given wings. I close my eyes, but when I open them, nothing has changed. I'm supposed to walk sun-wise around the well on May Day, but I can't get down to it. I walk to the nearest clothes shop, pick out the cheapest item on a hanger and take it to the till. I ask to keep the hanger, and then bring it back to the college entrance, throwing the oversized nightie in a nearby bin. The hanger is plastic—it will not be as good at divining as metal or wood, but I will make do. I stand at the railings and hold the hanger from the two ends in front of me. I wait, but the metal question mark doesn't tip down; either there's no water or I don't have the gift.

Tourists stream by me in bright raincoats. Some are large and wide and look like they have spent their waking hours eating. They all have the same expression: a hopeful, open expression that makes me want to dupe them, or hope that someone else will dupe them. The coffee is giving me bitter thoughts, as well as a thumping heartbeat and a raring to go, so I walk up Nassau Street and turn onto Kildare Street. I head to the National Museum, because sometimes nothing will do but to walk on a mosaic floor. I sit on a bench outside the museum to finish my coffee. At Leinster House, a man with a microphone is interviewing a politician in a suit. The politician has a round belly perched on skinny leg-stalks: from this angle he looks like a capital "P." I can't hear what he's saying from here so I add the words myself: "Implementing procedures . . . devising strategies . . . putting in place additional resources . . . going forward . . . facilitating job creation . . ." When I get bored of official language I imagine that the politician is talking about implanting puppies with duck genes so that they grow wings and develop a quack-bark, or funding research into the production of colour-changing carrots, or making it compulsory for school canteens to serve students two portions of sweets a day. I drop my empty cup in the bin and walk into the museum, heading straight for the bog bodies.

My favourite is the Clonycavan Man, who, the caption says, was found in a bog between the ancient kingdoms of Brega and Mide. It's that space between kingdoms where transformation occurs, that thin place that I am trying to find. I walk into the cubby to look at Clony. Only his head and torso remain, covered in mottled leathery skin, like cured animal hide. He has an upcombed Mohawk of gelled red hair, a bashed-up nose as if he was involved in some pre-Christian fisticuffs, and a tuft of hair under the chin, a *smigín*, my great-aunt would have called it. There is a single white tooth in his open mouth and a hole between the eyes. I sit facing him, cut off from the rest of the museum in the cubby, and listen hard, but I can't hear a syllable from two thousand years ago. I whisper, "Bye, Clony," blow him a small dry kiss and walk out of the room—I don't visit the other bog bodies in case he gets jealous. A small wooden door is almost hidden between two pillars at the bottom of a spiral staircase. The door is arched at the top and has a brass knob in the middle and requires a secret knock and a password to enter; I presume that's where the dragon guards the hoard of gold so precious it cannot be displayed.

I climb the staircase that leads to Ancient Egypt, closing my eyes and making a wish as I pass through the golden gate at the top, just in case. In the Ancient Egypt room, the mummies look placid and unquestioning, one of them looks surprised to be dead. I wonder if they get on well with the bog bodies or if there's too much of an age gap. I examine display cases of jewels and scarab beetles in Sinai turquoise—a turquoise the hiss of a boiling sea, a turquoise so smug it could be the only colour on earth—and go back downstairs to the main hall. A porter is putting chat on two American girls who look at each other and giggle. When the girls leave, I edge closer. He looks in my direction but he doesn't seem to see me. No matter, he will hear my voice.

"Hard to believe how old those bog bodies are, huh?"

I have learnt "huh" from American television programmes; I like to vary it with my "wha's."

"Yeah, they're old alright," he mutters, and barely makes eye contact before moving off. I'm pleased that I've said my sentence, but it could have gone better. Clonycavan Man would have been nicer to talk to. I walk around the gold pieces and write their names in my notebook, in case my next friend is a tycoon with a taste for old treasures: "Gold Dress Fastener, Torc, Gorget, Ring-Money, Bulla, Lunula, Lock-Ring, Ear Spool, Sun Disc, Basket Earrings, Folded Rod, Armlet, Beads, Bracelet, Sunflower-Pin, Collar, Neck Ring, Sleeve Fastener, Nine Hollow Gold Balls."

When my eyeballs are brimming with gold and I'm beginning to lose sight of whether gold is a good or a bad thing, I make for the carved stone head from Corleck, County Cavan, which sounds like an archaeological tongue twister. It's a whole other heap of "C"s in Irish: *ceann cloiche snoite*. I would like *snoite* to be a word in the English language. It would be pronounced "snuteh," and it would mean a snooty person in a snit. The head has three faces: one face looks placid, one looks gormless, one is planning cruel mischief. There's something frightening about three noses on one face. One of the mouths has a pencil-top-shaped hole in it, which must be where the magic spills out. I walk around the stone head seven times, making a wish on the seventh turn, but nothing happens. If I made the wrong wish, I could grow a beard instead of wings, or if it was raining when I made the wish, I might turn into a mermaid.

I leave the museum and head to College Green. I cross the street to the island with the disused public toilets, which might be as enchanted a water source on May Day as a holy well. There are two entrances with steps leading underground. The steps are covered with dead leaves, empty crisp packets, cigarette butts and half a bottle of cola. The toilets are surrounded by iron railings and padlocked iron gates. An electrical box stands on the western end, with a picture of a ballerina crossing her legs in a pirouette. It looks like she needs to go to the toilet. There's a strong smell of piss; I'm not sure if it's recent or if it's the ghostly smell of pisses past or if the ballerina hasn't succeeded in holding it in. I walk sun-wise around the toilets three times and toss some coins down the steps, but I don't shut my eyes because I'm on the edge of a traffic island in the middle of a busy street, and being flattened by a bus is a miserable way of getting to the otherworld. I cross the road, passing the hotel that used to be a bank, and stop to look in the window of the Irish Yeast Company. There are silver cake trays and cake decorations and three-tiered polystyrene wedding cakes with sun-faded figurine couples on top. Miss Havisham must haunt this shop by night. I walk north, and cross O'Connell Bridge. I look around O'Connell Street for a makeshift maypole, but the bus-stop poles are too yellow, and the road-sign poles are too grey. I head down Dorset Street, and pass a barber shop with a red-and-white pole: it's short and stumpy but it's the right colours. The pole hangs above my head, so I jump and wave my arms in a horseshoe shape around the pole. The barber and the man under the scissors stare out the window at me. I do three more jumps, giddy jumps, and shout "Happy May-Day!" before walking home. I have one last tradition to try.

I bring a bundle of cardboard packaging and old newspapers out to the back garden, pile them in a heap and set it alight. I'm supposed to lead a cow through the flames but I have no cow, so I take some beef burgers out of the freezer—dead minced cow will have to do. When the first flames appear I stand back, hold a burger in each hand and take a running leap over the fire. Nothing happens. I jump over the fire three times, then seven times, then I'm wondering whether to do another three jumps and whether the unluckiness of thirteen is cancelled out by May Day, when Mary's head appears over the wall.

"What are you doing, Vivian?"

I fling the burgers into the fire.

"I'm having a small barbecue."

"Why are you jumping over the fire?"

"I'm training to be a firefighter," I say. "I'm going to practice carrying a hose next."

She narrows her eyes.

"Is everything alright?"

"Everything's alright," I say.

Mary looks at me again and shakes her head slowly before moving off. The flames of my bonfire have almost died so I go inside and take off my shoes and socks. My feet are white and soggy, they look bare and uncooked. I sniff one of my socks: it is hard and crisp and smells of processed cheese, which makes me think of how cheese provokes dreams, possibly the kind of dreams that reveal a singular truth. It's nowhere near bedtime, but I make for the fridge and hack into the block of cheese. I eat as I cut and soon I have eaten it all. I need to sleep immediately after the cheese but it's barely evening, so I resort to chemical means. I go to the medicine cabinet in the bathroom and put three of my great-aunt's sleeping pills into my mouth. They taste bitter and nasty. Then I cup my hand and scoop some water from the tap and swallow them. I blink three times, but my eyes stay open. I go downstairs and put on the television. I can't decide which chair to sit in—they're all facing me with their hands up, hissing, "Teacher teacher pick me," but it's too hard to choose, so I stand in front of the television and watch a nature programme about a shark. The screen shows an ocean scene, with fish darting every which way to escape the shark. When the fish start to slow down and the shark stops swimming, I know this isn't right; if sharks stop swimming, they will die. I turn away from the television and now the floor is up and the ceiling is down and my head is awhirl like the ocean. I shuffle to the stairs and start to climb. There are sacks of potatoes tied to my ankles dragging them down and my head is in bogland sludge. My hand tries to connect with the banister, but the banister moves and, oh look, somebody else's hand has been attached to my body. I lean forward and put my head on a step because I just need to rest awhile . . .

I WAKE UP, but it feels more like waking down. I was on top of a steep mountain in my dream, looking down and knowing in my stomach that I would fall. I feel tired, so, so tired, as if I spent the night climbing the mountain but my head doesn't remember the climb, only my body does. I look around. I'm sprawled the length of six steps on the stairs. I need to do something; I can't figure out exactly what that something is, but it needs to be done right now. When I stand up, the walls wash over me and the chairs on the landing swirl around to greet me. I try to wave at them, but my arm is numb. I feel a pressure in my lower belly and realise that I need to go to the toilet. I walk heavy-legged to the bathroom, and go to the toilet. The mirror is covered in a white sheet, so I run my hands over my face and find puffy eyes with more lid than ball, and a carpet dent on my right cheek. My mind is afug. I need some kind of clarity elixir, so I go downstairs and take a bottle of cola from the drinks cupboard. I pour it into a glass, take some frozen peas from the freezer and plip the peas into the cola.

I sit on the brown swivel chair in the living room and drink, looking at the bookshelves; there might be a book in there that could tell me the world. The colours of the spines are faded into muddy reds and greens and browns, like autumn on a shelf. I take down the copy of Irish Mythology. The cover is moss green, a few shades darker than the spine. I start to read the book, but it's tough going. The print is small and tightly packed, as if paragraphs hadn't been invented when the book was written. I sift through the pages until I come to "The Children of Lir." I like this story because it's short and simple, and there are chocolates named after them.

King Lir had four young children called Fionnuala, Aodh, Fiachra, and Conn. Their new stepmother, Aoife, grew jealous of the love their father bore them and ordered her servant to kill them, but the servant refused. Aoife did not have the courage to kill them herself, so she used her magic to turn the children into swans. As swans, the children were condemned to spend 300 years on Lough Derravaragh, 300 years in the Sea of Moyle, and 300 years on the waters of Erris near Inishglora. Until Saint Patrick came to Ireland, and until they heard the Christian bell, they would not be changed back into human form.

I close my eyes and swivel in the chair. If I find four adult swans and bring them to a church bell, they could be returned to human form and I could be returned to fairy form. I stand up. I don't have to get dressed because I slept in my clothes, and there's a warm soft feeling of day-old cloth against my skin. I look in the kitchen cupboards and find half a chocolate Swiss roll with my toothmarks on one end—I like to pick up a Swiss roll and eat it like a hot dog so that I don't have to wash a plate or knife. Swans like bread, and if they like bread, they'll love cake. I put the cake in a brown paper bag, pack it into my handbag with my notebook and pen and leave the house. I pull the door softly behind me to get away unheeded and take the road at a run, but my head is eight steps behind, banging slow and thuddish.

I walk through Phibsborough to Crossguns Bridge and turn left onto the canal bank. I watch the gush of the water in the locks until my bladder starts to complain, then I walk west along the canal. The children of Lir heard St. Patrick's bell and were transformed, but the only St. Patrick's bell I know of is the one at St. Patrick's Cathedral in town. I don't know how to get my swans to follow me into town, across the Liffey and up the hill to St. Patrick's, and I fear these Royal Canal swans will be mocked by the Liffey swans if their accents or feather-styles are different. A shopping trolley half-sunk in the canal looks like a huge silver weed with water flowing through the holes. Empty cans of beer and cider bob about the surface. Along the banks, there are patches of burnt grass scattered with coloured strips of wire. A black plastic bag tied to a tree puffs up like a sailboat in mourning, and a rat scuttles along the bank and drops (plop) into the water. There are patches of white ahead, like chunks of cloud on the surface of the canal, and I make for them. The swans are parked near a bridge—maybe they too like edges and corners and chair cushions over their heads. I break off a piece of cake and throw it to them.

"Hello!" I say, "Hello, Fionnuala, Aodh, Fiachra and Conn."

There are only three swans, but I say all their names because I don't know which one is missing. One of the swans gazes at me so I address it.

"Fionnuala, if you come with me and eat cake, you'll change back into humans."

Fionnuala swims off to join her brothers. I throw more cake, and one of them beaks at it. This must be Fionnuala because any friend of mine is also a friend of cake. I throw more pieces in a trail leading to the canal bank, but the swans ignore me and float off in the other direction. I sit on the damp bank and eat the rest of it myself. The water is so still it makes me think of the lines from that poem I studied in school:

> *O commemorate me where there is water;*
> *Canal water, preferably, so stilly*
> *Greeny*

I would also like to be commemorated where there is water, but I'd prefer seawater that's roughy bluey, with fewer shopping trolleys and rude swans.

I walk back down the canal towards Drumcondra, and sit beside the statue of the poet on the bench. The statue is mottled with shapes the size and colour of flattened slugs, which, it seems when I try to rub them off, the sculptor did on purpose. The poet is staring at the statue of a pigeon over my shoulder, but he sets me on edge because he seems to be staring straight at me.

"What?" I ask him. "What do you *want*?"

I get up and walk towards the bus stop on Dorset Street, my head still soupy from the sleeping pills, my legs in glue. When the bus comes, I sit near the back and listen to two teenage girls behind me.

"Did you hear Amy Credden's pregnant?"

"No?"

"Yeah, and she's depressed."

"Why's she depressed?"

"She thinks she's too old to have a baby."

"What age is she?"

"Nineteen."

"Oh."

They drop into silence after the "oh," as if nineteen is so far in the future, it's beyond contemplation. I try to remember being a teenager but all that comes to mind is hand-me-down school uniforms with my name already sewn on them, faded from so many washings. I get off the bus on Dame Street, and turn into Dublin Castle at Palace Street. I pass the Sick & Indigent Roomkeepers Society, and wonder if "indigent" means a native or annoyed, or a native who's annoyed. I like this street; there are only two buildings facing it, I can take it all in in an eyeful. I cut through the castle, and come out the Ship Street Gate. An arch on my right leads to the Castle Steps, which look like they should be taken in leaps and bounds. A plaque states that: ". . . about 100 feet NW of this spot it is reputed that . . ." Jonathan Swift was born. I want to change the "about" to an "exactly," and the "reputed" to a "known." I can't add such uncertainties to a notebook of certainties.

I head towards Bride Street, and read a plaque on a building about a ragman who used to give goldfish to children in exchange for their parents' clothes, which the children took on the sly. I would have given away my parents' clothes for a goldfish in a jam jar; I would have given away my parents. I turn onto Bull Alley Street and into St. Patrick's Park. To the left of the entrance is a crescent-shaped stone outline containing clumps of blue and white flowers, non-committal kind of flowers that look like they were planted with indifference and a shrug. A small plaque amongst the stones reads: "Near here is the reputed site of the well where St. Patrick baptised many local inhabitants in the 5th century AD." The "near" is as vague as the "about" in the Jonathan Swift plaque, and the scourge of "reputed" strikes again: more uncertainty that can't be noted. A large sign states that: "Tradition has it that Saint Patrick baptised the first Irish Christians in a well, situated here in St. Patrick's Park, with water from the River Poddle, which still flows underground." All these "tradition has its" and "reputeds" and "near heres" are unsettling my sense of certainty. The clock on the cathedral clock tower tells the right time in gold numerals, which goes some ways towards settling me, and I walk through the park, looking at the stone heads carved into St. Patrick's Cathedral. A head in a curled ruff like an unbroken pencil paring makes stony eye contact with me. He looks like a George; George has very high standards and no sense of humour, but at least he's fair in judgement. Against one wall of the cathedral there's a concrete pouch of a house, about knee-high to a tall man, with a pointed roof and a black padlocked door. I wait for something or someone to come out of this little house, but nothing happens, so I follow the path of the park to the far side, and read the old plaques stating park rules.

"A person shall not consume intoxicating liquor or inhale, inject or absorb controlled drugs or solvents."

I'm impressed by the glut of verbs, and try to imagine how someone would absorb a drug, but all I can picture is a woman reading the word "DRUG" written in large letters on the page of a book, or a man bathing in drugged water, which seeps through his pores. I move on to the next sign: "Where a dog fouls a public place, the person in charge of the dog must remove the faeces immediately." I like the certainty of these words, there is no dithering behind vague words for the sake of politeness. I take out my notebook and write out the words from the sign. A herd of tourists gathers around me. One of them reads aloud the sign in accented English, stops reading, and looks at me and my notebook. The tourists' feet waver, and they drift away from my sign to find the plaques of famous writers along the park's edges. I return to the buried well. It's so near to a busy street with traffic vibrations that I haven't a hope of feeling the pull of the Poddle beneath. I leave the park and walk back into town, sniffing the air. There is a fierce bang of hops from the Guinness factory, a smell somewhere between meat and toffee that gives me a hunger but I don't know what for. I cross Dame Street and head down Cow's Lane into Temple Bar, stopping in a souvenir shop to buy a box of Lir chocolates. I stand outside the shop, peel off the wrapping and stuff the chocolates in threes into my mouth. There are eight chocolates in the box, but eating the last two would cancel out the magic of the six I just ate. I walk down the cobbles and turn into Merchant's Arch. A man is sitting under the arch, with a blanket on his knees and a paper cup of coins at his feet.

"Spare change for a hostel?"

"No change," I say, "but here's two chocolates."

I hand them to him and he mutters a thanks and examines the box.

I walk up the quays towards O'Connell Bridge, and turn onto O'Connell Street. A bus that will take me some ways home is pulling into a stop, so I get on. We veer left at the top of O'Connell Street, passing the theatre that used to be a cinema and is currently hosting an exhibition of dead bodies in living poses. A man is pissing against the railings between this building and the maternity hospital, possibly in an attempt to destroy the divide between birth and death. We pull into a stop on Parnell Square, opposite the maternity hospital. Two women with huge bellies stand outside the glass doors, sucking on cigarettes as if they're oxygen tanks. High on the walls above the doors, the remains of unknown words read "ERFTE PLIVET" in huge letters. If I had a baby in this hospital, I'd call it Erfte Plivet. The "T" in "ERFTE" is hanging upside down, which makes it difficult to pronounce, and the capital "I" in "PLIVET" could be a small "I," but a vowel in third place is easier to pronounce than a consonant. I believe that capital "I" is a confusion of a letter, and should be given a top-dot to differentiate it from its lower-case counterpart, but who is in charge of deciding such things? Do upper-case letters feel superior to lower-case letters? Which would come off best in a game of thumb wrestling? The uppercase letters have pointed edges and size on their side, but their lower-case rivals are bendy with attitude. The bus rounds the Black Church and turns right. The legend requires a person to walk three times anticlockwise around the church at midnight to summon the Devil, but it's unclear whether a bus semi-circling it once in daylight has the same effect. We pass Devlin Terrace: the street sign is blue-ed out to read "IN TACE," which sounds like the name of a company that supplies office stationery or slick advertisements. When I get home, I unfurl the map on the kitchen table and run a pencil through my adventures. Today's routes have more bus journeys than walks, so I leave their mapping to the drivers themselves, and add nothing to the traced shapes lining the kitchen table.

14

THE SKY IS dark with a lump of rain in it; this is good. There will be fewer people in today's thin places. I'm going to visit the National Botanic Gardens and Glasnevin Cemetery, but "cemetery" sounds too clean and functional—I prefer the vague foggy sound of "graveyard." I make a flask of coffee and let myself quietly out of the house. I walk through Phibsborough, following the curve of the road around to Glasnevin. When the watchtower looms into view, I look for Rapunzel at its window, a mummified Rapunzel with snakes for hair and rats for eyes, but not even a tormented squint conjures her into being. I pass a woman selling flowers at the entrance to the cemetery. The flowers look so perfect, packed together in their buckets. I consider getting some, but taking just one bunch would be like trying to separate puppy brothers, and buying flowers from a graveyard for personal use could put the hex of death on me. I walk to the old part of the cemetery and look at the headstones. Every dead person is "Dearly Beloved" or "Sadly Missed," but that can't be true for all of them; death brings out the worst of lies. I weave through the headstones, imagining what kinds of lives these people really had. Maybe

Edward Neary beat his wife and Mrs. Neary doesn't sadly miss the beatings. Mrs. Honor Cole might have been dearly beloved not only by her husband, but by a stream of other men too. One tombstone holds an upper-case bellow of a prayer: "MERCY JESUS MERCY." I'd like to know what badness this man did, or thought he did, in his lifetime. I pass the grave of Alphonse Hazard, who, with a name like that, had to have been a stunt double in Hollywood. I write his name in my notebook, along with any other names from tombstones that look like they could form a pattern. Several of the larger graves have iron cages around them; I don't know if this is to keep the dead in or the living out. Some of the tombstones on a grassy slope are cracked or knocked flat, the aftermath of a violent fight among the dead. Near them, a huddle of tombstones slants backwards and forward, like a chatter of people leaning back in their chairs saying, "Wait till you hear, c'mere till I tell you."

I walk up the slope towards the fresher graves. The flowers lining the path droop as if they were looking for their dead friends under the soil. The only sounds are the distant *vrum* of traffic and the rustle of trees in the wind and a bird with a chirp like the creak of a swing. I come upon a muted fuss some ways off the path: a new body is moving in. I sneak up slowly and hide behind a tree. An elderly woman stands at the open-mouthed grave, flanked by two younger women. The priest calls out a drone of words, and the women look at the coffin and cry. I didn't cry when my father died; I cried while he was alive. I leave the mourners and make a wide skirt around the row where my parents are buried—my sister is the only loving daughter on that tombstone. I walk past the famous dead to-wards the office to buy my plot. Buying a plot sounds like buying my story: I wish I could buy a story-plot to tell me what action to take next. A black clock with gold numbering above the door tells the wrong time; it's out by an hour and eighteen minutes. I go up to the woman behind the counter. She smells like a washed version of my great-aunt.

"Excuse me," I say, "how much does a plot cost?"

"Here," she says, "have a look at the price list."

She hands me a page. It costs €2,030 for a double plot.

"Can I borrow a pen?" I ask.

She gives me a pen, and I write "2030 ÷ 2 = 1015." The division sign is so perfect and symmetrical, it's a joy to write. I write the percentage sign next to the division sign "÷, %," it looks like its poor slanted cousin.

"Don't you love it?" I ask.

"Love what?"

She eyes my sums with wary in her voice.

"The division sign," I say. "It looks like a man trying to give a straight-armed hug to another man. Maybe he has unbendable elbows. What does it look like to you?"

"Like a division sign," she says, quietly. "Now how can I help you?"

"I'd like to buy a single plot for €1,015."

"It's €2,030 for a double, that's the cheapest."

Her voice is firm now that we are back on grave soil.

"But I'm going to be buried alone. This is like a single supplement, even when I'm dead."

She sighs from her belly and hands me a card with a name and phone number on it.

"You can discuss this further with my manager."

"Okay," I say.

I point to the price for three plots on the pricelist.

"If it's €2,030 for two burials and €2,680 for three, that's half a corpse thrown in for free. Do you think I could ask Penelope and David to be buried with me? I've only met David once and Penelope three times."

The woman's face slackens a little.

"Have you no family that you'd like to share your final resting place with?"

"I have a sister," I say, but she won't want a double Vivian on the tombstone.

I write "Vivian x 2" on the price list. If only I liked the multiplication sign as much as the division sign: "Vivian ÷ 2" eliminates me.

"Is your name Hannah, by any chance?" I ask.

"No," she says, "it's Maura, why?"

"I'm hoping for a palindrome of a friend, but she would have to write her name all in capitals like this."

I write "HANNAH" on the page.

"Or in small letters like this."

I write "hannah" underneath.

"Only then would she be symmetrical. We could have a picnic in Navan, but we'd have to shout it—NAVAN!—so it would be in capital letters."

Maura's top teeth bite down on her bottom lip. She looks like a disgruntled beaver.

"That sounds nice," she says quietly. Although her voice is kind, there's no truth in it.

"If I buy my plot now, is it officially my land?"

"How do you mean?"

"If I want to have a picnic on my plot, can I?"

"That'd probably be fine."

"Great. And if I haven't finished my picnic when the cemetery closes, can I stay, if I promise to stay only on my grave?"

"You'll have to ask my manager," she says, "if you give me your number, I'll get him to give you a ring."

I write it down for her, and say, "I remember the 087 by thinking of an eighty-seven-year-old sighing, *Ohhh*, because an eighty-seven-year-old has lots of aching joints and dead friends to sigh about."

"I see."

I lean over the counter.

"How do you do your sevens?"

"Excuse me?"

Maura looks startled, like she has been pulled out of the sea on a hook.

"When you write the number seven, do you add the slash across the middle, or do you leave it out?"

She looks at the freshly written number.

"I leave it out," she says, so quietly that I have to strain for the consonants.

"So do I! I fear it looks unfinished without the slash, but it looks too much like a mustachioed man frowning to justify putting it in."

"How true," Maura says, in a voice thin and transparent as cling film.

I point to the "Additional Charges" section on the sheet.

"If it's €395 extra for a Saturday burial, I should probably try to die early in the week."

Maura examines my face like it's an especially difficult maths test.

"Is your passing imminent, I mean . . . all these preparations . . ."

Her voice dwindles, the question mark forgotten.

"I don't know how imminent it is, but I'd like to be prepared. Is it possible for me to be buried with a reading light and a book, just in case? It might be a good time to tackle *War and Peace*."

"You'll have to ask the funeral director about that, I'm afraid it's outside our remit."

The door opens behind me and someone else comes in, so I say goodbye and fold up the price list and leave the office. Now that Maura has my phone number, she might call and invite me to her house for tea. I feel part giddy with the success of my dealings with Maura: "gid" I'll call it.

I make for the gate leading into the Botanics at the back of the cemetery, and head straight for the wallflowers, my favourite flower. They smell so sweet, I want to put my whole face in their velvet petals and breathe their pollen into my lungs and cough it back up as sweet-smelling phlegm. I like the depth of their reds and their yellows and their names that sound like Gothic romance novels: "Cloths of Gold, Blood Red, Giant Pink, Tom Thumb, Ruby Gem, Vulcan, Scarlet Bedder, Harlequin Mixed." The wallflowers are bedded with clumps of *myositis*, an eye disease of a name but a blue wonder of a flower. *Bellis Pomponette* sounds like a glossy cheerleader, but looks like fungoid forms or spiny creatures or things going wrong in my cells.

The Rubus have funeral Mass names: *odoratus, inapertus, plicatus, inominatus,* so I head toward the tulips which are in flower and make me think that good things are possible. Tulip Daydream is an orange and yellow open-petalled belly laugh of a flower that reminds me of a fire in a hearth, but I wish it had a more original name. I walk through the overgrown part of the gardens, to a tree with strips of cloth and ribbons tied to its branches. It must be a wishing tree, maybe a hawthorn. There's no spare cloth in my bag, so I use my pen to poke a hole in my vest, which is old and frayed. Then I tear a strip up the cloth, across and back down, and tie it to the tree. I circle the tree three times clockwise, then three times anticlockwise. I would like to incant a spell but I don't know the words, or how to speak them. I walk on, a draught running up the bare strip of my belly, to the path through the peony flowers. Their names might be heroines from fairytales and poems, and I'm a small part glad they aren't in flower because their appearance might not live up to the name. I write them in my notebook: "The Moor, Beatrice, Marie Crousse, Victoria, Ducesse De Nemours, Surprise, Edulis Superba, Kelway's Queen, Asa Gray, Bowl of Beauty, Pink Hawaiian Coral, Gertrude, Grisselle, Fair Rosamund, Venus, Purpurea, Dorothy, Reevesiana, Graziella, Marie Jacquin Paeonia Paradoxa, Blanda, Sabinci, Anemoniflora, Northern Glory, Obovata, Chinese Dragon, Banquet, Harvest, Leda, Marchioness, Vesuvian, Roman Gold, Zephirus, Splendens, Peregrine, Dreadnaught."

I write "Dreadnaught" on the inside of my notebook, because I think it's a word to live by: I would like to dread naught. I would also like a flower named after me; when I find out my true name, I will befriend a botanist and ask him such things. I follow the curve of the path to the trees and step onto the grass, looking for a circle of trees that could be a fairy ring, or a tree with a door to a whole other world. I pass a gnarled yew that could be the Magic Faraway Tree, and a weeping beech with coins for leaves, probably used as currency by the pixies living in the tree hollow. I sit at the base of the trunk, which is separated like a giant's toes, and sup from my flask of coffee. A man drives by in a buggy. He parks near me and heads for the trees.

"Morning," he says.

"Morning," I say, "I like trees."

"Well, you're in the right place, then."

I try for a casual chuckle, but it comes out too high-pitched and keen. The man nods toward my notebook.

"Studying the trees?"

"No, I'm looking for a specific tree."

"Oh," he says, "what kind?"

"I don't know exactly, but I'll know when I find it."

"Oh?"

"It will have a doorway in the trunk large enough for me to enter but small enough that nobody else can see it."

He clears his throat.

"Right, well I'd better get on with it, no rest for—"

"*The Wicked!*" I shout, but the man takes fright and gives a little jump backward before walking away. He has left quite abruptly, but he has given me six sentences, if I count "Morning" and "Oh" as full sentences. I walk over to the buggy and write on a blank page of my notebook: "GUESS WHO? HINT: I LIKE TREES."

Then I tucked the note into the windscreen wiper and hurry off before he sees me. I head for the rose garden and read the rose captions; some of the names might be racehorses or cocktails or the answers to bad jokes: Lovely Lady, Just Joey, Disco Dancer, Simply the Best, Dusky Maiden, Absent Friends, Tequila Sunrise.

I only write the fictional heroines or delicious food names in my notebook: "Ice Cream, Zépherine Drouhin, Dawn Chorus, Peamight, Robin Redbreast, Honeywood, Gertrude Jekyll, Constance Spry, Sweet Juliet Aussleep, Spinossissima Fruhlingsgold, Ausblush, Othello, Anna Livia, Frylucy, Oranges + Lemons, Iceberg, Peer Gynt, Starlight Express, Lady Macrobert, Clarissa, Mary Rose."

I cross the little bridge over the stream, climb up Pond Walk, and sniff the rhododendrons. *Boddaertianium* smells like edible perfume, but *Sheltonae* smells like a wet bed. Near the water, a clutch of bamboo stands tightly bundled. I squeeze into the middle; it feels like I'm in a wigwam. This could be my portal, a still-growing wardrobe door to Narnia. I feel around, but the bamboo doesn't part, and it's too tightly packed to go any further. I walk on toward the glasshouses with their bulging roof-bellies, and go into the hothouse. There are banana trees and huge jungle palms and it smells of warm, damp earth. I feel like a midget in a primeval forest. A woman is watering the plants with a yellow hose—this seems like cheating somehow. A sign on the step reads: "Ludwig Wittgenstein (1889–1951) Viennese Philospher. Stayed in Dublin in the winter 1948–1949 and liked to sit and write at these steps."

I sit on the steps, but the only grand philosophical thought I have is whether Ludwig got piles from sitting on damp concrete for so long. I look through the lists of flower names in my notebook, but I can't see a pattern or a code or a hidden anagram so I walk home. The house feels empty, as if there is too much air and not enough substance. I tuck my head under my jumper and sniff. I smell like overripe meat—this must be what my coffin will smell like. The chairs in the living room seem a little hostile: eleven chairs heaped together all facing the same way, like a particularly ineffectual firing squad or an interview panel of invisible mutes. I pull the two nearest chairs towards me and turn them around. Then I squeeze through the rest of them and turn them to face in different directions; now they look less accusatory. I go to the kitchen and trace the route from my house to the cemetery and back through the Botanics. I don't know how to map my routes within the cemetery, or the gardens, or how to draw maps within maps, so I draw symbols to mark those minor walks. Today I walked a winter-bare tree that was knocked to its knees in a storm, with a coffin and a flower suspended between the branches.

I HEAR A small beep from my bag and think it's a bomb, but no, it's my phone. Penelope has sent a message: "Going to visit my mother tomorrow. You are invited. Pack for the weekend."

I read the message again and again, and even after six reads, it's still an invitation and Penelope still wants me to come. I go upstairs to my great-aunt's bedroom and take down an old brown suitcase from the top of the wardrobe. There's a sheet of dust on top, thick and greyish white, like dandruff from an unwashed scalp. It seems a shame to disturb something that has been so many years a-growing, so I snap the locks gently to one side. Inside, it's lined with faded stripy wallpaper and smells like old feet and talcum powder. I bring the suitcase to my bedroom and start packing my things.

15

I WAKE UP excited like it's Christmas and nervous like it's exams. Penelope is picking me up at eleven to drive us to her mother's house on the left thumbnail of County Meath. I get out of bed and put on a white top and blue bottoms because I want to look like a crested wave. I eat breakfast and shake some fish food into Lemonfish's bowl.

"Morning, Lemonfish, here's today's food."

He bobs up and gulps down the powder. I shake some more into the other side of the bowl.

"And this pile is for Saturday and Sunday."

His eyes bulge, and he swims over to his weekend rations. "No, Lemonfish, this way."

I tap the other side of the bowl to encourage him back to today's breakfast. The doorbell rings and Penelope's voice squawks through the letterbox, "We're all going on our summer hol-i-days!"

I drop the fish food, grab my suitcase, and run to open the door. Penelope looks surprised by the suddenness of my face.

"Morning."

I close the door quickly behind me and hurry her along. "Morning, Vivian, are you excited?"

"Yes."

I follow Penelope to her car. It's an old car, the kind of car that I used to draw in school, a boxy square on top of a boxy rectangle. It looks more definite than the other curved cars on the road. Penelope unlocks the boot and I put my suitcase next to hers and get into the passenger seat. The inside smells of old skin and warm petrol. The other door opens and closes (*clunk*) and Penelope gets into the driver seat. She breathes out as if the effort is over when it has only just begun.

"Are we ready to roll?" she asks.

A baker is flattening us into a Swiss roll in my head.

"Yes."

She turns the key in the ignition, the car sputters and gasps like a hospice breath.

"What will your last words be?" I ask.

"Vivian, now is not the time to indulge such morbid thoughts, we're going on our holidays!"

I'm not indulging anything; these thoughts come unbidden and stay until they're answered. I try telling her the sound of the engine is like death, but she shushes me with a song that sounds more like death than my talk of death. The sound of beeping begins to drown out her singing.

"Why are they beeping?" I ask.

"I don't know. Other drivers can be so rude."

Penelope sighs and swerves to avoid a cyclist, who roars something I can't hear. She drives like a Don't Drink and Drive ad, she drives with a rattle and a wallop and a clang and a bang. When she doesn't like the feel of a lane or the colour of a puddle or the shape of a pothole, she glides into the other lane. I've never seen cars driving straight at me before, the drivers' mouths forming into cartoon "O"s before beeping and swerving. The road is straight, but we veer from side to side like a boat on a rough sea. Penelope keeps up a word-clatter about her mother from Dublin to Meath. I half-listen and half-count the dead birds on the side of the road. Soon we pass through a small seaside town with a train running through it. A huge plastic ice-cream cone outside a shop gives me a hunger even though I don't like soggy wafer or runny ice cream. We round the bend and turn right opposite a pub onto a bumpy lane.

"Home sweet home!" Penelope says, with one of her fake shrill laughs. I hate when she says meaningless things she has heard other people say.

"It should be home salty home because it's beside the sea," I say, but Penelope has gotten out of the car, and I follow her down a cracked path to the front door. The cottage is small and white and sits on rocks jutting out to sea. The sea is the front garden, back garden and side garden, with the cracked path connecting the cottage to land like a three-quarter island. The door opens and Penelope's mother comes out. She has short white hair and is wearing a navy housecoat with flowers on it. I would like to wear a housecoat, it would cover my whole body and put an end to the morning foostering in the wardrobe. Penelope and her mother eye each other warily, muttering stilted sentences. I turn to the sea. The strand is long, the tide is out, the rocks seem over-prepared for something that might never happen. The sea churns white foam like it's beating egg whites.

"Vivian!"

Penelope waves me over. She introduces me to her mother and we shake hands. Mrs. Drysdale's hand is soggy dough and her mouth curls downwards like a tortoise but she says, "Welcome," and leads us inside. The hall is dark and cluttered with holy water and pictures of the Pope and Padre Pio. It smells of salt and damp. I follow them into the kitchen and sit on an old brown sofa covered in red crocheted cushions. Mrs. Drysdale bustles about making tea and putting scones on the table. I should learn to bustle so I don't look like an imposter in my kitchen. Penelope and her mother keep up a strange twittering sort of chatter that doesn't include me and seems to be loudening into an argument, so I turn my ears to deafness and examine the walls, which are white and mottled with warty bulges of damp. A grotto of the Virgin Mary sits on a small altar in the corner lit by a blue bulb, and a framed picture of the Sacred Heart hangs on the wall lit by a red bulb. It's like being in a room with a fire engine and a traffic light. I turn my attention to the scones. I can't decide between butter and jam or cream and jam, so I choose butter and cream and jam, and I manage to get two eaten as the sentence pitch climbs higher and higher in the background. Soon I hear the thud of words descending and the squeak of a chair on the linoleum floor. Penelope gets up.

"I'm going to unpack the car," she says, "you two can get to know each other."

I don't know how to get to know somebody; I haven't brought my notebook of friendship questions. Mrs. Drysdale sits across from me with a face that says, "Well?" I feel bare and hunted.

"What's your favourite insect?" I ask.

She sniffs. I attack the silence alone.

"I like ants—I like how busy they are and how they can carry away breadcrumbs twice their size . . ."

She cocks her head to one side.

". . . and how they follow each other to their secret den. I want to shrink and visit their den to see if they have a map of Antworld and magazines with advice about investing breadcrumbs in ant banks."

Mrs. Drysdale hasn't moved her face since I started talking. Sweat runs down my back and is diverted by the waistband of my jeans. Somebody somewhere has just pierced a voodoo doll of me. We sit in a thick, wadded silence until Penelope comes back with the suitcases.

"Come on, Vivian, I'll show you to your room."

I pick up my suitcase and follow her to the room that faces out to sea. It's white and bare with a single bed, covered in a dark green eiderdown. A crucifix hangs above the bed and there's a dark wooden wardrobe in the corner. As soon as Penelope leaves, I check for Narnia, but the back is solid. I look out the window. The sky and sea and sand are all the same shade of grey; only the wave foam tells them apart. I put my things in the wardrobe quickly and hurry down the hall to the kitchen.

"I'm going for a walk on the beach," I say.

Penelope gets up and peers out the window.

"I don't know, Vivian, it's a bit damp."

"I don't mind, I'll go on my own."

The two women murmur a bit but I put on my coat.

"I won't be long," I say, and I walk quickly out the door before the tide rushes in and takes over my walk. I clamber down the rocks, skidding on black seaweed that looks like strips of bloated beetles. I pop them (*squelch squelch*) and start walking the strand, looking at all the treasures the tide has brought in. There are shells and starfish and crabs and stones, and I take out my notebook to write a list:

1. *A piece of orange rope, barely long enough to hang an elf*
2. *A black tyre, half buried in the sand (I step inside in case it's a fairy fort, but nothing happens.)*
3. *A rusty fridge that could be a retirement home for magnets*
4. *A child's car seat face down in the sand, that looks like it tipped the child out and shunted it to a world beneath*
5. *A dead sheep that could be a mer-sheep from the sea depths*
6. *Blue rubber gloves.*

Every few feet there are blue rubber gloves on the strand—a container must have been lost at sea. Some are buried palm down, only the wrists showing; some are reaching up, a finger or two visible from the sand; others are gathered together in a menacing huddle. When darkness falls, they move so slowly, so calmly, pulling their blue bodies out of the sand, taking over the village with their rubbery ways.

I walk up a concrete slope into the village. An ice-cream van at the entrance to the beach looks forlorn and misplaced in the grey mist. I find a supermarket that has a family name on the sign instead of a brand name I can sing from radio ads. In the baking section, I pick up red and blue food colouring. The bottles are such perfect miniatures, they look like quarts of coloured whiskey for a pixie. The woman at the till scans the bottles and smiles.

"Baking for a children's party?"

I look at her. Why does everyone in supermarkets think I'm having a children's party?

"No, I'm going to colour in the beach."

"Well, I hope they're magic bottles, you won't get far with those!"

She laughs. I would like to say a sentence and end on a height and laugh at my own joke.

"I'm just doing the patch in front of my window to improve the view."

"Oh, right."

She has lost interest and starts a conversation with the girl at the next till about her husband's coeliac attack. I walk back to the beach, picturing a giant loaf of bread punching a man in the belly, and head in the direction of the cottage. Now I can't see the sand for blue gloves. I pick one up and put it in my pocket to dilute their power, and I'm so engrossed in keeping my mind off a potential blue takeover that I almost walk into the moat of a sandcastle. A boy and a girl are kneeling beside it, adding stones to the curved path.

"I like your castle," I say, and I kneel down beside them to examine it more closely. There are four high turrets, four shell windows, a stone door and a stone path, with a moat guarding the outside. A frond of tea-brown seaweed hangs from a stick in a turret as a flag. The children barely glance at me and keep adding stones to the path.

"Where does the path lead to?" I ask.

The girl looks at me and points to the gate behind her. "That's our house."

I take the food colouring from my bag.

"Do you want to colour in the turrets?"

They eye the bottles warily as if they were black magic potions.

"What's turrets?" the boy asks.

"These."

I point to the sand cubes on the top.

"This is where the princess would stand and wave."

The girl looks at the food colouring.

"Pink!" she says.

"It's actually red," I say, "but maybe it'll come out pink."

I open the red bottle and pour a few drops on the turrets, but a shout goes up and I take fright and spill the bottle. A woman walks quickly from the children's house shouting their names. The girl suddenly starts to wail: "She put blood in the moat!"

I look at the moat. A streak of red is running down the front of the castle, and there's a splash of red in the moat.

"Why are you crying?" I ask. "We killed the troll who lives in the moat."

The boy looks thrilled but the girl's face scrunches up and she shouts: "She killed the troll!"

The mother has reached the gate and I don't want to take part in a botched explanation, I don't want to waste words that will be flung back at me, so I get up quickly and half-run half-walk, until I'm sure they aren't following me. Then I slow down to look at the shells. I used to bring home damp and gleaming shells, I used to think if I found the perfect shell I would find the shape of the world, but I was always disappointed. When I washed them later, their sea-gleam would trickle down the sink, leaving a dull sheen the colour of dry lament.

I pick up the skeleton of a periwinkle shell, examine the whorls and put it in my pocket. This one won't betray me, it holds no promise of gleam. Then I pocket a dog whelk shell that's dull alabaster, an honest colour that won't disappoint. I find two shards of pottery and a grey oval stone wrapped by a narrow white band, like an unfinished American football, and add them to my collection, hoping they don't have an inter-substance squabble in the darkness of my pocket. A man with a metal detector and earphones walks slowly along the strand, moving the detector from side to side before him like a grass strimmer. I follow him in case he hits treasure, but there's no beep. I'm surely more of a beachcomber than he is, even though he's looking for precious metals and I'm looking for broken treasures and shells that will keep their colour in the dry. A blotch of pink near the shoreline becomes a partially deflated balloon when I get closer. It says "Happy 60th" on it. I wonder whether I'll live till sixty and, if I do, whether anybody will throw me a party. I would like a birthday cake big enough for everyone at the party to have a slice but not so big that there's lots left over the next day and I doubt whether anyone came to my party.

When I reach the cottage, I pour the food colouring onto the patch of sand in front of my bedroom window. The blue and red meet in the middle to form purple: three-sevenths of a rainbow. A shopping trolley has come to a bad end near the rocks, its nose in the sand and two back wheels jutting into the air in an awkward dive. I consider bringing it home for Mrs. Drysdale, but up close, it's dirty and rusty so I leave it be. I climb back up the rocks to the cottage, and Penelope opens the door.

"How was your walk?"

"Good," I say, "look at my fresh hoard."

I pull out the shells and pottery and stone and blue rubber glove from my pockets, along with clumps of wet sand. The kettle on the range is already whistling, and Mrs. Drysdale gets up to make more tea. I don't want another hot drink, but it seems as if this is a ritual I must take part in. I wash the shells under the tap while Penelope hangs my coat on a hook by the range. Her mother puts the teapot on the low table in front of the sofa and sets out a plate of biscuits. I sit down. The biscuits, oh no, the biscuits are the soft beige not-quite-biscuit not-quite-cake atrocities with an almost burnt taste that I hate; they make me retch beige vomit. Penelope puts two cups on the table, sits beside me, and hands me the plate of biscuits. I take one.

"Have another," she says.

"No, thanks," I say, "I'm grand."

"Ah, you have to have another, we're on holidays," she says, and she pushes the plate towards me.

I take another biscuit and bite into it. It's as awful as I remember. Penelope starts talking about the games she played on the beach as a child, and I nod "mmm hmm" and "really gosh wow," and while she's gazing out the window I stuff one of the biscuits down the back of the sofa. If there are mice living there, they can feast on my leftovers. I pretend to nibble the other biscuit and then stuff that one in the same place. Penelope looks at my empty hands.

"You're a big fan of the biscuits, huh?"

She shoves the plate at me again, and I take another biscuit and stuff it behind the cushions. There would need to be whole teams of mice living in the sofa to get through so many biscuits. Penelope and her mother have started to argue again. I can't make out their words, it's all dry snarl and wet hum, so I get up and look at my hoard. I've left the shells to dry around the edge of the sink; they too hate the arguing and are about to creep down the steel sides and escape through the plughole. I pick up the dog whelk and put it to my ear. I can hear the fizz of the ocean even though the tide is still out. Now I stick the periwinkle skeleton in my ear, but the sea must have passed right through the bones; I can hear only the hiss of Penelope and her mother, a live version of the soap opera on my television at home.

The walls start to press in on me so I climb onto the counter, open the window, and squeeze out. A seagull on the rocks shrieks like it's being pinched, then laughs like it's being tickled. The tide has gone out so far it's hard to believe that it will ever come back. I'm glad the tide is out. I hope to die without ever having to set foot or hand in seawater again. I hunker down at the wall under the kitchen window. Life feels narrower in this cottage, hemmed in by questions and tea routines and constant word-spatter. I realise that I don't miss being in a family, the clutch and the cling of it, the hold they have over you, but I probably should go back.

I get up, walk around to the front door, and let myself in. Penelope is standing staring at the wall, and her mother is scrubbing a pot with steel wool. Her fingers have worked up a pale pink foam, they're moving so fast they're in a blur. The air is so stiff, it makes me want to back into a corner and climb under something.

"Grey and pink go well together," I say.

"Sorry?" Penelope turns to me.

"The grey pad and the pink foam," I say. "It's a sporty combination."

"Vivian, we have to leave now. I'm sorry."

"I don't mind," I say.

"You're very kind."

I'm not kind at all; I'm glad I got to unpack my things in a strange room, but I don't want to stay over. Mrs. Drysdale looks at me and sniffs in Penelope's direction.

"Elaine's in one of her moods."

"Who's Elaine?" I ask.

Penelope's head jerks from her mother to me.

"Pay no heed to my mother, Elaine's my middle name, she just doesn't like to call me Penelope. Isn't that right, Mother?"

Penelope's teeth are almost bared at the old woman, she looks like she could make a leap and a snarl and a lunge for her throat. Mrs. Drysdale spits red fury; if her eyes could froth they would. The heat in the room seems to have been turned up to the highest setting, and I begin to sweat.

"I'm going to pack my bag," I say, and I run to the bedroom.

I snatch my clothes from the wardrobe and stuff them into my suitcase. Then I tiptoe through the hall and out the front door, before realising that I've forgotten my shells. I don't want to go back inside, so I crawl around the house and poke my head up outside the kitchen window. Penelope and her mother are standing with their backs to me. I reach in to grab the shells and pottery and catch fragments of shouted sentences, but I throw them right back and keep only my sea hoard. I creep back to the car and sit on my suitcase holding the dog whelk to my ear, the ear not facing the sea, so I have the real sea in one ear and the shell-hiss in the other. I root in my suitcase for the food stash—travelling without backup snacks is like getting into a coffin without dying first—and eat two packets of cheese-and-onion crisps. I'm breathing out through my nose in loud sniffs to appreciate the violent aftertaste when Penelope comes out of the cottage carrying her bag. Her mouth is set in the same tortoise line as her mother's.

"Hello, Vivian."

"Hello, Penelope."

She unlocks the car, and I put my suitcase in the back seat and get into the passenger seat. When Penelope gets in, the car sinks and I bounce—*oh*—in my seat and bash my head—*ow*—off the ceiling. She slams the door and the car shakes, nervous of her bad mood. She tries to start the car, but she's holding the key like a knife and digging furiously into the ignition, so it takes a while. Then she turns the car around quickly and I'm slammed—*oof*—into the passenger window. Penelope sits hunched forward in the seat, her fingers white and clawed around the steering wheel. She drives fast so fast I close my eyes, because if I'm going to be slammed into something else I want it to be a surprise. The car makes a sudden swerve and we come to a stop. I open my eyes. We're parked on the side of a road and Penelope's head is bent over the steering wheel. She's had an accident, I think, this is what people look like when they're freshly dead, but she starts sobbing and gulping, *oh no.* I pat her back and stare straight ahead.

"Viv, I'm sorry, I'm so sorry."

"There's nothing to be sorry about, please just drive."

My hands start to sweat and shake; Penelope's shaking is contagious.

"I shouldn't have pretended my name was—"

"It's fine," I say, "everything's fine."

I put the whelk against my right ear and Penelope keeps

talking, which spoils things. Why do people insist on giving explanations that make everything more complicated? I squeeze the shell against my ear and block out the words, needless tanks of words that sound better in a muffled hiss outside the shell. From here, I can choose the syllables I like and let the rest trickle down my face. When her words slow to a dribble and sobs take their place, I put the shell in my lap and pat her back again. My hand is trembling so hard, I only need to rest it against her back and it goes *pat pat pat* all on its own.

"Let's go," I say brightly because that's how leaders sound when they're motivating their charges.

"Let's go!"

"Vivian, you're a true friend, thank you. I've never told anyone what I've just told you. And to forgive me for pretending—"

"It's *fine!*" I shout, and I smile so hard my cheeks don't know what to do with themselves. I turn the radio almost the whole way up, and we drive back to the city in the crescendo of a power ballad.

16

When I wake the next morning, my dream is so close, I can smell the overripe fruit at the edge of it. It's a recurring dream about a bowl of fruit that's on the verge of rotting. When the bowl appears, I realise I ignored it for weeks and now it's too late. There's no story in this dream, just a thick dark sense that I've wasted things, and this sense lingers in my stomach when I wake, like a kick wrapped in spinach. I get out of bed, jump on the spot, throw my hands over my head, and roar *"Ararararararara!"* Then I slap my head until the dream has faded and my head can only think of the pain. The church bell chimes nine times—but "chime" is the wrong word for this bell's sound. "Chime" sounds thin and tinkly—this is more of a "chowm" or a "choym." I close my eyes and scrabble in the wardrobe until my fingers land on a jumper that feels like today. I pull it out. It's a green glittery cardigan of my great-aunt's that makes me look like an overdressed Christmas tree.

I rush my breakfast because I'm fed up of eating breakfast with spoons and dinner with forks and washing cutlery that just gets dirty again. I put my bag over my shoulder—I was going to say "sling" my bag over my shoulder but that makes me think of an injured soldier—I'll stick with "put." I walk to the supermarket and make for the fruit section. My dream has reminded me that I should eat more fruit. The Pink Lady apples are the colour of rhubarb-and-custard sweets. I believe I have enough green foods in my life, I should eat more pink. I turn the apples over in my hand, seeking out the most bruised fruit because nobody else wants them, like nobody wanted me on their team in PE class in school. I walk to the far side of the supermarket to the party section and gather armfuls of paper plates and plastic cups and cutlery. I bring them to the checkout and lay them on the conveyor belt but, *oh no*, it's the girl who thinks I have boy twins in wheelchairs alone at home. She picks up the apples and scans them.

"Have you got a club card?" she asks.

"It's okay," I say, "they're being minded by a childminder. I pay her to push them round in their wheelchairs, and if they need to eat or go to the toilet, she'll help them, they're alright."

I say my words at a rush, I say them like they're paining my mouth and I need to get them out. The girl blinks at me like she has just come out of the cinema into the sunlight.

"What?"

I realise, *oh no*, it's a different girl.

"No," I say, "I don't have a club card, my great-aunt warned me about the satellites."

"The satellites?"

"Yeah, the satellite beams read your supermarket preferences and the government takes the information and uses it against you."

"Oh, right, yeah. Do you need a bag?"

"No, thanks," I say.

I pack the apples and plastic things quickly into my bag, take my change and run out of the shop. My feet turn townward so I follow them, heading for Berkeley Road and then Eccles Street, where nurses and doctors spill out of the hospital. I used to think I'd like to be a nurse, but my hands are graceless clods, and needles and scalpels require steadiness. Also, people don't respond well to my words, and the right words are important for a nurse. A woman with a small child sits next to a parking meter asking for money in a voice like an old song. I walk on to the private hospital and go inside. There are people waiting in a line near the entrance and I join them; it might be for something nice. When I reach the top, I realise it's a queue for the toilets. I don't need to go, but I've come this far, so I go inside and wash my hands without looking at the mirror.

I head for the canteen because I like canteens. I like the routine of it, the pile of damp trays, the helping myself. I like the drinking water spout, the metal tubs of hot food, the rows of yoghurt, the heaps of pastries, the bowls of fruit, the piles of chocolate bars at the till. I especially like the tub of baked beans, all orange and smug like best bean-friends. My biggest achievement so far has been adding the final piece to a baked-bean jigsaw. It might still be in the hoardroom if the mice haven't mistaken it for a real plate of beans.

I take a tray from the pile and look at the hot food but I don't know what anything is. I peer at the menu board behind the counter, but I'm not wearing my glasses and the chalked words are white fuzz. The queue presses forward, and I don't know what to eat, I don't know how to ask what the food is, what animals it comes from, what the sauce words mean. My heart thuds and my ears seem to have a pulse of their own:

thuh thoink thuh thoink. When I'm next, I step out of the queue and make for the fridge. I pile cartons of yoghurt—all three flavours—orange juice, apple juice, an apple, an orange, some pastries, a packet of nutty looking biscuits and two chocolate bars onto my tray. While the man rings up the total, I open my purse. There are a few coins wrapped in a supermarket receipt and a ragged, Sellotaped €5 note. I rummage around in the bottom of my bag, but all I come up with is fluff and a couple of raisins. I wait for the final sum like it's a court ruling.

"That's €12.46, please."

I hold my money in my outstretched palms.

"That's all I have."

The man stares at the coins and fluff.

"If you don't have enough, you can put some of it back."

I look at my tray. The green apple and the orange orange and the purple and gold chocolate bars look so perfect on the off-white tray that I can't separate them.

"I won't take any of them," I say, "but I just need to draw them so I'll remember them in this exact position."

I take my notebook and pencil out of my bag and draw a big rectangle, for the tray. Then I sketch the food and drink. I'm not so good at drawing, so I label each item, just to be sure.

"Have you got any colouring pencils?" I ask the man.

He shakes his head slowly.

"Crayons, even? Although it's harder to stay inside the lines with them."

"No."

The silence after the "no" is still and full, as if the air has been let out of the man's lungs and he's waiting for me to leave before he can draw breath again.

"No matter. I'll colour it in at home," I say, then I turn and walk very quickly out of the canteen and out of the hospital. At the traffic lights on Dorset Street, I push the pedestrian lights button again and again and again. Across the road, the clock in the tower of St. George's Church tells the wrong time. Sometimes I feel that if I could walk around Dublin and set all the clocks to the right time, the world would be in the right order. When the green man appears, I cross the road and walk through the flats onto North Frederick Street. I head for the Garden of Remembrance and walk the length of the water feature and up the steps to the Children of Lir statue. Their heads droop and their arms dangle; if they walked, they would walk like zombies. I toss in some coins and circle the statue three times, then I walk back down the steps and sit on a wooden bench among the pigeons and lunch-eaters. I empty all the gold and copper coins from my purse onto my knees, and run them through my fingers like a fairytale miser. It seems strange that if I don't have enough of these small discs, I can't have all the food on my tray, when there is no real connection between the two. A wiry man dressed all in blue lopes over to me. There's a layer of grease on his face, as if he had slathered it in butter. I rub a finger across my own forehead and it comes away shiny; maybe he's thinking the same thing about me.

"Have you got forty cents for a hostel, love?"

"A hundred years ago, you'd have asked me for a farthing," I say, "although that would only get you a piece of bread. Maybe it'd be better to ask for a ha'penny. That'd get you two sweet biscuits."

"What?"

He shifts from foot to foot and looks at the money on my lap.

"In the museum, there was a list of the values of old Irish currency," I say. "A florin would get you a pair of moleskin leggings, or a crown would get you three waistcoats—which would you rather?"

"Eh, I never really thought about it."

"I'd say go with the three waistcoats—you could swap two of them for a pair of moleskin leggings; then you'd have a full outfit."

"Yeah, yeah."

He pulls his jacket forward and hunches his shoulders. Then he scratches his head, glances around quickly.

"I didn't think the old punt would lie down so easy," I say. "I spent a year multiplying euro prices by 0.8 in my head to keep my sense of the punt, in case it came back."

"Yeah, yeah, listen, can you spare some of that change for a hostel?"

He points at the hoard on my knees, which looks like Ebenezer Scrooge's counting house. I scoop up a fistful of coins and put it in his hand.

"God bless you, love."

He makes some kind of blessing gesture as if he was a track-suited butter-faced priest and walks away quickly.

I put the remaining coins back in my purse and walk south to the Chester Beatty Library to look at pictures of magical things. A fifteenth-century encyclopaedia shows drawings of mermen with monkish tonsures, a mermaid with nipple-less breasts and a spiny fish with the head of a bear and the teeth of a dog. The seventeenth-century Persian book *Collection of Things Strange and Rare* shows a creature that will appear on the Day of Judgement. It has the spotted body of a leopard, the shorn head of a human and antlers. I envy students of those eras who were taught these things as fact, I think I would have more in common with people who are hundreds of years dead than with people who are alive now. I move on to a nineteenth-century Iranian barber-surgeon toolkit. It contains a set of beautifully symmetrical drug scales that I would like to give to the next drug dealer I see, because ugly things should be done beautifully if they are to be done at all.

The Middle Eastern paintings have magical-sounding titles, full of apostrophes and "I"s and "Z"s and "Q"s; I could win Scrabble outright if I used only Arabic words, and if I had people to play Scrabble with. The names of the different Islamic scripts dance on my tongue when I say them aloud and spring off the page when I write them in my notebook: "Sini, Sudani, Maghribi, Nasta'liq, Thulth, Muhaqqaq, Naskh, Kufic and Ghubar."

I like that the makers of Arabic didn't insist upon a "U" after a "Q": "Muhaqqaq" looks fearless, undaunted, unencumbered by "U"s. The Ghubar script is tiny, with letters no bigger than specks—the caption says it means "dust" in Arabic. I would like to learn this secret script and send a message in Ghubar from a bottle in a Middle Eastern sea.

A caption says that paintbrushes were made from the hair of squirrels or goats, the inside of a calf's ear, or hair from the throats of two-month old white kittens. How did the paintbrush-makers know that black kittens just wouldn't do, or that three-month old kittens were past their primes? I write the names of the components of Islamic calligraphy ink and paint pigment in my notebook; they might be the words of an incantation, or the ingredients of a magic potion: "Lampblack, Gum

Arabic, Saffron Water, Myrtle Leaf Water, Rosewater, Narcissus Liquor, Pulverized Pearl, Gold, Cinnabar, Lapis Lazuli, Ochre, Orpiment, Indigo, Silver, Red Lead, Malachite and Vitriol."

If vitriol was used in ink today, I could blame it for any malice that came from my pen.

A Japanese print called "The Lucky Dreams" contains images of Mount Fuji, a hawk and eggplants. The text says that if you dream of any of these items on the night of New Year's Day, good luck will follow. January is a long way off. I'll try to dream of all three tonight because I need three times as much luck as good luck. I need the mightiest luck in the world.

Upstairs, I read about the dance of the whirling dervishes, which is, according to the caption, the circling of the spiritual around the material world. I don't know what that means: the word "spiritual" makes my skin weep because it seems to say so much but really says so little. The text continues: "The upward pointing right hand and the downward pointing left hand symbolise the passing of knowledge from one world to another."

The whirling dervish dance could transfer the knowledge of how to return from my original world to this one. I hurry down two flights of stairs to the ladies' toilets. There's nobody here. I can't cover the mirrors so I close my eyes, raise my right hand, and point my left hand down. I stretch each index finger out like God in the Sistine Chapel painting or ET's glowing finger. Then I swivel myself around and around, my arms taut in a diagonal line. I spin faster and faster until I don't know if I'm spinning or standing so I open my eyes. I'm still moving; the row of toilets swirls into my vision, then the mirror: *no, no*, not the mirror. I turn from my reflection and plant both feet on the ground. My body has stopped but my head's still awhirl. I look up. Nothing has changed; the doors and tiles are still red, the toilets are still toilets, I'm still me. I reverse the dance by switching the position of my arms, close my eyes and twirl faster and faster, using my right foot as an anchor and tapping the ground with my left. I feel I'm about to lift off somewhere, some place that's not here, when I hear a rustle and a shuffle and a "What in the name of Christ?"

I open my eyes and bring my spin to a stop. The toilets swim back into focus. A woman with grey hair and a face like wet cement stands at the door, staring. Behind her, a tourist in a bright pink jacket points her camera at me. I don't think I could begin to find the sentences that would explain my dance to this audience; years of words would need to be spoken and none of us has the time. I blink to steady my eyeballs and walk past the women to the door. The tourist is filming my exit so I point my nose in the air and give a queen's wave: a small tilt of my upright hand as if I'm waiting for a mitten to drop from the ceiling. When I get outside the toilets, I walk quickly, so quickly that my feet lift clear of the ground; if I was an Olympic race-walker, I'd be disqualified. I leave the museum at a rush and head for Dame Lane, where I slow to an amble. There are green-framed windows in cages and an orange letter box on the wall with a sticker saying: "Rob a Bank Today." I don't know where to get a gun and I'm sure I should have principles against such things, but if I robbed big, I could leave €50 notes in cardigan pockets in every charity shop in town. When I reach South Great George's Street, I think of other streets that have north-south pairings: North/South Great George's Street, North/South Circular Road, North/South Frederick Street, North/South King Street, North/South Earl Street. These street-namers seem to have been influenced by the unimaginative bird-namers, when they really should have paid more heed to the moth-and-butterfly-namers. I wonder how many city-centre meetings started with empty chairs because of the omission of a north or a south in the address. Meetings, I think. Meetings. What actually happens in a meeting? I wonder if I could call one, and with whom. I could serve bottled water and coffee from a plunger. I could write an agenda and take minutes and propose things, but I probably couldn't second anything if I was on my own.

A clock sticks out of a red-bricked pub in the laneway across the road. It tells the wrong time. A band of mischievous clock-makers must sneak around the city at night with a ladder and screwdriver, tweaking clocks until they run slow. They share tips on ladder safety and clandestine urban high jinks with the Smurfs painting the street signs. I cross the street and stand under the neon "Why Go Bald?" sign, looking at the soot-streaked backs of the buildings at the junction of George's Street and Dame Street. They're all edges and angles and juts, the kind of discordant imperfection that makes me feel I can breathe—unsymmetry at a symmetrical T-junction. I walk the length of the lane to Andrew's Street. If I had a friend for all the first-named streets of Dublin, I would be so popular. There'd be a Leo in my address book, and a Geraldine and an Andrew. There'd be a John, Anne, Thomas, Henry and a Mary. There'd be two Georges. I walk up the slope to Suffolk Street, past the green pub with the hanging baskets and the smell of cooked dinner. There isn't a bus for ten minutes, so I follow the curl of the road back around the tourist office that used to be a church. I walk to the far end of the car park to look at the decrepit statue of St. Andrew. There's a look of pure torment on his face, but I suppose I'd be tormented too if my face was almost worn away. I walk back to get my bus and stop in the supermarket on the way home to buy an eggplant. I'm tempted to buy three to triple my luck, but then I'd need to triple the hawks and Mount Fujis to balance the ratios. When I get home, I trace the walking part of my route onto greaseproof paper. Today I walked a squinting side profile of a cat with an upturned collar and a stalk on its head.

I take a book about birds from the shelf and open it on the hawk page. Then I find a picture of Mount Fuji on the Internet and print it out. Now I have all the components of a lucky dream except the timing: it's not the first sleep of the new year, but it's surely the first sleep of a new baby somewhere. When I go to bed, I stare hard at the hawk and Mount Fuji and the eggplant, making sure I spend equal amounts of time on each. Then I put the book and the picture under my pillow, hold the eggplant in my hands and will myself to dream correctly.

17

I WAKE UP in a frown. Things don't seem right already and I've barely opened my eyes. I'm lying on a squelchy mush; the eggplant has burst and is mashed into the sheets. I sift through my dreams—I seem to have had more dreams than sleep—but none of them featured vegetables or mountains or birds. I duck under the blankets and sniff, but a vegetal smell has taken over my own smell. I scrape the worst of the eggplant off the sheets and throw it down the toilet, then I put on some clothes over my pyjamas, eat breakfast and pack my bag. I take the street map down from the bookshelf. Today I will visit Middle Third. There are three branches of Middle Third on the map: a straight line and two curved lines attacking it at an angle like a Chinese symbol. The three branches don't connect at a point of concentrated magic so I will need to walk the whole area. I put on my great-aunt's green coat because hobbits like green, and leave the house.

"Ah, Vivian, how are you?"

Bernie's sitting on her doorstep smoking a cigarette, her right elbow cupped in her left hand.

"Fine, thanks," I say and keep walking.

"Where are you off to in such a hurry?"

"To Middle Third to find a hobbit."

"Where?"

"Middle Third in Killester," I say. "If hobbits live in Middle Earth, then every third person in Middle Third should be a hobbit."

She coughs up a puff of smoke and shakes her head.

"You'd do better to find a husband, never mind your hobbits."

I walk quickly on. A roar hits me square in the back of the head: "About time you got the ring on the finger, a woman your age."

⌾

I WALK THROUGH Phibsborough and Glasnevin to Collins Avenue. It takes me an age to walk the length of it—there are so many houses, it's hard to believe all these people exist without my knowing them. Just before the road ends, I turn left and follow the road to Middle Third, which opens out onto a large triangular green with clumps of trees. I wander among the trees looking for the entrance to a hobbit hole and find a beer can and some empty crisp packets. Hobbits love their food and ale; they may have left a trail of crisps and beer drops. I walk the different prongs of Middle Third looking for signs of a trail, but all I find is a cigarette butt, and hobbits prefer pipe-weed. The houses are mostly bungalows, but it's underground dwellings that I'm looking for. A short man walks towards me, about the height of a tall hobbit. He's wearing shoes, so I can't see if he has large hairy feet; he's wearing a cap so I can't see if he has pointy ears; he's wearing a black coat which is the wrong colour—unless he's coming from a hobbit funeral. I stare at his face as he passes. It's mild and friendly and he nods at me—he has given me the nod to follow him to his hobbit hole, so I turn around and follow. He walks quite slowly, and I have to be careful not to catch him up if we are to keep up this pretence for the human world. He enters the driveway of a house. I look behind me for potential spies before following him. He is putting his key in the front door when he turns around to face me. He looks surprised.

"Can I help you with something?"

"How come your door is rectangular?" I ask.

"Excuse me?"

"Oh, this must be the decoy door—where's the round door to the underground part?"

"I'm sorry, what's this about?"

"The quest to find my way back," I whisper. "I'm looking for a hobbit to guide me."

The man stares at every piece of my face as if he's trying to suck it all in. He speaks in a low voice full of corners.

"If you don't get off my property right now, I'm calling the guards. Now get *lost*!"

I turn around and leave the driveway, leave Middle Third, leave the chance of a hobbit guide. He was a hobbit for sure, but a reluctant one who didn't want to leave home, just like Bilbo Baggins. Maybe if I wait, he will change his mind and seek me out, especially if he suspects how much cake there is in my cupboards. I walk to the Howth Road and get a bus into town, then I get another bus home from town because I don't trust my feet to lead me to the right place. On the way home, I send Penelope a message: "Please come over. Bring shovel."

Penelope replies: "Okay."

I stop at the supermarket, and take a great big sniff of a breath as I walk in. It settles something inside me to see so much stuff in one place: the tins of food all piled up, the stacks of frozen food in the freezer, the pallets of produce waiting to be shelved, the crates of fruit and vegetables, the heaps of toilet rolls, shelves of cakes, buns, biscuits, cereal, soup. The things that contain the food interest me the most: the tubs and packets and bags and boxes and cartons and bottles. Whoever thought to put different foodstuffs in different kinds of packaging? I stroll around stroking the packaging and looking at the contents. I buy three cartons of mushrooms and seven mesh bags of chocolate coins wrapped in gold foil, caught like chocolate fish in their nets. When I get home, I map the walking part of my route. Today I walked the hood of the Grim Reaper with a giant ladybird clinging to its underside.

I get up and empty one of the dead plants from its earthen pot into the bin. The smell of dry clay is delicious and I bend down and sniff the bin. Then I rinse out the pot, dry it and empty the gold coins into it. When I cut the nets open, they leave tiny yellow pieces of netting on the counter—I could glue them to Lemonfish as new scales. I scoop up the pieces and bring them over to his bowl. Things are not looking good. His white beard has grown longer, like a water-goat, and his stomach is an angry bloat. He's listing to one side as if the water under him is the floor that he's dragging his body across. Poor Lemonfish. I knock on the bowl and wave, but he ignores me. I throw one of the gold coins into the bowl so that he knows what he should look like. It sinks slowly and he doesn't seem to care.

∞

I GO UPSTAIRS and scoop out the unflushed eggplant from the toilet with my hands. When I sniff the toilet bowl, my eyes burn; it must be time to clean it. I spurt some toilet cleaner into the bowl and swoosh it around with the brush until it smells of swimming pool and lime. The doorbell rings and I come down the stairs at a leap and a run. Penelope seems to be inside before I have opened the door and my mouth to say hello. She's carrying a shovel with a plastic bag wrapped around its tongue.

"Hi, Vivian, what are we digging?"

"Just a hole."

She has already pushed past me into the kitchen.

"Do you want to go to the toilet?" I ask.

"No, I'm fine."

"It's clean."

"I don't need to go."

"Oh."

Penelope leans her shovel against the counter and sits down at the table, but I pull her up and bring her outside. I put her shovel in her hand and take up my shovel and scrape out a circle on the grass.

"Here's where we dig."

"Okay," she says.

We slice into the earth, which is soft and spongy on top. The going is easy until we hit gristle and mean little stones; the sound of metal on stone is terrible to my ears. Penelope stops digging and leans on her shovel.

"Where will we put the soil we've dug?"

"Around the edges is fine."

The smallness of our progress is surprising. I had expected boggy softness and squelch but this is dry hard work; the soil doesn't want to come up. Penelope grunts with every movement of her shovel. It's like listening to a tennis match with the grating of metal on stone instead of the *puick puick* of a tennis ball. Every time she puts her foot on the shovel, her skirt catches under the heel of her shoe, and I hear "*Feck*" and "*Balls*" and "*Why me?*"

"Because you won't hoist up your skirt," I say.

"What?"

"You asked 'why me'—if you pull your skirt up higher, it'll be out of the shovel's way."

Penelope stares at me, her forehead creased into a question mark. She has the look of someone who has something big to say, but she purses her lips and tucks in her skirt and slashes the earth with her shovel. We've hit a pocket of worms, which burrow furiously under the soil when they're exposed. I never knew so many worms could exist—this wriggling brown world under my feet is terrifying—but I understand why they stay so secret and safe and hidden. When two mounds' worth of clay have built up on the sides, the hole still doesn't seem so deep. Penelope sighs.

"Hard to believe all that came from this small hole."

She sneezes, but I'm so caught up in my soil-world that I

forget to say "bless you" for a few minutes. I want to ask Penelope whether the "bless you" still counts if it's late, or whether it counts towards the next sneeze, but she seems tired and bothered and closed to my questions. Her face is red and puffy, a burst sandbag of a face. I worry she'll sicken and die into the hole, and that's not what this hole is for.

"Do you want to rest for a bit?" I ask.

"Jesus, I thought you'd never ask."

She sits down on the mound she has dug up and sinks back into it, her legs dangling in the hole. Her feet in her sandals are grubby and the toenails have a black rim of dirt under the tips, like a soil pedicure. I go into the kitchen and bring out mugs of milk and the biscuit tin.

"Men who work the fields drink milk when they take a break," I say.

Penelope takes two biscuits and eats with her mouth open; I wish she would keep the biscuit mush private.

"So when do we stop digging?" she asks, biscuit particles firing from her mouth.

"I don't know yet."

We eat in silence because Penelope is out of puff and I have nothing to say. When I've finished my milk, I take Penelope's mug from her hands and stand up.

"Up and at 'em, rise and shine," I say, and I clap my hands because this is how armies and boarding-school children are put into action.

Penelope climbs to her feet in a low grumble. She has clay streaks on her face, under her fingernails, on the back of her skirt. I look into the hole.

"If we keep digging until the hole is my height, I can be

buried here standing up, with the grass lid pulled over my head like a stopper."

"I'm not sure that's allowed, Vivian. I thought you'd already bought your plot in Glasnevin?"

"Not yet, I'm considering my options."

We dig for a bit.

"You could do it," I say.

"Do what?"

"When I die, you could come over and drag me into the hole."

"How would I know when you were dead?"

"I could ring you if I think I'm dying. You could walk me out to the hole and I'd die in there—but just in case I go suddenly, we should practise now."

I drop my shovel and lie down on the grass a good distance from the hole.

"Okay, pretend I'm dead and you drag me to the hole."

Penelope lays down her shovel and runs over to me. Even though it's a straight line, she runs zigzagged like someone in a film trying to avoid getting shot. I close my eyes and feel a sudden wrench to my armpits, I had expected a more dignified death-pull.

"What are you doing?"

"I'm dragging you by the oxters. Jesus Vivian, you'd want to lay off the cakes, you're a ton weight."

I dig my bottom and elbows into the ground to add more tonnage. Penelope tugs and heaves and grunts. She doesn't get very far, even when I raise myself as much as possible off the ground.

"This isn't working," I say. "You'll need to devise some kind of system using pulleys and ropes."

"How?"

"I don't know, I'll be dead."

Penelope's face is blotched pink and white like a mutant Friesian cow, and she's panting so hard I fear she'll be the first to die. I get up off the ground.

"Okay, back to the digging."

I dig until my legs and arms stiffen up and feel like they belong to someone else. Penelope's grunts have arpeggioed into moans of rage and horror, as if she has reached an outer circle of Hell. I tell her to stop digging and I climb into the hole, which is only thigh-deep but fairly wide. I kneel down and duck my head.

"Can you put the lid on?"

She slides the grassy top over my head, and a darkness consumes me, a dense darkness that smells more alively damp than any daylight I have known. A muffled voice barges through the hole like the click-stop of a CD player at a funeral ripping me out of the music and spoiling the magic. The lid slides off and Penelope looks down. Her skirt is bunched up, showing a strip of dark hairs down her shin that the razor forgot. A fierce, meaty bang from her sends my nose in the opposite direction. I climb out.

"When I die, you've to come over before my body sets and put me in the hole."

"Okay," she says.

Her dug-up earth is mashed down, mine is formed into a tall peak. It looks mystical and full of mountain promise. Penelope has recovered her puff and lets out a gush of words, enough to fill ten bedpans, but this is no time for listening to outside sounds.

"You have to go home now," I say.

Her face empties and sinks; it looks like a diary with only January filled in. She shrugs and nods her head.

"I'll get my things."

"You have to go because I'm going to visit my sister," I say. "Thanks for your help, though."

Penelope's face perks up.

"You're welcome, Vivian, and I'd be honoured to drag your body to the hole when the time comes."

"Thanks."

Now forms a silence clogged solid as old concrete, the kind of silence in which physical contact is made or serious words are spoken. I clap my hands three times to break the spell, and I move towards the hall. Penelope's words have restarted. I open the door as loudly as I can and wave goodbye. She chatters on the doorstep and I say "yes yes oh indeed yes" and move the door slowly to a close, until I'm peeping through a narrow chink, and the word "goodbye" has been uttered. When I close the door, I lower myself into a squat against it and listen to the sound of peace and nothing. The house looks different at this level: The walls are higher and the doors are giants' doors and I am a shrunken Alice in a not-so Wonderland.

I crawl through the house to the kitchen and take the packets of mushrooms out of the fridge. I pierce the film and empty them into a glass bowl, because surely natural materials hold more magic than man-made ones. Then I bring the bowl outside and start planting the mushrooms in a ring around the unmashed mound of earth. I leave small gaps between each mushroom but when I start to run out, I space them further apart. I consider uprooting the ones I've planted close together but that might cancel out the fairy magic, so I try to ignore the lack of symmetry. The smells of earth and fungus are so damp and inviting that after my fort is planted, I climb back into the hole.

"Hello!"

I lift my head. Mary's head is peeking over the garden wall.

"Vivian, what in the name of God are you at?"

"I dug my grave and now I've planted a fairy fort," I say.

"Ah, Jaysus, Vivian, you need to get a hold of yourself."

This sounds like something I could try, and I wrap my arms tightly around myself.

"What are you at now?" she asks.

"I'm trying to get a hold of myself but I can't reach all the way around."

"Ah, Vivian."

She shakes her head slowly. I feel New Year's Eve kind of lonely, the kind of lonely that throbs and grinds, until I remember Penelope.

"My friend dug it with me," I say, "it was fun."

"That's good. I haven't seen your sister about recently . . ." Her voice trails into an ellipsis and, although there's no question mark, she seems to expect a response. Well, two can play the punctuation game.

"She's very busy," I say, "she has lots of children . . ."

"Two, isn't it?"

"Two what?"

"Two children; I thought your sister had two children?"

"Yes, but they seem like a lot when they're together."

"Ah."

She smiles. Lines around her eyes form like wings when she smiles, etched so deep they almost bleed. She gives a half-wave.

"I'll let you get back to it, then."

"Okay, bye."

Her head disappears. I climb out of the hole and go into the house. I look at Lemonfish; he might benefit from a change of scenery. I bring his bowl outside and empty the contents into the hole. The water level drops so I refill the bowl a few times and empty it in. Lemonfish bobs about near the surface—I haven't seen him move so much in weeks. I say goodnight to him and go inside to eat cheese: tonight I hope to dream of the little people who will come out of my fairy fort. I picture them pulling themselves out of the earth wearing the mushrooms for hats and coming into my bedroom to lead me away. The more cheese I eat, the more little people I conjure up, so I chew as fast as I can before my brain catches up with my stomach and tells me to stop eating. When I've eaten my fill and beyond, I pour a gulp of whiskey into a saucer. I would like the fairies to get sufficiently tipsy that they're happy to come fetch me, but not so stewed that they get angry and shouty, even if a fairy shout is quieter than a human whisper.

18

I LIE IN bed awhile trying to figure out why I'm excited, and then I remember: my appointment with the hairdresser is scheduled for mid-morning. I have never been to a hairdresser before; my great-aunt used to cut my hair when it got ragged. I need to look my best, so I put on my great-aunt's tweed suit and frilly white blouse, and go downstairs and out the back garden to check how Lemonfish got through the night in his new home. When I reach the hole, I look in. The water has vanished, oh no, and Lemonfish is lying motionless on the dry soil with one eye staring up at me.

"Lemonfish, no!"

I lower myself into the hole and squat down and blow at him, but this doesn't seem to be the best way to perform mouth-to-gill resuscitation. I climb out and run to the kitchen for a jug of water, which I pour into the hole. The bottom fills with water and he rises—Lemonfish Lazarus I'll call him if he survives—but when the water settles, he floats still and glassy-eyed on the surface, not moving a fin. Suddenly my breakfast of cornflakes no longer seems appetising. Lemonfish ruled a kingdom no bigger than a fruit bowl, but he deserves to be treated like an ancient Egyptian king and buried with his treasures. I go inside and take his carton of food from the kitchen counter, along with some chocolate coins and a lemon from the fridge, to remind him of his first friends in this house. Then I go into the hoardroom and pick out a notebook with an ocean scene on the cover (I make sure there are no sharks because I think that would scare him), and some marbles. I bring the after-world treasures out to the garden and arrange them in the hole around the deceased. Then I run back inside for his bowl and place it upside down around him so he's on show in a glass case, like a famous saint or a dictator. I get the shovel from the shed and scoop some of the soil from Penelope's mound and scatter it over the bowl. I shape it into a pyramid fit for an Egyptian king. I try to think of what is said at burials on television, and I say in my most solemn voice:

"Scales to ashes, fins to dust."

Now I feel ripe for a poem so I finish with, "Your death is untimely, it's so unjust."

I balance one foot on the lip of the shovel and clasp the handle with both hands and bow my head. This feels sombre and fitting, like a scene I once saw in a painting.

I brush the soil from my hands, leave the house and walk through Blessington Basin. The pigeons are out in force, a kind of feathery force that could inflict real damage if they acted as one. They gather around the sign saying "Please Don't Feed the Pigeons" and produce a communal guttural "coo" that sounds like an impassioned protest about workers' rights. I loop to the left around the basin. Two men are sitting on a bench and two are standing facing them, hunched into each other. Their voices seem strained, pained, pushed from the depths of their bellies, as if the effort of making sounds was just too much; the pigeons have more vocal force. The man supping from a gold and blue can steps into my path.

"Excuse me, love, have you got any spare change?"

The "U" in "Excuuuuse me" takes up a sentence of its own.

"No, sorry."

I use the same two words when I'm asked if I have a light, a smoke, or money for a cup of tea. I walk down O'Connell Street and pass Prosperity Chambers, which makes me think about money, so I go into a newsagent to buy a scratch card, and walk back to scratch it under the word "prosperity." I fail to prosper. I walk on past Hammam Buildings, which has two large wooden doors that should be swept back by two butlers with elegant bows. I walk up to the doors but no butlers appear. If only they would add another "mah" at the end to make it "Hammammah," and spell it in capitals, "HAMMAMMAH." It could be a palindrome of a curse, a symmetrical curse against a mother.

I cross O'Connell Street at the Spire and walk up Henry Street. It's early, so the delivery vans have control of the street. Men jump in and out of vans and wheel boxes of goods through doors that I don't notice when the street is thick with shoppers. The street thrums with the engines of delivery vans and trucks, the roll and thunk and click of van doors, the beeps of reversing trucks, the squeaks of trolley wheels. I walk up Mary Street to the traffic lights, but crossing at the lights seems too fierce a jolt after the shock I had this morning, so I go into the shopping centre that used to be a hospital. It's supposed to be haunted, but I don't believe it because the clock above the entrance tells the right time; if I was a ghost, tampering with the clock would be the first item on my mischief list. I cut through the shopping centre to the supermarket that leads to Liffey Street, holding my nose so that I'm not tempted by the sweet buttery smell from its bakery. A lady in a hairnet and white coat is giving out free egg cups of fruit juice. I take one and she turns her smooth-tipped words on me about the health benefits of the juice. I nod—"yes, that sounds healthy alright"—and take a carton of juice. I walk to the next aisle and stuff it behind some crisps, then I leave the shop and wander around the small paved park behind the shopping centre. Old headstones line one wall, from the pub that used to be a church. I love buildings that used to be something else and that look more like the thing they used to be than the thing they are now. In the middle of the park, a bronze cow looks contented even though there is no grass to chew. I walk back through Liffey Street. The street sign for The Lotts has been completely blue-ed out. I step onto The Lotts and close my eyes but nothing happens, even though I'm off-map, on a street that doesn't exist, as close to another world as I can be. I walk on. The sign for Hotel Yard, another lane off Liffey Street, hasn't been greened-out, because the leprechauns prioritise sleeping over making their mark. I walk down Hotel Yard. I can't find a hotel or a yard, only a pair of women's underwear. Proby's Lane, further along Liffey Street, has been blue-ed out to read "PLAN." I write "PLAN" on the inside cover of my notebook next to "Dreadnaught"; it seems like a word to live by.

I go into the huge mostly-clothes shop halfway down Henry Street. It's so big it never feels crowded, it's so bright it almost feels gloomy. If I stand at the Henry Street entrance, I can see a whole building's length through to the Ilac Centre behind.

I come here when I need to know there are piles of umbrellas and shoes and candles and pillows and bread and meat to be had. I like to imagine being locked in here overnight. I'd start by running laps of the place—it looks like a football pitch worth of space—then I'd raid the supermarket downstairs. I'd cram cake and sweets and crisps into my mouth, then I'd take the halted escalator upstairs. I would take heaps of women's clothes, men's clothes, large children's clothes to the changing rooms and try them all on together. I'd run in and out of each changing room and then up to the homewares department, where I would set up a bed with piles of pillows and cushions and blankets. By now, I'd have worked up a second appetite, and I would raid the café on the top floor. I'd bring a bale of towels to the toilets and wash my face and dry each part of my face with a different towel: a pink towel for my nose, yellow for my eyes, green for my cheeks and, of course, a purple towel for my forehead. I would go to the ladies' and piss a dribble in each toilet and flush them all mightily. Then I'd turn on all the taps and the hand driers and blow my nose hugely with toilet paper from every stall. I'd light lots of candles and settle into bed, leaving the candles burning all night around the bed like Sleeping Beauty's byre (I would find out what a byre is first) and fall into a deep deep sleep. I don't know what would happen the next morning; this is where my imaginings end.

I leave through the shopping centre and walk to the hair salon. I was picturing a cowboy saloon with swinging wooden doors and sawdust floors and spitting and fighting, but this salon has a tiled floor and girls dressed in black with lots of big shiny hair.

"I'm Vivian, I ordered a haircut."

"Hi, Vivian, I'll just take your jacket."

One of the girls gives me a laminated card with the number forty-two on it. We seem to be having a raffle.

"Is the prize a bottle of shampoo?" I ask.

The girl looks at the other girls and gives a half-snort.

"No, that's for your coat."

"Oh."

I look at the card. Two twenty-ones are forty-two, but three fourteens is even better, and seven sixes is best of all.

"You can follow me, Vivian."

I walk behind the girl into a long room with mirrors on either side. It smells hot and clean, the hairdryers are hoover-loud, and there are small piles of hair on the floor. I press my eyes onto the back of the hairdresser until she comes to a stop and points me to a chair. I sit down, and she pushes a lever with her foot "*squeak squeak*," I feel like I'm being milked or inflated but it's only the chair rising upwards. The mirror in front of me takes up my whole front vision—this seems to be the way I talk to the hairdresser. I stare at my knees until a voice says,

"Just lean forward there and we'll get this on you."

I look up to a black cloak enclosing me. I could be a witch or a melancholic wizard or a puffed-up professor in this cloak, I could deliver pronouncements or cast spells or make impassioned speeches. A different hairdresser puts a batch of magazines on the ledge in front of me.

"Would you like tea or coffee?"

"Coffee, please, with lots of milk foam."

I'm being tended to by a team of black-clad angels, and I don't know where to look because hands are coming at me from all angles and different voices are saying my name. A girl brings coffee, and, finally, the girl who took my coat sits in the chair beside me. It's a relief to be at eye level with someone.

"So what can we do for you today?"

"You've already given me coffee and magazines and a cloak," I say, "it almost seems rude to ask for a haircut."

She gives another half-snort, closer to a whinny this time. "Are you looking for a trim or something totally different?"

"What would be totally different?"

"Well, you could go for a choppy bob or a slanted fringe or a . . ."

She seems excited by the thought of breaking my hair into pieces, but my neck already feels cold at the thought.

"I just want a trim," I say.

"Okay, how many inches will we take off?"

"One, please."

"Okay. And will we colour your hair today too, cover those greys?"

"There are greys?"

"Yeah, the grey hair coming through, did you not notice?"

I'm so surprised I almost look at myself in the mirror but I avert my eyes just in time.

"Like badger stripes or zebra stripes?"

"Have you not seen it in the mirror?"

Her voice is a long dose of surprise.

"I don't like mirrors."

"We could do a semi-permanent colour at the roots to hide the greys, something that will blend in with your natural colour."

"I don't want to be coloured in, I need to stay the same colour I started out."

"Okay, let's get your hair washed first."

"You're washing it?"

My hair hasn't been washed in a long while, it feels like a sticky paste at the top of my head with straggles coming out.

"It's a wash, cut, and blow-dry—it's included in the price."

I look over to the basins where a woman is sitting with her head leaning back. Her head is being hosed, and her neck looks long and exposed and vulnerable—if a knife-killer came in this minute, he'd go straight for her neck.

"I don't want to get hosed, can you cut my hair when it's dry? Please?"

"Alright."

She stands up and starts scissoring my hair, a miniature sword fight around my head *squang squang squang*. I squeeze my eyes shut in case the scissor-swords pierce my eyeball.

"Up to anything special tonight?" she asks.

"No, I buried a loved one this morning."

"Oh God, I'm so sorry, were you close?"

"Yes, he lived with me, but I could never tell what he was thinking."

"Yeah, they're all like that," she says, throwing her eyes to the ceiling. "Was it a nice funeral?"

"It was. I recited a poem and buried him with his favourite things."

"Ah, that's lovely, what did you bury him with?"

"His food and his bowl."

"Oh. No football jersey or anything?"

"No, I don't think he liked football, he didn't seem to care if it came on TV."

"Ah, it's terrible all the same. No kids?"

"What?"

"You didn't have kids together?"

"I don't think that's possible."

"Oh, I'm sorry."

"That's okay, I'm more upset that he's dead."

"Oh God, yeah, of course. What did he die of, if you don't mind me asking?"

"He had a fungal growth. And he was falling apart, he kept losing bits of himself."

"Jaysus, that sounds serious," she says, removing her hands from my head and wiping them on her skirt. "Are you not afraid it's contagious?"

"No, I never usually touched him, but sometimes he nibbled my fingers when I fed him."

"Oh."

Now there's a silence, a happy silence for me because I've had a to-and-a-fro of a conversation like I haven't had in a long time, but there's a tense quality to her silence that I hope the scissors don't catch. When she has finished snipping, a different hairdresser comes over to wipe the hairs off my cloak.

"Are you off out anywhere tonight?"

"I might go out the garden and check on my fairy fort."

"Oh."

Her "oh" sounds like she wants the conversation to end, but I've had such a successful conversation with the other girl that I want to continue.

"Isn't hair great all the same?" I say. "Where would we be without it."

"Bald," she says.

I hadn't expected an answer, I thought I was uttering one of those half-joke half-question sentences that produce laughs not responses.

"What would you do if a bald man came in and asked for a haircut?" I ask.

"He's not going to come in, is he, if he has no hair."

"But what if he hadn't looked in the mirror and didn't realise he was bald?"

"I don't know."

Now the silence has teeth in it. I pick the dirt out of my fingernails.

"Are you going anywhere nice on your holidays?" she asks.

"No."

"Oh."

She sounds like she really wants me to go somewhere and I've disappointed her.

"Oh, I forgot," I say, "I'm going to the Isle of Man. I've been learning Manx and I'm going to bring home a cat."

"That sounds nice. What's the weather like there?"

"Temperatures hit close to fifty, I hear."

The highest temperature I've seen is thirty degrees, but when I lie, I like to lie big.

"Oh."

Her voice is doubtful, but she ends the holiday conversation and holds a mirror behind my head.

"Now, what do you think?"

I raise my head and focus my eyes to the right of my reflection—seeing part of my behind-head is alright. It's lank and striped with frizzy white hairs and looks like the head of a stranger.

"It's lovely," I say, "just what I wanted."

"Good, good," she says, and she's already undoing the Velcro of the cloak at the back of my neck with a rip. Her head has moved beyond me and my holiday to the next cuttee.

"I'll get your coat for you," she says, snatching the number tag from my hands.

"Wait," I say (for I am brave with words now), "what does the number forty-two mean to you?"

Her face looks pained.

"Nothing, it's just a number."

"I think the 4 looks very unstable, only one leg holding up a chair of a number. The 2's leg is flattened so that it's more balanced, but 2 keeps looking backwards and I fear it's living in the past."

The girl is holding the gown and mirror with a strength so fierce that her knuckles are white, and there are white crescents on the tips of her fingernails like tiny onion slices.

"Is there such a thing as an onion manicure?" I ask.

She looks quickly to the reception area, her eyes bulging and pleading like a cow I saw on television that was about to be slaughtered. The phone rings and she breaks into a run and shouts "I'll get it!" I don't know where to be now: I've gotten up from the chair so it's not my chair anymore; I can't go to reception because I would be eavesdropping on the phone call. I stand in the middle of the salon looking at the floor, trying to avoid the mirrors. When the hairdresser ends the call and hangs up, I walk over to her, but she quickly disappears into a room behind reception. She comes out and pushes my coat into my hands and then goes back to the till.

"That'll be €45, please."

"Forty-five is even more unstable than forty-two, don't you think?"

"No, I mean yes."

She holds out her hand for the money.

"The 4 might be doing a one-legged flamingo act, but at least it's got one straight leg. Look at the 5—it's balancing on a curve, the kind of curve that won't straighten and could (if it wanted) keep curling around and topple the whole thing."

She stretches her arm out further for the money, and I hand it over.

"Just one more thing," I say. "Have you ever thought about what numbers would look like if we put them flat on their backs? It seems cruel to make them stand up straight all the time. Maybe when night falls, we should allow them to lie down."

The girl rummages in the till.

"So here's your €5 change, bye now—"

Before I can respond, she has run into the cloakroom and shut the door.

Wait, I want to say to her, if the coats go in the cloakroom, do the cloaks go in the coatroom? I look around, but the other hairdressers seem to be too engrossed in their work for such a topic, so I say a small quiet goodbye to the room and open the door. The building lets out a deep hot breath that whooshes me onto the street.

I walk north from O'Connell Bridge and head down Moore Street, where the smell of ripe fruit mixes with the smell of curry and spices from the Asian and African shops. I pass a woman selling fruit.

"Bananas there, ten for a eurrrrro!"

The woman drags the "R" into the "O" as if the "R" is an older cousin being forced to play with the younger "O." Her call is so strong and pure it's as if generations of effort went into a single word. I repeat the way she says *"eurrrro"* in a mutter to myself, but it sounds like a misbegotten croak from my mouth. I need to develop an accent, I need to feel at ease with my syllables, but I haven't used enough words aloud and I don't know what kind of accent I'd like, or if I get to choose. If I could find the perfect combination of words in the right accent, a portal would surely open up. I walk over to the banana-lady's stall.

"I would like some fruit, please."

I put a vowel between the "F" and the "R" in fruit and another vowel between the "P" and the "L" in please so it comes out: "I would like some feroot, pihlease."

"What would you like, love?"

"What would you recommen-ed?"

She stares at me like I'm an unpicked scab.

"I've got some lovely peaches and grapes."

"I'd like some gerapes, pihlease."

"Any peaches?"

"No, I don't like peaches, they're like juicy velvet. Velehvet."

The words are taking too long to say. This won't do as an accent. I hand over the money.

"Where are you from, love, with an accent like that?"

"I'm not quite sure—that's what I'm trying to find out."

She narrows her eyes and stares hard at me; her face is a criss-cross of dents and clefts like a bashed-in car door. I say good-bye and walk down the street. The stalls sell flowers, fruit and vegetables or fish. They have striped awnings and two metal doors at the back, like portable kiosks. The fruit and vegetables are displayed on metal steps, as if they are singers in a chorus. In a fruit choir, the apples would have chubby rounded voices and the lemons would reach the high notes. The pears would do their best but they'd always be a little off key. The raspberries would twitter in squeaky voices, and the grapes would be impossible to train—they'd huddle in bunches and mock the choir mistress.

The shops on this street are packed tight together like a large family. A large yellow sign above my head says "Lucky Four Bingo," but surely there'd be no bingo if four always won. I pass the yellow-and-blue supermarket with uniformed staff outside smoking. When I reach Parnell Street I cross at the lights and walk up Dominick Street. Dominick Lane has been blue-ed out to read "DOM," which I write in my notebook, humming the "Big Bad Dom" tune from the bleach ad on television when I was small. Two mannequins lean against the upstairs window of a disused warehouse near the top of the street, as if they're taking a break from a naked aerobics class. Opposite the concrete Virgin Mary at Broadstone Station, I pass a petrol-puddle rainbow on the side of the road, a display of fairy firepower that shouldn't be ignored. I bend down and sniff: it smells chemical and dreadful and gorgeous, like garden sheds and garages and uncooked cement. The rainbow has formed full circle, and the uncoloured inside is small so I step gently inside, perch on my tiptoes, close my eyes, and wish hard. It would help if I knew what I was wishing for. I open my eyes because I'm losing balance and now, *oh no*, I drop flat-footed into the rainbow and the colours re-swirl. I squeeze my eyes shut and wish hard, because a reforming rainbow must be one of the most magical things that can happen to tarmac. When I open my eyes, nothing has happened. I walk the rest of the way home and turn on the radio. The news is being read by a woman with a steady accent who spends a good measure of time on each syllable. I sit and repeat words after her: "tribunal," "hearing," "recession," "high court ruling," "shortage of hospital beds," "suspended sentence," "death by misadventure," which makes me think of Huckleberry Finn's raft overturning on the Mississippi. The words she uses are not words I use, so I change the dial. I pause between stations where there's a bristle of static, the wordless gush of it settling something inside me. I trace my route onto greaseproof paper. Today I walked a Turkmenistan with a tail.

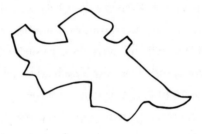

KIOSKS. KIOSKS. KIOSKS. Kiosks." When I say the word over and over again it stops making sense as a word so I write it down on a piece of paper and put it in my pocket to make it real. When I was small, I used to watch a television programme about a man who wore forty coats with fifty pockets. He owned a flying sweet shop that was shaped like a kiosk, and I wanted, more than anything, to live in that sweet shop. If there is one thing I could do now, it would be to stand behind a counter and measure out sweets. I don't like calculating sums of money, so it would be a charity sweet shop with sugary donations for the poor.

I walk down the North Circular—I would like to call it the Norrier, but I don't feel I have the right—to the Phoenix Park, and follow the path to the Tea Rooms in the kiosk. It's white and octagonal with a red roof almost half the size of the building. If the witch in "Hansel and Gretel" had a holiday home in Dublin, this would be it. Inside, there seems to be a kiosk within a kiosk containing food items, with a hatch in front of the inner kiosk to order from. I ask for coffee and a slice of chocolate biscuit cake. A pair of swinging half-doors lead to the kitchen; I have an urge to hurl myself through them with my hands shaped into a gun, shouting, "Put your hands *UP!*," but that might jeopardise my cake order. I bring my food to a table in the corner and bite into the cake but, *oh no*, they used ginger biscuits—how unwise to put such a divisive biscuit in a cake without warning. I pick at the chocolate parts surrounding the biscuit and think about kiosks, hatches, cubby holes, booths, pavilions, gazebos: cosy, odd-shaped structures halfway between a piece of furniture and a room. When I've finished my coffee, I walk out of the park to the bus stop. A snail trail loops and swirls across the path as if somebody took a silver-inked pen for a walk. I imagine a giant snail that could tuck the kiosk onto its back and carry it off, teapots, cups and all. At the bus stop, a middle-aged woman comes over. She's holding a newspaper and mumbling to herself. She stares at me.

"When's the next bus?"

I look at the electronic screen.

"Three minutes."

"Why do they make newspapers like this?" she asks. "They're impossible to fold."

"Maybe they're allergic to staples," I say, "but if you ironed it, it might fold better."

She looks at me suspiciously.

"I'm not allowed to iron."

"Oh, I don't iron my clothes either, you're not missing much."

She shakes her head fiercely from side to side as if she's trying to get rid of some especially tenacious lice.

"How many minutes now?"

"Two."

She puts her face closer to mine.

"I'm having lunch with the president. Where can I buy new shoes?"

"Henry Street has lots of shops," I say.

"Am I?"

"Are you what?"

"Am I having lunch with the president?"

"You said you were."

"Oh, right."

I'm not sure how to fill the silence that follows until the electronic screen changes.

"One minute now," I say.

"One minute of what?"

"One minute of time until the bus comes."

"Am I getting the bus?"

"I don't know. I am."

"Oh."

The bus roars up the slope. When it stops, I put my arm around the woman and bundle her on. She stands beside the driver.

"Where are you off to, love?" he asks.

"I'm going to dinner with the president," she says.

"I thought you said it was lunch," I say.

"It's dinner," she says, glaring at me.

The driver snorts.

"I don't care if you're going to breakfast with the pope, where are you going to?"

"I told you, I'm going to meet the president."

"The president lives in the park," I say. "You have to go back that way." I gently shove her out of the way and pay my fare.

"Oh, right," she says, and she shuffles off the bus with another shake of her head.

The driver smiles at me.

"Mad as a bag of cats, wha'?"

"Completely loo-lah," I say, and I twirl my finger around my temple.

Then I say "Leeson Street, please," in my most superior voice because for once I'm not the mad one, I'm the person who puts mad people on buses and pushes them off again. I look down the bus. I'm the first person on and it feels like *my* bus; I have the pick of the seats. I sit in the front seat, but I might have to make way for old people, so I get up and sit in the double seats at the back, but someone opposite me could ask me for the time and I don't have a watch, so I move to the second seat from the back. I am the Goldilocks of Dublin Bus with my just-right seat. When we reach Leeson Street, I push the bell and walk the length of the bus without clutching the yellow poles because they're usually sticky. A gang of guerrilla passengers with glue on their hands must get on every bus in Dublin and spread the glue from pole to pole.

I look at the driver in the mirror.

"She was really for the birds, wasn't she?"

The driver looks at me in the mirror.

"What?"

I repeat my sentence. I wonder if the driver notices that I used a phrase involving birds after he used one involving cats. He turns his gaze back to the road and says, "Yeah," but he has cut the word as short as it will go, his throat wrapped tight around it. The bus stops and the doors open.

"Thanks, bye now," I say, "see you again."

I give him more words than I usually give drivers, because I was the first one on and it really was my bus.

I cross Leeson Street to the red-brick kiosk on an island in the middle of the road. It's a rectangular shape, with the occasional bulge and jut and a large circular window almost the size of the front wall, like a see-through door to a hobbit hole. A red-and-white striped awning hangs over the window, but *awning* is such an ugly gape of a word, I'll call it a "pluice." If I tried to enter "pluice" in the dictionary, I'd have a fight on my hands to keep it from being spelled "ploose," but I am up to the task. I walk around the building. It used to be a public toilet, so I give a few great sniffs, but no smell remains. Inside is wooden, with snacks and fruit for sale. I get coffee, and bring it to a silver table outside. When I look around, the streets come at me at odd angles: everything seems at a slant, there is no symmetry, no order, no system. A blue clock at the top of a large, ivy-covered house tells the wrong time. I need to be in symmetry, so I get up and cross over to the canal. The canal flows in a straight line, and a duck leads two ducklings in a neat triangle; all's straight in the world. I walk towards the statue of the poet on a bench—he looks so calm and serious compared to the poet at the other canal. The long grasses on the canal bank rustle in the wind; if they're not grasses but wheat or oats, then I'm witnessing the prequel to bread or porridge. I turn onto Northumberland Road and look at the brass plaques outside gates, which wouldn't be so grand if they were brass placks. And "plack" would suit the ugly tooth-coating better. I pass by embassies in quiet buildings that look as if they're locked into a deep sleep. They should keep in mind that the hero from an action movie could blast in at any moment.

At the junction with Lansdowne Road, I see my next kiosk. It's a neat hexagon, decked out in shades of brown and cream like a chocolate bar. I circle the building but the shutters are down, and a notice tells its "Dear Valued Customers" when it will reopen. If I bought coffee here every day, I might have value, but I would never be worth as much as the kiosk, which I heard is on the most expensive piece of land in Ireland. I don't know how land value is decided—I'm imagining gold ingots or silver bullion buried beneath. I'd like to live in this kiosk because it looks the cosiest, but I'd rather carry it off somewhere first because these roads are too busy and the big grey building nearby looks unhappy. To find out if my bed would fit in the kiosk, I lie flat on my back and stretch my body along the length of one side. It's difficult to see if my feet are within the line of the kiosk. A man in a suit walks by.

"Excuse me," I say, loudly, because he's wearing earphones.

He pulls out one earphone and looks at me a little anxiously. "Are you alright?"

"Yes, thanks. Could you tell me if my feet are sticking out?"

He stares at my feet.

"Well, they're sticking out at the ends of your legs."

"I mean, are they sticking out beyond the kiosk."

He looks at the kiosk and then at my feet.

"It's hard to say."

"Have you got any chalk?"

"Sorry?"

"If you had some chalk you could draw a line from the edge of my feet to the edge of the kiosk, and then I'd know."

"Know what?"

"Know if I could fit inside lying down."

His face puckers and he brings the earphones up to his ears again.

"Thanks for your help," I say quickly, because it's okay if I end the conversation first. He nods and walks off. I sit up, keeping my legs stretched out, and open my bag. I take some copper coins out of my purse and start throwing them gently, until one lands just where my heel ends. This is my marker: I crawl forward to the coins but, *oh no*, there are lots lying around, and I don't know which was the deciding one. The copper pattern the coins have made looks like a trail from a snail with digestive problems.

"Is everything alright there?"

I look up at the sudden thud of a voice; a guard is standing over me.

"I'm fine, I'm just looking for my money."

I gather up the coins, trying to remember their pattern to map them later.

"Would you mind telling me what you're up to?"

He speaks in italics, all slant and emphasis. I climb up off my knees with a *creck crick crack* and look at him. He wants nice tidy reasons for concrete problems that are solvable in this world.

"I was playing," I say.

"Right, well next time, play in your own home."

"But there's no kiosk at home," I say. "If only there was a flat-pack kiosk I could buy and set up in the garden."

The guard's face is set hard, so I say, "Thank you, officer," and scuttle off. I wish people would ask the right questions; everybody wants to know if I'm alright, nobody wants to know how to sleep in a kiosk.

I walk back into town. Stephen's Place has been blue-ed out to read "_ _ _ PHEN'S PLA_E." I write it down in my notebook, relieved that the Smurfs left in the apostrophe. Apostrophe. I repeat it aloud: "apostrophe, apostrophe, apostrophe."

It could replace "achoo" as a sneeze-word, if the sneeze has more than two syllables—but who would I write to suggest such a thing? I walk to the gazebo by the duck pond in St. Stephen's Green. It's open on all sides, the kind of place a singing couple would haunt, not cosy and enclosed enough to count as a kiosk. I leave the green and walk down Dawson Street to my final kiosk of the day: a telephone kiosk with one green side and three cream-coloured sides. The roof is turret-shaped, with a knob on top like a lid that you could pull off. I step inside with my eyes closed, and when I open them, I'm facing a battered blue phone. The smell of piss burns my eyes. I close the door behind me and pick up the receiver.

"Hello?" I say. "Hello?"

But there is only a dull beep, and the screen tells me to pay a minimum of €2. Even if I had a €2 coin, I wouldn't know who to call or what to say to them. I replace the phone in its cradle quickly—someone might call with a message and the line shouldn't be busy.

I TURN ON my computer to research how to get a new word into a dictionary. If I could invent a new word and get it going a bit in the world, speaking might come a whole lot easier. I read: ". . . the process of adding any new word, or a new sense of an existing word, is long and painstaking, and depends on the accumulation of a large body of published (preferably printed)

citations showing the word in actual use over a period of at least ten years . . ."

I may not have a decade to work on squeezing my new word into print, and "painstaking" has too many harsh consonants, so I give up on this. If it was a simple process, I'd like to introduce positive versions of negative words: "thinkable, bridled, gusted" and "gruntled" would all be put into use without their nasty uns and dises. I would also ask the dictionary to spell "coax" as "coaccs," because the half-looped "C"s are softer than the harsh intersecting lines of the "X." I would request that a new letter be introduced: an "N" added to an "M" in words with a double "M," so that an "M" and a half—a triple horseshoe shape—would replace "MM." And, while I was on the subject, I'd throw in a request for the letter "K" to be abolished. I feel it's ugly and overused, when a good "C" or a double "CC" would do nicely. (I would like to write a book without using the letter "K," but then it would just be a "boo.")

Now I move onto my job search. After keeping Lemonfish alive for so long, I should be qualified for some kind of goldfish care position. I type "Goldfish" into the search box, but all that comes up is a sales-and-marketing position in Goldfish Marketing. Much as I like Lemonfish, I don't think I could find fulltime employment in talking up his good points. Next, I search for "Reader." An ad for "Psychics, Tarot and Angel Card Readers" comes up. The job description states that "Good Computer Skills are necessary and Experience in Tarot is vital." It seems strange that "Psychic Abilities" are not under "Skills," and that "Computer Skills" are placed ahead of "Tarot Experience." Even stranger is the industry category the job is placed in: "Miscellaneous, Call Centre/Customer Service, Sales." There must be no category for magic. I scour each category looking for something suitable. A company is seeking an experienced beef slaughter and deboning operative. I think I'd like to be an operative of something; it sounds meaningful. An ad appears for courses in manual metal arc welding or oxy-acetylene welding. I would like to be able to say I'm a welder. It sounds substantial and useful, and being an elder with a "W," it sounds wise.

A sudden, shrill noise jolts me and sends me into my standing position, but I don't know where to rush to. The screen on the house phone flashes; someone is calling me! I pick up the receiver.

"This is Vivian speaking. Who is calling?"

"Hi, I'm Peter, I wonder if you have a few minutes to answer some questions about your service provider?"

Peter sounds like someone who would have his lunch eaten at his desk by 10 a.m.

"I'm very busy, Peter, but I can spare a couple of minutes."

"Great, thanks. Firstly, what age bracket do you fall into?"

He lists chunks of numbers, and I picture my age in curly brackets {}, then straight brackets [], then circle brackets (), all of which look like the start and finish of something.

"I can't put my age in a bracket like that," I say, "I'd be frozen in that age group on your survey forever."

A silence falls on the other end, but it's more of a rise than a fall; it rises through the receiver and pinches my earlobes.

"Also, I say, what exactly do you mean by years?"

"Sorry?"

"Have you ever thought about a place where a year is not 365 days?"

"No."

His sentences are shrinking, he can barely tap out the consonants.

"Have you ever thought: what if we all got together and decided that we wouldn't let May turn into June just yet, that we'd hold onto May for another couple of days?"

"I can't say I have."

"Or if we decided to double up on December and skip January altogether—January's a right sulk of a month, it has far too many days."

"Indeed. Can you tell me what Internet provider you're with?"

"Can you give me a hint?"

"Eircom, Imagine, UPC, Magnet . . ."

"UPC."

"And what's your mobile provider?"

"UPC."

"UPC isn't a mobile provider."

"Oh. Eircom?"

"Okay."

He asks lots of multiple choice questions with four answers about things I have never thought of, things I know nothing about, and I choose the third option for each one. Surely I will be right one-quarter of the time.

"Right," he says, "what do you use your phone for most?"

"Sending messages to Penelope."

"Okay, anything else?"

"Sending messages to my sister, but she rarely replies."

There is a strange noise on the other end of the line, some ways between a gurgle and a choke. I fear this survey could go on until winter.

"Peter," I say, "do you ever go to fancy-dress parties?"

"What?"

"I was just wondering if I could come along sometime. I've never been to a fancy-dress party, but if I did go, I'd dress up as a migraine. What do you dress up as?"

There's a silence, and Peter's voice, when it comes, is full of knots.

"Right, I think we're done here, thanks for your time."

"Wait," I say, "you haven't told me your favourite costume," but he rattles through a paragraph about confidentiality and how this information will be used, and then he unplugs his voice and hangs up. I press the phone hard into my ear. I think I can hear the sea in the distance, in a crackle and hiss beyond the beep. Peter might not have invited me to a fancy-dress party, but I have the sea in my ear and my words for the day spoken and it's not yet midday.

20

I WAKE IN a lunge, grasping at the air in front of me. In my dream, there was a wall, a solid grey wall that would not budge when I shoved against it, and I was held back not just by the wall, but by something pulling me from behind. Now the wall is gone, however, and I'm sat in the bed with a low dismal feeling that there's a ferocious amount of work to be done. Oh yes, my sister is coming, with her husband and children. For dinner, I said I would cook them dinner. They will produce whole continents of words between them, but few will be directed at me, so they don't count. I get out of bed and put on my great-aunt's tweed skirt suit with a white frilly blouse underneath. Then I pull on two pairs of tan tights to cover the gap between skirt and ankle, and lace up my great-aunt's grey, thick-soled shoes. The skirt is loose, so I find a hair elastic in a drawer, gather up the excess fabric at the waist and tie it. The jacket has padded shoulders that stand out stiffly from my body, and the knotted ball of waist material bulges into the jacket but no matter; I am dressed up for visitors. I eat breakfast standing up because I'm sure that's what busy career women in suits do. Then I gather up my shopping bags and walk to the butcher's. The butcher is a fat man with a red meaty head that I'm glad of—it wouldn't do if he looked like fish or lentils. When I enter the shop he nudges the young lad beside him, and the pair of them look me up and down as if my outfit is not quite the thing.

"Your arms aren't folded," I say.

"What's that?"

"In photographs of butchers, their arms are always folded, like this."

I fold my arms across my chest. The men look from me to each other and back to me. They have no answers, it falls to me to kill the silence.

"I would like some meat," I say.

"Well, you're in the right place, then," the butcher says, and they both snigger.

"I'm cooking dinner for five people, what would you suggest?"

He points to a large creamy hunk of flesh with red peeking out from the top, like a paper cone with a sweet red jelly treat inside. "I've a lovely leg of lamb there—three hours in the oven and you're good to go."

"I won't be going anywhere," I say. "I'm hosting today, but I'll take it."

I'm pleased the process has been so simple. One piece of meat is simpler than finicking with five smaller pieces. The lamb costs more than I spend on my weekly shop, but I hand over the money as if I do this all the time. It's heavy, so heavy that I wonder how a chunk this big could be less than a quarter of a baby sheep. I leave the butchers and walk to the fruit-and-vegetable shop. I want to ask if the shop could be called a producery, but the lady behind the till looks short on temper.

"Hello," I say, "what kind of vegetables would I cook with a leg of lamb?"

"Potatoes, peas, and carrots," she says.

"Okay."

I scoop up those items in my arms and bring them to the till. "It's my first dinner party," I say, "I want it to be special."

"What are you doing for dessert?"

"Oh, I hadn't thought about that."

I don't know why; my head is usually in the pudding before I even think about the main course.

"Do children eat dessert?" I ask.

She laughs, a scratching raucous laugh that could scrape chips of paintwork off the walls.

"Is the Pope Catholic?"

I force a laugh, but it sounds like it came from a bottle. I pay for the vegetables and cross the road to the bakery. The glass shelves display mounds of pastries and cakes and buns. There are: chocolate eclairs, coffee slices, custard slices, tiffin slices, meringues, fancies, cupcakes, fairy cakes, chocolate biscuit cake, gingerbread men, cream doughnuts and other spongy cakes, in muted colours that I don't recognise. There are also large cakes: black forest gateaux, lemon drizzle cake, lemon cream cake, coffee cake, chocolate fudge cake, fruit cake and tea bracks.

I don't know in which direction my niece's and nephew's sweet teeth veer, so I buy two of every bun and walk home with cardboard boxes dangling by twine from my fingers, sticking out a ways on either side of me like I'm peddling cardboard boxes. When I get home, I put the cakes on the table and the lamb on a baking tray in the oven.

"Goodbye," I say to the lamb, and I wave.

It feels like waving goodbye to a child at the school gates who will be killed in school later that day. When it comes out it will look completely different, so it really is goodbye forever. The butcher didn't say what temperature to cook it at, and I don't want to poison my guests with half-cooked meat, so I turn the oven to the highest setting and close the door. I put the potatoes in one pot and the vegetables in another and cook them in a boiling fury. Then I lay the table for five people. I am so wiped clean by all this grocery shopping and boiling and roasting, I feel like I could start anew. I tuck my nose under the collar of my blouse. It smells a little like the butcher shop under here: a dull meaty thud of a smell. If my guests get a whiff, they'll think it's uncooked lamb. I'm not sure what to do with myself while the food is cooking so I take out my notebook and pen and start a list of conversation topics:

1. *The Children*
2. *Politics*
3. *Penelope*
4. *Holidays*

There's something on the list for everybody. I take some sticky tape from the drawer, cut a piece, stand on a chair, and stick the list to the wall near the clock. Then I sit and watch the oven, but I don't know what I should be watching for. Food cooks in such a silent, devious way; I wish it screamed when it started to burn.

THE BLEAT OF the doorbell surprises me out of my sitting. I turn my face into a smile and tug myself out of the chair to open the door.

"Welcome," I say, "do come in."

My sister is wearing a red top and a purple skirt: she looks like mixed berries. I'd like to pour yoghurt over her head. Her husband, Pat, is wearing khaki, even though he's not in the army or the jungle.

Lucy and Oisin have mashed their faces into their parents' legs.

"Children, I have cake!" I squeak, because people talk in high voices around children. Oisin's face unfurls from my sister's leg.

"Cake?"

Vivian looks as if she's dropped her toast butter-side down.

"Don't mention cake until they've eaten their dinner," she hisses.

Oh no. The children have already gone into the kitchen and spotted the plates of cakes. I run after them and grab the plates and put them in the cupboards. They both start to cry.

"Don't worry," I say, "we're having lamb—you know, *Mary had a little lamb, little lamb, little lamb.*"

I sing but I only scrape the high notes, so I clear my throat to start again. Oisin's eyes grow large and he looks from me to my sister, who silences me with a fierce stare.

"Don't worry, kids," she says, "we're not eating any little lambs."

Pat is staring at the books on the shelves as if the secret of the universe was written on the spines.

"Tell it to me when you find it," I say.

"Tell what to you?"

"The secret of the universe."

He eyes my sister past my head. My words are the wrong sort, so I close my mouth and go to check on the meat. I wrap a dishcloth around my right hand, open the oven door and pull out the tray. The lamb has shrunk, wizened brown and hard: this is some brand of fleshy alchemy. I put it on a plate, then I scoop out the potatoes and carrots and peas—they're as soft as the lamb is hard—and put them dripping and soggy onto plates. I bring the plates to the table. Vivian and Pat stare at the meat like it's alive but it's the opposite of alive; it's even deader than it was earlier. I start hacking at the meat with a sharp knife. The going is tough, so I saw the knife into the joint in an L-shape and pull out chunks with my hands. I divide these chunks among the plates until the bone is left bare like a pale truncheon. Then I spoon out a mush of potatoes and vegetables onto each plate and set the plates in front of each person. Oisin is sitting in the chair opposite my list.

"Oisin, that's my seat."

I tip his chair forward a little.

"*Aaagghh!*" he screams, a sound that can't occur in nature.

"Vivian, can't you just let him stay there?"

My sister is hissing at me again, what a snake she is.

"I need to see the clock," I say, "it's important."

I tip Oisin all the way forward until his small head cracks like a soft-boiled egg on the edge of the table. Now the screams are three-dimensional: they reach great heights and stretch great lengths and span large breadths; they suck the air out of the room and fling it back, giving back less and less with each scream so the air gets tauter and leaner and meaner. My sister rubs the child's head and makes soft murmurs, but at least he's on her lap now and not on my chair. I sit down and look at my plate; it's an assault of a meal. When the screams die down to a whimper and Oisin has scuttled over to the chair beside his father, I clap my hands three times.

"Eat up," I say, "it doesn't look like much but maybe it will taste alright."

Pat mutters something and Vivian elbows him and says, "Come on, kids, eat up."

I lean forward and squint at my list of conversation topics. "How are the children?" I ask Vivian.

She smiles—her first real smile since she came—and empties packets of stories onto the table, stopping every now and then to say, "Isn't that right, Lucy?" or "Do you remember that, Oisin?" I try to eat, but the meat is leathery and I can't progress beyond chewing. If I swallowed, there would be meat-shaped bulges in my throat like a rat in the gullet of a snake. I look around the table. Pat picks at the meal with his fork but doesn't bring the fork to his mouth. The children haven't touched theirs, and Vivian is talking so much she isn't eating. I lean and squint for the next conversation topic.

"Pat," I say, but it must be too loud or too sudden because he jumps in his chair, "Pat, do you believe in politics?"

He leans forward, "That's an interesting question, Vivian. I suppose politics is a necessary . . ."

He continues talking as I pile all the uneaten food onto my plate, gather the plates and put them in the sink. Then I bring the plates of cakes to the table. Oisin reaches out to take one, but my sister holds his wrist.

"Vivian, can you bring over some plates, please?"

"Oh no," I say. That would be needless washing-up. "The table is clean enough to eat off."

I reach in and take an eclair, and the children grab a bun each and stuff them in their mouths, grab and stuff again. My sister's forehead puckers into a frown, and she hisses a *fffff* of a breath between her lip and teeth. Pat is still talking about politics in a low-grade background hum. I listen for every third word and try to make new sentences from them: "negotiations . . . constituency . . . forward . . . votes . . ."

"Where did you get the suit, Vivian?" my sister asks.

"It's Great-Aunt Maud's," I say. "Do you like it?"

"It makes you look like a—"

Pat leaps in.

"—like a lady, Vivian, you look lovely."

"Thank you," I say, and I stand up and do a small twirl, and I keep twirling faster and faster like a whirling dervish. I point one arm to the ceiling and another to the floor and twirl as fast as my feet will let me. Beyond the swish and tap of my feet on the tiles I feel a terrible silence, a vacuum of a silence that threatens to pull me into it. I slow to a halt, and meet eight wide eyes.

"It's my whirling dervish dance," I say, "it connects me to different worlds."

"Walling dawvis," Lucy says and she slides out of her chair and starts twirling around. I show her how to point her arms, but before she can learn the dance properly my sister is out of her chair and scooping Lucy up. I sit down again. My head has been emptied of thoughts and filled with air pockets. I lean for another bun and sneak a squint at the list. When Pat takes a breath from his politics, I shout, "*Penelope!*"

Pat and Vivian turn sharply to me.

"What?"

"I have a friend called Penelope and she isn't pronounced Peeny-Lope."

Vivian's face shoots up.

"A friend? Where did you meet her?"

"I advertised," I say proudly; my sister always tells me to be more proactive.

She and her husband exchange a cautious little glance.

"Where did you advertise?"

"On a tree, I didn't need to use an agency."

"Oh, Vivian," she says, and there's more sigh than voice in her words.

Pat sits forward. "What's she like, this Penelope?"

"She's an artist," I say, "and she likes cats and cake and biscuits. She paints cats, but she doesn't paint cake or biscuits."

"I see," he says, and he turns to my sister and gives a small shrug.

"I like her a lot, except for her breath."

My sister looks at me with a grave expression like she's deciding what to wear to my funeral.

"I'm sorry about the burnt dinner," I say, because my sister likes to be apologised to.

"You should really use a cookbook," she says, and she tinkles some names that sound like church bells: Delia, Nigella, Lily.

"I would like to learn to cook something in a big pot," I say, "A whole meal in one pot that I could watch and know when things were starting to go wrong."

There is no response, so I start the next topic.

"Are you going on holidays this summer?"

Vivian sits forward.

"Yes, we're going to our villa in France. It feels more like a home from home by now, doesn't it, Patrick?"

She calls him Patrick when she's showing off, as if she thinks an extra syllable adds importance. Pat's cheeks turn pink, and he shifts in his chair.

"Yes, we'll go over for a couple of weeks in July."

He leans backwards while my sister leans forwards.

"I didn't know you had a house in France," I say.

"We've had it for a few years," she says. "The children love it, they just run around barefoot like little savages."

I look at the children. Lucy is wearing a stiff dress with frilly ankle socks and pointy-toed shoes, Oisin is wearing slacks and a shirt and tie: they look less like savages and more like a Victorian princess and midget businessman.

"Oh, did I mention there's a pool? We have the neighbours in for wine and cheese by the pool—such a civilised way of life."

"I have wine!" I shout. "And cheese!"

I run to the cupboard and pull out the bottle of white wine, then I take a butt of orange cheddar and a tub of cream cheese from the fridge. I set them on the table and skim the blue fur from the top of the cream cheese. There is a rush of murmurs from my sister and her husband.

"No, no, I'm driving, I'm not drinking, thank you."

"But it'll be like France," I say, "we'll drink wine and eat cheese and I'll turn up the heating and we can pretend we're in France."

My sister stands up and scrapes her chair back.

"I'll just bring Oisin to the toilet, then we should go."

Oisin's face is in his cake and he screams when she picks him out of it, covered in white cream like an albino minstrel. She brings him upstairs, and Pat leans forward to Lucy.

"Are you ready to go soon, Lu?"

Lucy doesn't answer. I don't know how he can subtract a syllable from his daughter's name, especially after he has been given an extra syllable by his wife. The room falls into a hush; the only thing breaking the silence is Pat's foot jiggling against the table leg. He flattens his hands on the table, arranging them symmetrically with the tips of his thumbnails touching.

"Are you making a 'W' for yourself or an 'M' for Lucy?"

He turns slowly to me.

"I'm sorry . . . ?"

"The point where your thumbs join is either the centre peak of the 'W' or the centre trough of the 'M,' which is it?"

"I don't know," he says in a voice like threadbare socks.

A silence follows that rips at my ears with its intensity, it feels as if pots and kettles and other metal objects are being hurled across the room in a clanging free-for-all. Eventually my sister descends the stairs with a thud and a creak, and she storms into the kitchen carrying the boy.

"What in Christ's name is the meaning of this, Vivian?"

She points at Oisin's trouser leg with the potential squirrel tail stuck onto it.

"You have a tail, Oisin," I say, "like a bunny rabbit."

He grins.

"What are you *doing*, what *is* this?"

My sister's voice contorts to match her face. She is all atwist.

"I was trying to make a squirrel out of a mouse," I say, "but I've made a rabbit out of a child instead: a wonky rabbit with a tail on his leg."

I stroke Oisin's tail and he giggles. My sister sticks her face in mine.

"Do you know how much these trousers cost? He was supposed to wear these trousers in France."

"But barefoot savages don't need trousers," I say.

Pat snorts.

"Patrick," she barks, "we're leaving."

He picks up Lucy, who screams, which sets Oisin off again.

The noise crumples my sister's mouth into a purse, like she has drunk orange squash without adding water, but I'm happy because the children want to stay here with cake and the chance of rabbit tails. Pat and Vivian leave in a rummage of children and bags and coats, and I wave goodbye at the door. It would have been nice if they'd left with smiles on their faces and thanks on their tongues, but I consider the visit a success because only 50 percent of the guests left in tears. I go into the living room, fold myself onto the blue velvet armchair and breathe in the silence. My lone silence has the quality of marshmallows, padded with sugary dough, but other people's silence is punctured with pointy, jagged blades. I feel like I have filled a pocked tray with plastic buttons or built a tower of beakers without toppling them; some of my sister's words may have been hissed or shouted at me, but they count as words nonetheless. I put my arms out on either side of me and waft the air towards me. Then I tuck my nose and chin under my collar and breathe in my great-aunt's smell combined with my own: if the scent of lavender and beef and cobwebs was ever bottled, this would be the result. To quiet the clamour of family noise in my head I turn the radio dial to static, and listen to the surge and crackle from beyond.

⌒

I LEFT THE country once, when I accompanied my great-aunt to Paris. The streets in that city were wide, and the buildings looked like paintings of themselves. I had learnt French in school, but I don't like saying the French "R"—it's a gag of phlegm in my throat—so I used only words with no "R"s, and avoided red wine and oranges and crêpes. I thought that the next time I went abroad I would visit all the countries in the world with stars on their national flags. The number of days that I would spend in each country would be in proportion to the number of stars on its flag. Visiting my sister's holiday home in a country with a starless flag would not be ideal, but it could be the making of me. Two Vivians in one house seems like a lot, two Vivians out of five people, but I could take the children for walks in the forest and we could make breadcrumb trails to find our way back. We could hunt for fairies in the woods and mermaids in the swimming pool—mermaids with hair frizzed green by the chlorine. We could buy cakes topped with glazed fruit in the bakery and have pastry picnics in the garden. These plans make me so giddy, I pick up the phone and call my sister, even though she only left a few hours ago. She answers with a double serving of cream in her voice.

"Hello?"

"It's me," I say, "I have an idea."

"Oh?"

The voice is semi-skinned milk.

"I'll come to France with you and mind the children while you spend time with Pat—with Patrick."

There's an intake of breath on the other end.

"Well, Vivian," she says, her voice thinned to water, "we usually use that time to spend just as a family . . ."

"I'm family," I say, "it's perfect!"

"Let's talk about this another time, Vivian. I'm tired, the kids are tired. I need to go."

"Okay, *bye*!" I shout, and hang up before she does. It's important I can claim some small victories.

21

I'M POURING A glass of water at the kitchen sink when I notice the arch of a rainbow outside the window. It's a perfect bow, the edges of the colours barely blurring into each other. I recite "Richard Of York Gave Battle In Vain" and, sure enough, the colours match the rhyme in the right order: red, orange, yellow, green, blue, indigo violet. It's always a surprise when these things work out right. The "In Vain" colours— indigo and violet—blend in disappointingly with the sky, so I focus my gaze on the "Richard Of York" end, which seems to meet the earth nearby. I snatch up my keys and the closest im- plement for digging—a bread knife—and hurry out the door. As I pass Bernie's garden, she pops up from behind the wall.

"Where are you off to in such a hurry?"

"I'm looking for the end of the rainbow."

"You're what?"

She stands up with a heave and a grunt.

"I'm just looking for someone."

"Vivian, sometimes I think you're away with the fairies."

I tear off down the street in the direction of the rainbow. It's fading quickly, there's barely a shade of colour left, but it ends in the ruin of the psychiatric hospital. The building is large and grey and looming; a rainbow is exactly what it needs. When I look up again, the rainbow has vanished; all I can see is a clock tower and weather vane. I walk under a stone arch into a courtyard surrounded by windows that could be rectangular eyes—many are broken or boarded up, with pigeons flying from ledge to ledge. I turn in slow circles. There's no sign of there ever having been a rainbow in here, maybe the grey stones didn't like the look of the colours and sent them back to the sky. I make for a corner—it feels safer here—and comb the edges, thinking about how to dig the concrete for gold when I hear whistling. It must be my leprechaun; they whistle as they mend shoes. I creep along the wall and peer around the corner. A man in a blue jumper and fluorescent vest appears. Leprechauns are supposed to wear green or red, but maybe Dublin leprechauns wear blue. I balance on my right foot like an unpink flamingo and pick at the laces of my left foot. I need to throw my left shoe at the leprechaun so that he drops whatever he's holding. I overbalance and topple onto the ground with a *whoof.* I'm still on the ground, pulling at my shoe, when I hear steps and a "hello" spoken like a question, like an answer to a phone call.

I look up to see the leprechaun-man standing over me.

"Are you alright?"

"I'm okay, I'm just trying to take off my shoe."

"Why?"

"You'll see."

I loosen the lace, ease my foot out and fling the runner at him, hitting him in the chest.

"Ow, what the hell did you do that for?"

He rubs his chest and I watch his hands; nothing falls from them—no gold, no half-made shoes, no answers.

"I'm sorry, I thought you were somebody else."

"Who?"

"A smaller person. About thigh-high. Did you see the rainbow in here?"

"Never noticed. Looking for a pot of gold, are you?"

He smirks.

"Yes," I say.

He stares hard at my eyes as if he can see something there that I can't.

"Are you looking for it too?" I ask.

He laughs.

"If you find it, love, keep me in mind."

His voice has softened, and he gestures to the ruin of the hospital.

"Were you in here before?"

"A couple of times."

I don't tell him that I often peek in when I'm passing to get my dose of creep and spook, I don't want him to think I'm odd.

"I see, were you in for long?"

"Not too long," I say.

I don't want him to think I'm a trespasser. His face settles into a grave expression. I look at his feet. He's wearing black boots. If he was a leprechaun, he'd be wearing buckled shoes. I look at his jacket.

"Would you say your jacket is more yellow than green?"

"Definitely yellow."

"Oh."

A leprechaun in blue and yellow is just no good, unless blue + yellow = green, and he's undercover. I stand up to my full height. The man is taller than me.

"Have you ever taken growth hormones?" I ask.

He sputters a laugh, all spit and honk.

"Can't say I have."

I can't think of any other way a leprechaun could grow so high. I look down his body to make sure there isn't one leprechaun standing on another's shoulders, but there's no awkward bulge or join.

"Did you eat a whole chicken for lunch?" I ask.

"I had a chicken sandwich, why?"

"Was there a wishbone?"

"No."

"Oh. Leprechauns use the wishbones to douse for gold."

He laughs.

"You're not going to dig through concrete with your bare hands are you?"

"No," I say, "I've got this."

I pull out the knife. He jumps back a little and raises his hands.

"Whoa now, love."

"I hadn't time to get the shovel," I say, "this will have to do."

"Why don't you give me the knife," he says, his voice containing tremors and quivers and shakes and shivers—a whole range of notes in each word.

"Are you looking for the portal too?" I ask.

I hand him the knife and he takes it with quaking hands. "Have you told anyone you were coming here?"

"No," I say. "Penelope would have come but I hadn't time to ask—I was in a hurry to catch the rainbow."

"Okay."

He says it like it's the only word in the dictionary.

"Can I have my knife back?" I ask. "I'm going to look elsewhere for the rainbow."

"How about I mind it for a while."

"Okay."

I suspect he's going to dig for gold and is too embarrassed to admit it.

"Is there anyone else at home?" he asks.

"There used to be Lemonfish, but he died of fungus and drought."

"I see. No one else?"

"My sister came over with her family, and Charlie and Sharon called in the other day. And Peter might take me to a fancy-dress party, I'm just waiting for him to call back."

"Good, good."

His face looks more settled now, it has evened out like a thick spread of soft cheese.

"Bye for now," I say, because I need to return to get my knife back.

"Bye, love," he says, "I'll say a prayer for you."

I'm not sure a prayer will open rainbow portals, but he probably wouldn't agree to chant a spell or incantation for me. I walk back home. A girl passes by on a bicycle, raising one leg over the crossbar and slowing to a halt. She balances so elegantly she glides: if it was yesterday she did it, I'd say she "glode" because "glided" is a worthless past tense. Every other step I take with each foot, I kick the ground with my sole. It makes a satisfying scratch-scrape, like a *tch* in a strop.

When I get home, I map my short route. I walked half a teacup. I turn on the television.

A newsreader announces that a man has been shot in a case of mistaken identity. I fear that if a criminal has the same house number as me, the hitmen could mistake street for road and shoot me. I should write to the government and suggest that hitmen be issued with GPS so they get the right houses. I change channels to a documentary presented by a giddy young man jumping around a cliff and waving his arms. He says things like "First time ever this has been done . . . biggest . . . greatest . . . never seen before." So many superlatives uttered with such enthusiasm become boring, so I change the channel to an interview with a sweating man in a T-shirt. He has just won a tennis match, by the looks. He is asked how he feels about winning and what this means for him and what happens next. Interviewers never ask the questions I want to know the answers to, such as: if a cup of tea was put in his hand right now, what would his ideal biscuit be? If he could invent a new type of bed, what would it do? If water had a colour, what should it be? If he could have nine toes and eight fingers or eight toes and nine fingers, which would he choose? The tennis player is giving all the right answers to all the wrong questions. I change the channel to a large woman singing a soaring tune in another language before an orchestra. I close my eyes and try to imagine living a life that demanded such climaxes, but my life soundtrack is more of a nursery rhyme with three repeated notes. I change channels to a man sculpting something out of stone. His hands move deftly, but deftly doesn't convey how skilled he is; I'm going to say deftfully.

I turn off the television because there are too many people doing things they are excellent at and I feel like a mediocre still life hung next to a Caravaggio. I go to make myself a ham sandwich. Sometimes I don't know if I like a food, or if I just know it so well that I assume I like it. I eat a piece of ham, its texture sweaty and thin. Next time I will buy ham from a butcher, a clump of thick slices in a brown paper bag, instead of misery sealed in plastic. I should vary my lunches more, but I don't know what else to eat. I used to have soup, but I didn't know what to do with my jaws, and I didn't know which verb to use: was I eating or drinking? I could call it "dreating," but that sounds like a weary farmer giving a dose of medicine to a sick sheep. I avoid jelly for the same reason—it's a semi-solid frustration of verblessness. I outwit candyfloss by twisting a hank of it into a knot of solid, chewy sugar. Vivian: one; candyfloss: nil. Today seems like a day to eat in bed, so I bring my lunch upstairs on a tray wordlessly, crumblessly.

22

I LOOK OUT my bedroom window and see a girl's hair sweeping into a capital "L," so I know that it's windy. The longer I stare out the window, the more of my nose I see from the corners of my eyes. It's going to be one of those days when I can't ignore the view of my nose, a constant triangle in my vision. Today I'm going to write a letter to somebody in a foreign country and send it in an airmail envelope. I like airmail envelopes: the blue and red diamonds around the edges, the words "Par Avion"—which sound like a cure for a common skin complaint if you push them together or an upmarket brand of water if you don't—and the thin paper that looks as if it wouldn't last a local journey, never mind an international one. I don't know how to find an international address when the phone directory only covers the Dublin area, and it's hard to write to someone when I don't know who they are or what they want to read about. I go to the post office to buy some envelopes. I choose some large brown ones for unfolded letters, thick magnolia ones for official-looking typed letters, ordinary white ones for ordinary letters, and airmail envelopes for letters abroad. I need to buy stamps too, but I will get more sentences out of more people if I go to a different post office for those.

When I get home, I go into the hoardroom and take the most recent telephone directory from the pile. I open it and crumbs of paper fall to the ground; the edges of the pages are jagged and frayed and bitten away. I take an unlined writing pad from the stationery pile, which hasn't been eaten. The mice must prefer the taste of printed words. I bring the mouse-bitten directory and the unmouse-bitten writing pad downstairs and put them on the desk. I sit down and rub my hands together, then I clear my throat and say aloud: "Right, then, better get started."

I take a black biro from the jar on the desk.

"No rest for the wicked," I say, and I point my pen at the blank page. The plastic biro seems feckless and not up to my task, so I take a gel pen from the jar and write "Dear" in the top left corner. This pen has giddy ink; it produces rounded vowels and words that bounce, but it doesn't look serious enough, so I pick up my great-aunt's gold-nibbed fountain pen and write over the "Dear." The ink is so thick and silky, the words will surely flow from my fingers. Now I open the telephone directory on the page with the most tooth marks: MacGillycuddy. One of the names is Ignatius, and I write "Ignatius" after "Dear," and then I think for a bit and write in large curly script: "If you eat ham sandwiches five days out of seven, you are more pig than human."

I read back over the sentence and it looks a bit accusatory so I add in "possibly": "If you eat ham sandwiches five days out of seven, you are possibly more pig than human."

"Possibly more pig" sounds like a tongue twister, so I paint a white line of correction fluid over "possibly." I lean down to blow on it and I breathe in the smell, which is like a painful sneeze. When it's dry, I write "maybe" on the rough patch: "If you eat ham sandwiches five days out of seven, you are maybe more pig than human."

My sentence takes up most of the page, but it still seems unfinished, so I draw a pig's head and write "Oink" at the bottom.

I choose a white envelope and write Ignatius's address on the front, tear the letter from the pad, fold it, and put it in the envelope. Then I close the phone directory and open it on Clarke. Maura Clarke sounds like somebody I'd like to meet; she would cook hearty soups and lamb stews and keep the chat going as she was preparing the food. On a fresh sheet of paper I write "Dear Maura," and I suck the metal top of the pen. I add: "Be careful what you put down the sink—it might come back to sink you."

I imagine heaps of tea leaves, globs of unused butter, lumps of meat and the odd pea, forming a mush and oozing up the sink through the plughole in vengeful mood. This letter also looks unfinished, so I draw a picture of a tap that looks more like a star with one fat leg. I take a magnolia envelope from the pile, and write Maura's address on it. I put a thick book from the shelf under the pile of letters so it looks as if I have even more letters written. Now I take a fresh piece of notepaper for my letter abroad. Instead of trying to find a foreign address to write to, I decide to put my letter in a bottle. That will save the price of a stamp and reach whoever should be reached. I go to my notebook and look for my List of Nice-Sounding Places That No Longer Exist: "Timbuktu, Peking, Ceylon, Persia, Byzantium, Abyssinia, Rhodesia, Bombay, Saigon, Bohemia, Mesopotamia, Siam, Numidia."

The names have been replaced by new names that sound duller and flatter; I would like to reintroduce the old names, but I don't know who to ask or how to begin. I look at the seas and oceans on the map of the world on the wall. I will aim my bottle for the Great Australian Bight because I've never heard of a Bight, and it sounds like a word I should have been using but have neglected until now. I write: "Ursula, Great Australian Bight" on the front of an airmail envelope because I'd like a friend with the same symmetrical vowel to consonant ratios as Penelope. Then I write my address in the top right corner, followed by:

> *Dear Ursula,*
> *How is life on the Bight? I would like an*
> *Australian pen pal. I watch* Home and Away *and*
> Neighbours *sometimes (with the sound down) so*
> *I know what Australia looks like but not how it*
> *sounds. Maybe you could come and visit sometime.*
> *Yours Sincerely,*
> *Vivian.*

I fold the letter and put it in the airmail envelope and seal it, though this really should be a watermail envelope if it's travelling by sea. Then I go to the kitchen and open the drinks cupboard. I take out a bottle of cola and pour what's left of it into three mugs. I rinse out the bottle and shake it, bring it to the bedroom, and dry it with the hairdryer. I bring the bottle back downstairs, roll the airmail envelope up like a sausage roll, tie it at either end with twine, and squeeze it through the bottle opening. It doesn't look like much; it could be ignored or discarded as rubbish, so I stick a blank white label over the red label and write "MESSAGE" in permanent marker. I put the bottle in my bag with the other letters, and take from a teacup on the bookshelf all the copper coins that my great-aunt had been collecting since the euro was introduced. Then I put on my coat, leave the house and walk into town. With all this communication potential in my bag I feel like I'm carrying a bucket of radar. I pass charity collectors, and a group of religious people with a microphone outside the GPO. Inside, it reminds me of an echoey Soviet building from a spy novel, with its railings and queues and grey-brown efficiency. In the middle of the floor stands a kiosk-shaped wooden counter, with silver shields on some of the panels that make it look like a solid wooden crown. Black and white triangles on the floor radiate from the counter, I wonder if the people addressing envelopes and licking stamps know that they're standing in the middle of a zebra sun. I walk to the counter.

"Two stamps, please," I say.

"Irish or international?"

"Irish. I'm sending my international letter by bottle."

"By what?"

"By bottle, look."

I take the cola bottle from my bag and show it to the man. He leans closer and laughs.

"Ah, here, Cathal, would you look at this."

Cathal leans over from the next counter.

"She's sending this by bottle instead of airmail."

Cathal grins and looks at me.

"Where's it going to?"

"The Great Australian Bight," I say.

I don't want them to think I don't trust their postal system, so I add, "It's cheaper than buying a stamp."

They both roar laughing, like I've said the funniest thing.

Maybe I am full of comedy and just don't know it.

"Recession postage," Cathal says, and goes back to his counter. I pay for the Irish stamps in small copper coins and say bye to the man.

"Good luck with the bottle," he says.

I leave the post office, cross O'Connell Street and walk down Sackville Lane. Taxis line one side of the street, and there's a smell of piss from the other. A group of men and women sit on the steps of a shop drinking cans. One of them is singing. I like daytime drunk people because they sing; maybe they only shout at night-time. One of the women steps in front of me.

"Have you got forty cents for a hostel, love?"

"No, sorry."

"What about forty cents for alcohol?"

"No."

Her friend shouts: "An alcoholic without alcohol is like a bird without feathers!" and they all laugh.

The first woman's face looks bald, and I feel sad for this featherless bird, but I can't spend my bus fare on hostels or alcohol. I cross Marlborough Street, turn left onto Abbey Street and join the queue for the bus that will take me to the nearest seashore on the northside of the city. When the bus comes, I get on.

"The seaside, please," I say.

"Whereabouts?"

Oh no, I have worn out my words for the day but this man wants more.

"The wooden bridge."

He says the price and I count out the fare in small coins. The driver tuts and sighs.

"Robbing the piggy bank, were you?"

"No piggy bank," I say, "just a teacup."

I cram the money into the machine as fast as I can and take my ticket. I sit upstairs and watch the sea begin. It's a grey squally day: the waves are bouncing over the wall, the seafront is empty but for a few people walking dogs. When the wooden bridge appears I ring the bell, twist myself down the stairs and get off the bus. I cross at the lights and walk down the bridge to the beach. I remember my father teaching me to swim here when I was small. I remember a hand on my back and a pushing and a shoving. I remember lungs of burning saltwater and stinging eyes and pain-cold skin. I remember staying home when they went to the seaside after that.

The tide is in, the waves full of gush and thud. I walk down the jut of land to the statue of the Holy Mary on stilts. Beyond her, a line of rocks stretches further out to sea. I climb down to the rocks and, when I reach the last dry rock, I fling the bottle with all I've got. It feels like my arm was ripped from the shoulder and flung to sea as well. The bottle bobs about on the wave-foam, uncertain which way to go. The surface of the sea is covered in shreds of dirty-beige foam. Mermaids who die in *The Little Mermaid* turn into foam; this must be a mermaid massacre. I climb down the rocks onto the strand and do little giddy jumps thinking of where my bottle will end up and how it will be received. A car is driving in squealing circles on the narrow patch of dry sand: two perfect circles connected in the middle like the number eight. This might be two fairy forts with the magic concentrated at the point where the circles meet. I walk to the dunes to wait for the car to leave. The dunes fling sand into my eyes, the long grass cuts my hands, the wind whistles through an empty glass bottle like a banshee with no heed for my ears; this is a stinging place. There are pieces of brown and green glass that I can't call shards because they're rubbed soft by the sea, and "shards" sounds sharp and mean. These pieces are scratched and cloudy and hold secrets of long sea voyages.

When the car drives off, I climb down from the dunes and make for the circles. They look perfect from afar, but up close, clumps of loose sand have sputtered out of the lines. I jump inside one circle, landing with both feet together. Nothing happens. I jump to the next one. Nothing. Then I jump for the meeting point that connects the two circles and stand still with my eyes closed. Nothing has changed in my ears, and I open my eyes slowly. I check my arms for wings and my horizon for height differences, but there's no change, apart from a small pair of feet near the circles, followed by a larger pair of feet. It's a little girl holding a plastic bucket and spade, with her mother. The girl stares at the circles.

"What are you doing?" she asks.

"I'm playing hopscotch," I say.

"Hopscotch is squares, they're circles."

She points at the circles with her spade.

"I don't like sharp edges, and corners can be so mean."

"Oh."

The girl understands my answers better than any adult. Her mother isn't quite so interested. The girl drops her bucket and starts to draw another circle in the sand with the corner of her spade.

"Stop!" I shout.

The mother jumps.

"What's wrong?"

"She's spoiling the magic."

"She just wants to play."

I don't want to play this game with a child who has ruined any chance of a portal opening up, I don't want to fake fun with a small person who has more chance of fitting through a portal than I have.

"Let's play hide-and-seek," I say.

"Yay!"

The girl drops the spade and claps her hands.

"You two count to twenty-five, now close your eyes."

They cover their eyes with their hands and start to count aloud. I run as fast as I can in the direction of the wooden bridge and I don't stop until I'm certain I've shaken them off. Then I walk back towards land. The houses facing the seafront look like Noddy's Toytown from this angle, all differently coloured and shaped and higgledy-piggledy. If I could connect all the lines where the tops of the houses meet, I might find a pattern and solve the world with it. As I walk over the bridge, I stop to watch the waves flinging themselves at the wooden posts beneath. What if the sea just stopped—what if the sea-motor under the sand stopped turning and the waves got tired of thrashing around? My bottle would have no chance of reaching Australia then. I erase that thought from my head by rubbing my forehead from left to right and from right to left, from up to down and from down to up. A girl passes me, swinging her arms and moving quickly. She's wearing an expression of pure fury on her face and a pastel-coloured tracksuit. There's something wrong with buying special clothes to walk in, instead of walking in old clothes that you already have: something wrong that I can't explain, like buying seashells instead of finding them on the shore.

When I reach the main road, I walk along the seafront to the disused baths. On one side of the baths the tide has washed in a faded pink armchair, a rusty cooker, an orange traffic cone stripped of its reflective band and three yellow-green tennis balls. While one of the mermaids cooks a meal, a second sits on the armchair juggling tennis balls and a third plays mer-guard, and puts the cone in the middle of the road to stop traffic for a caper. I follow the path around to the front of the baths. A rusted gate that used to be blue is padlocked, and the railings are overgrown with shrubs that smell damp and cloying and are preparing to take over the concrete. I feel as if I'm beginning to rust so I walk back to the road where cars are moving forwards not backwards and catch a bus into town. Then I take another bus home and come in the front door feeling like I've been declared a champion of something, some obscure sport that nobody has heard of. I map my walk but it's unsatisfactory—pieced together from chunks of walks between bus rides. I walked a length of twine with a small hook on either end, the side profile of an old-fashioned cash register, and one half of a cursive capital "T."

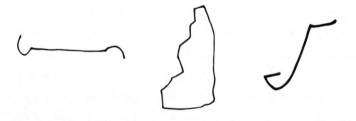

I MAKE A white-bread-and-butter sandwich, and pour some milk into a white mug. I put it all on a black tray and add a bar of chocolate to break up the monochrome. Then I bring my lunch into the living room and sit on a brown soft chair that smells of seeping body. When I pull a green rug over my knees, I might be in a particularly soft tree. During the chocolate course, I realise chocolate and milk are a good combination and wonder why quenching chocolate thirst with water feels thin and metallic and terrible. When I've finished eating, I look through the bookshelves and take down a couple of books. One has a red-and-white special-offer sticker on the cover. I fear the discounted books might be taunted by their full-price peers, so I take out the metal stepladder from under the stairs, open it against the bookshelves, and climb up. I lift out each book and peel off any labels I find, adding them to a small sticky ball. There are books about birds, flowers, the Arctic, the Antarctic, Africa, the Americas (my great-aunt stopped learning about continents after "A"), trains, medicine, war and make-believe things. My favourites are the make-believe books; I like to get lost in worlds inside other characters' heads, which is impossible if the writer slaps out hard cold facts that I can't retain.

A shelf at the top contains hardback books by famous people about how they overcame hardships to conquer their parts of the world: half-lies from gleaming smiles. I want to read the stories they left out: the childhoods with enough to eat, the friends in school not the bullying, the connections to power not the start-from-scratch. I decide to get rid of these books so I drop them on the floor in a heap of white teeth and red lips.

I pull my sleeve down over my hand like I'm cold or about to punch someone and sweep the dust off the empty shelf with my sleeve. The full shelves frown at the empty one, the pursed-lip disapproval of my great-aunt seeps through the urn on the next shelf, the famous faces on the covers turn into my great-aunt's face and the smiles twist into menacing grimaces. I pick up the books in clumps and stuff them back on the shelf; it was a bad idea to change anything, to get rid of anything owned by my great-aunt. I crawl in between the red chair and the cushion, and sniff the dust and feel the scratch of crumbs on my face. Although there is very little air, I feel like I can breathe for the first time today.

23

A S WELL AS cakes, the bakery nearby sells milk and eggs
and custard and digestive biscuits and packet soups and
tinned goods. I buy a dozen eggs and a coffee cake for Penelope's
visit. When I get home, I put the cake on a plate on the table,
and lay out cups and saucers. Then I take the biggest pot from
the cupboard, a huge stainless-steel pot that I set on the hob. I
put the eggs in a bowl beside the cooker. The doorbell rings, and
I hear Penelope's voice shriek "Yoo-hoo!" through the letterbox.
I would like to write a story called "Through the Letterbox,"
but it might be a very short, dull story, with only envelopes for
characters. I open the door and Penelope swoops in in a gabble
of words about a neighbour she met.

"She just never stops talking, I can't get a word in edgeways."

I look at Penelope. I can't get a syllable in edgeways or any
other which ways when she starts talking, but maybe in a
friendship you can't have two people who talk all the time. I
bring her through to the kitchen and set the kettle to boil while
Penelope stares about her.

"Doing some cooking, Viv? Some kind of egg stew is it?"
She laughs.

"When you call me Viv, could you either whisper the 'viv' in lower case or shout it in capitals, please?"

"Okay, VIV," she bellows. "Why?"

"It's more symmetrical that way."

"A truer palindrome."

"Yes."

She takes out her phone, fiddles with it and reads: "The longest palindrome in everyday use is the Finnish word '*Saippuaki-vikauppias*' for soapstone vendor."

When I try to wrap my lips around the word, it comes out sounding like a disease and its cure in one. I'm not sure of an occasion in which I could foist the words "soapstone vendor" into the conversation, but I must think further. I make tea in the teapot, bring it over to the table and start cutting the cake. There is a deep, finger-sized hole in the buttercream icing at the top. I look at Penelope but she is staring straight ahead with her hands on her lap. I cut the cake into quarters and push the fingered quarter onto Penelope's plate and an untouched quarter onto mine. We eat and drink in silence until Penelope speaks.

"What are you making with the eggs?"

"I need you to brew some eggshells."

She leans forward and stares at me. Shards of her breath dart my way, stale and wretched. I lean back in my chair.

"What do you mean?" she asks.

"You crack the eggs and put the shells in a pot of boiling water while I watch."

"Why?"

"If I'm a changeling, I'm supposed to say something like 'I'm as old as the forest but I've never seen an eggshell stew before' and then disappear up the chimney."

Penelope's forehead corrugates.

"But if you already know the words to say, how does this prove anything?"

"Oh. I don't know."

Penelope looks at the cooker.

"And there's no chimney."

"I might disappear up the extractor fan."

We look at the fan. It's covered in brown grease and the holes are so small, I would have to be pencil-thin to fit through.

"Maybe."

She gets up and switches on the cooker. The *swwssh* of the gas flame is very soothing, like a gentle breeze or a low brook. She sits again and we eat our cake.

"Is this a companionable silence?" I ask. "I've read about these in books."

"I suppose it was."

She smiles. I smile too.

"Have we just exchanged a grin? I've also read about exchanging grins in books, but you're not wearing my smile and I'm not wearing yours."

Penelope squawks out a laugh the size of India. I walk over to the cooker and dip my finger in the water, it's lukewarm.

"Penelope," I say, "picture a small boy called Luke who's just learning to speak."

"Okay."

"Now imagine it's hot and he wants to take off his jumper, do you know what he'd say?"

"No."

"Luke warm!! Like lukewarm!"

"Is that water boiled yet?" she asks.

"No, it's only lukewarm."

I stir the water with a wooden spoon. Why didn't Penelope laugh at my joke? I may have spent too long setting the scene, or I might have put in too many exclamation marks. I will study books of jokes and learn how to tell them; I will learn some of the lesser-known ones and pass them off as my own. I imagine a situation in a restaurant—no that won't do, the jangle of cutlery and clatter of delph is too loud to do justice to my joke-telling—a quiet pub perhaps: a quiet pub on a Monday evening. I'm surrounded by friends and I'm telling a joke, one of the jokes from the book. The scene I'm picturing is of the moment just after the punchline and people are laughing, they're laughing so hard that they're bent double and drink is pouring out their noses. I'm sitting up straight with a mildly amused smile on my face, but that is just the start of my jokes, there are more to come: funnier, better, cleverer jokes that will flatten these people, flatten my friends to the ground with the force of my humour.

"Viv? Sorry: VIV!"

"Yes?"

"It's boiling."

I blink and stare at the bubbling pot. Penelope comes over to the cooker.

"Right, what do you want me to do with these?"

She picks up the bowl of eggs. I put a second bowl on the counter beside her.

"You crack the egg, empty the egg-meat into this bowl, and then put the shell into the pot."

"Okay. How many eggs?"

"Half a dozen."

247

I sit on the rocking chair in the corner, but I can only see Penelope's back.

"Can you turn to one side so that I can see the eggshells going into the pot?"

She moves to the counter and turns.

"Like this?"

"Yes, carry on."

She cracks an egg on the side of the bowl.

"Stop!" I shout. "I've thought of something."

Penelope pauses, lifts her hair from her eyes and slaps at a thin yellow worm of egg yolk running down her wrist. "What is it?"

"I should be in a cradle. Or some kind of baby's cot."

"Why?"

"In the stories, that's where changelings were when they watched the eggshells brewing."

"But that's because they were babies."

"Oh, oh right."

I pull the rocking chair over to one side and lean out to get a better view. Crack goes the egg on the side of the bowl. "Feck," says Penelope when the shell smashes in her fist.

"Don't mind it," I say, "there's more, keep cracking."

She cracks an egg, empties the insides into the bowl, throws the shell in the pot, and does it all over again. On the sixth egg, I watch closely and wait for the voice of a thousand-year-old fairy to come burbling up my gullet, but nothing comes. Penelope turns to me.

"Do another one," I say, "maybe seven's the lucky number."

She does it again: nothing.

"Eight could be a lucky number in some country," she says hopefully.

I shake my head.

"Let's stop now."

Penelope walks to the sink and rinses her hands.

"I didn't know you washed your hands," I say.

"I do on special occasions," she says. "What are you going to do with the eggs?"

I get up and look into the bowl. The yolks are suspended in the whites; some whole and smug, others gaping and disappointed, oozing slowly into the clear liquid. Bits of broken shell hang in the mess, like fractured stars in a gluey galaxy.

"I'll make poached eggs," I say, "crunchy poached eggs."

I dip my finger into the yolk-stream and lick it. It tastes like I shouldn't. Penelope sits in the rocking chair and I eye her, feary that she might be the one to go shooting up the extractor fan while I'm fiddling with the eggs—who's to say she doesn't belong to another world? I throw the egg-meat into the pot and swirl it into a whirlpool with the wooden spoon. This, I presume, is poaching. It feels good to cook eggs with such a dishonest verb. There isn't a peep from Penelope, and when I turn around to look, she's running a finger around the rim of the cake, scooping icing into her mouth. Faster and faster I stir the water until the eggs seem on the verge of taking flight like so many squashed flying saucers; faster and faster they whirl until I feel like I'm in the water with them, I'm spinning around and around and *"Um Gottes willen, es brennt, es brennt,"* the only phrase I can remember from German class in school, "Oh my God, it burns, it burns." There are flames: orange-red-purple-green up-close flames that don't look real, they're so bright. I'm straining, pushing, pushing back back back against hands that are pushing me on on on. I try to scream but my throat clogs and holds it so I push I push I push my body back and my voice up until the scream emerges, and even though it's from my mouth, even though it's my scream, it's so far beyond me and so far above me that I scream again, wondering what I am taken over by.

"Vivian," comes a voice, definitely not my voice, "Vivian, are you alright?"

I realise it's dark, and it's dark because my eyes are closed. I open them and Penelope's face is hovering over me. Her cheeks hang down like empty balloons, her eyes are so huge and bulging I fear they will fall from their sockets into my mouth, and her breath—her breath is fit to wake the dead let alone the fainted so I quickly say, "Yes, yes, I'm alright," and I sit up. It's only then the pain hits, a sear across my chest and down my left arm, a mean, petty kind of pain that stings, but isn't brave enough to go deep, deep as the flames.

"Viv, I mean VIV! The water spilt and scalded you, let me take a look."

I snatch at her hand but it's too late, she has pulled the top of my jumper aside.

"What are those scars, what happened to you?"

She is all gasp and stutter, she sounds like she could keep spilling questions at me in higher and higher pitches if I don't answer.

"My father tried to send me back, he wanted to swap me for his human child."

The new pain has mounted the old pain; it's deep and all-consuming, a constant bass-note throb. I pull my jumper back over the pain and look around. The floor is scattered with ragged chunks of egg whites and gleams of yolks. It's a pity my skin doesn't look so perfect when it's poached.

"How?" she asks.

"Twice through the fire, once through the sea."

"The sea?"

"He said that if fire didn't work, water might. It didn't."

I get up from the floor and sit on the rocking chair. Penelope rinses a dishcloth under the cold tap, I take it from her and lay it on the scald.

"I like scaldy mots," I say.

"You like what?"

"Scaldy mots. It was written on a building in town. I wonder who wrote it and if they mean it. Near that was written, 'The army are coming.' I wonder if they were done by the same person or if they were linked in some way."

Penelope pulls a chair opposite me and sits down. I don't know where to put my knees.

"Viv, when I told you about my mother . . . when I talked about what happened . . . why didn't you tell me then?"

She is not making full sentences; she is not making sense. I get up and walk to the table.

"It's a pity the poached eggs are ruined," I say, "but we can have cake instead."

I cut another slice. I skim off the smoothed outer rim of icing that Penelope has run her finger around and take a bite. It doesn't taste as sweet as before, and the coffee flavour leaves a bitter tang in my mouth. Next time, I will try a different flavour; next time I will buy a plain sponge.

24

I WALK TO Penelope's house in the belting heat. Summer has landed overnight, and the street is full of arms and legs that are not usually seen; they seem detached from their owners like so many piles of limbs in the death scene of a war film. I ring Penelope's doorbell. The door opens after a clatter and a thump, and her face appears, a yellow splodge on one cheek and a blue swash across her forehead.

"Come in, Vivian, I'm just finishing off a painting."

"Oh," I say, "I thought you were dressing up as a rainbow."

I follow her up the stairs to the living room. She's wearing a T-shirt with thick pastel-coloured stripes, she could be a block of ice cream. The cats are arranged in different poses on the sofa like a greeting card. I take the list out of my pocket.

"Right," I say, "we need white walls and a full glass of water and a small mirror and a torch."

Penelope goes to the cupboard, takes out a wide glass, and fills it with water. She puts it on the table, then she opens a drawer and foosters around until she pulls out a torch. Finally, she goes into the bathroom and comes back with a small rectangular mirror, puts it on the table and looks at me.

"Now we need to close the curtains," I say.

I sit at the table while she closes the curtains to the small windows and the patio doors. An envelope on the table is addressed to Miss E. Drysdale. I look quickly away: it's not good to snoop in other people's things, and anyway, "E" has far too many rigid lines and corners for an initial. When Penelope sits down, I put the mirror into the glass of water, turn on the torch and shine it onto the mirror. I move it around, until rainbow swirls of colour appear and Penelope shrieks and claps her hands. I hold the torch in position for a while, but no small man appears. Penelope yawns.

"Remind me what you're looking for?"

"A leprechaun," I say, "but I don't want his money, I want to ask him to guide me to the nearest portal. I'll tell him he can keep his crock of gold if I can pick his brains."

"I wouldn't use that expression, Vivian," she says. "Leprechauns take things very literally, he'll think you're going to partially lobotomise him."

I stare at her. Sometimes it's hard to know if she's very strange or very clever. Sometimes it's best to stick to practicalities.

"Will you hold the torch?"

Penelope takes it from me and I knock on the table and under the table, looking for a hollow which could hide a portal.

"Can I put the torch down now?"

"No, wait."

I get some thick books and set them on the table and put the torch on top. I stare at the colours, Penelope stares at the colours, but nothing happens. She yawns like a bored lioness and lays her head on her arms. The breath of the yawn catches up with me, it smells heavy and sleepy, like the dregs of old milk in an unwashed cup. I stare at her face, her head, her body, her entirety. I'm not sure if I genuinely like her or if it's the shape of her name that appeals to me: all rounded smiling letters and soft consonants like the theme tune of a children's television programme.

"Let's have a drink outside!" she shouts suddenly, her head popping up sharply with the force of her idea.

"But there's no rainbow in the sunshine," I say.

"Ah, Vivian, leprechauns like the sun too, they make flip-flops instead of shoes when it's sunny."

I stare at her. Penelope may look like an ice cream but she acts like a cone. She jumps up from her chair and foosters again in the cupboard, taking out two glasses. Then she opens the fridge and pulls out a bottle of wine, unscrews the top and sloshes it into the glasses. It sounds like a giant swallowing a waterfall. She hands me a glass and leads the way onto the balcony. There are two chairs and a table facing the sun, as if they were bought especially for this occasion, this exact hour. The drone of a lawnmower next door sounds like a snore without breaths. We sit. Penelope holds her glass up and says, "Cheers," and I do the same. I take a gulp and the cold shock of it on my throat is a welcome, it feels like the only thing that could be done right now. We sit and drink in a silence that I hope is comfortable, but I'm not sure, so I start using my words in case it isn't.

"I might be drinking wine in France this summer."

"Oh?"

Penelope turns her yellow-and-blue face to me. I take another slug of wine.

"I'm probably going to France with my sister and her family. They have a house there."

"Oh . . . ?"

This "oh" has the power of a question in it, and she barely misses a breath before asking,

"Can I come too?"

"Let me think."

I close my eyes and think about my sister and her husband and their two children; it will be like Noah's Ark with them all marching two by two and me trailing behind them alone.

"Yes, probably, I'll just check with my sister."

I sup more wine. The sun has melted its gaze a bit, it seems hazier and less direct. My tongue feels thick when I try to form my *S*'s, so I focus on using consonants with a tougher coating. Penelope stretches out her arms in front of her. They are eggshell-beige except for the white crooks of both elbows.

"I can paint the sea in France," she says.

I picture her in a swimsuit and beret holding a palette of paint and a brush, swashing stripes of pink and yellow and green onto the waves.

"As long as you don't paint it blue," I say, "it's blue enough already."

"Mm."

Her voice sounds like it's under the sea already, and when I look at her face, it's full of bliss and waves. She is draped back in her chair, her body looks looser somehow.

"Would an older mermaid be called a *mermissus*?" I ask.

"An older Irish mermaid, perhaps," she says.

"We'll see *mermadames* in France."

"And *mermonsieurs* too."

Penelope winks at me, her mouth falling open at the same time. She can't go looking for monsieurs in France, "mer-" or otherwise; she's my friend and not Monsieur's. She refills our glasses, and I take two big sups to put the thought out of my mind.

"Leprechauns like to drink," I say. "Whiskey's their favourite."

"Let's try him with some wine," Penelope says.

We go inside. I bring the glass with the mirror to the sink and pour out the water. Then I pour in some wine, and we remake our rainbow. Nothing happens. Nothing happens when we close the curtains, nothing happens when we open the curtains, nothing happens when there's water in the glass, nothing happens when there's wine in the glass: nothing *happens*.

"Cheer up," Penelope says, putting her arm around me. Even though she looks thin, she feels soft and pudgy, as if she moved from babyhood to adulthood in one step. Her armpit is resting on my left shoulder and I shrug, trying to shake it off. I don't want her smell mixed with mine, I don't want to be diluted or contaminated with the odour of someone else. She doesn't heed my shrugging so I duck and run outside, saying,

"Let's go back to the sunshine."

LATER THAT NIGHT, I walk home on two fizzy legs. Never has the North Circular looked lovelier. The trees are grand and high, the bumps on the footpath are fairy mounds, and I imagine a horse-drawn carriage pulling me along the curve of the road. A group of bare-chested teenage boys pass, their calls to each other like cheers after the end of a long drought. I let myself in the front door with my key and think what an odd thing it is to do, to let yourself in, as if you needed permission to enter your own house. I go into the living room, take the urn from the bookshelf and knock on the lid.

"Hello, Maud," I shout.

I was never allowed to call her Maud when she was alive. *"Maud, Maud, Maud!"*

I give the urn a shake, and shove it back between the books.

Then I pick up the phone and dial my sister's number. She answers with a hushed urgency.

"Hello?"

"Hi, Vivian, it's me, Vivian!"

She gives a monstrous *tut* that's almost a *THUTH*, and a sigh that could scatter a plastic army.

My sister's relationship with me is one prolonged sigh.

"It's after two, Vivian, why are you calling?"

"I want to let you know that Penelope can come too!"

"Who's Penelope—come where?"

"Penelope's my friend I told you about. She can come to France too!"

There's a low muttering in the background and a growl from my sister's husband, followed by a rustle and a soft thunk. She returns with a hiss.

"Vivian, have you been drinking?"

"Yes, we were practising drinking wine for France."

"It's gone straight to your head."

I picture a bottle of wine dressed as a rocket spearing into my brain.

"Yes, I am speaking wine-words," I say. My speaking is more of a "thpeaking."

Her voice drops to cold menace. "Listen to me and listen carefully: you are not coming to France, Penelope is not coming

257

to France, I don't want to ever hear about France from you again, understand?"

I repeat the sentences in my head and my mood drops a thud down a concrete staircase with each one.

"I understand. No France."

"Good night."

The line goes dead. I hold the phone to my ear awhile and listen to the *beeeeeeeeeep*. It's a soothing even tone, unlike my sister's north-facing voice. I raise my shoulders slowly. I feel as if I don't fit into my body, as if there's a gap between me and my skin. I don't know what to tell Penelope—she has almost grown fins in anticipation of the sea—where would I find the words for such a conversation? I wish there was a shop where I could buy buckets of words; I would cut them out from a numbered sheet, arrange them in order and recite. I climb upstairs and get into bed: clothes, shoes and all—this is no time to be undressing. I pull the blankets over my head and huddle under, making sure that all my fingers are inside the blankets and nothing is peeping out, not even the tips. My head feels swimmy, and I repeat "No France No France No France" over and over in my blanket tent until they stop making sense as separate words and become "nofrance," the name of a magic spell. I don't know when I drift off to sleep but I must have, because I wake up the next morning and I'm still not going to France.

I DON'T KNOW how to tell bad news. A doctor told me about my great-aunt dying and I try to remember how he put it: the words he used and the way he used them. I'll telephone Penelope because I don't want see her disappointed wail of a face;

bad enough to hear it. I dial her number, and she answers on the first ring with a "hello" that's beyond frightened. This is good; if she expects bad news, my task is easier.

"Penelope, it's me."

"Oh, hi, Vivian, how are you?"

"I'm afraid I have some bad news."

"Oh?"

"We did everything we could, but she was very old."

"Sorry?"

"In the end, her heart just gave out."

"Whose heart?"

"Sometimes even the most advanced medical equipment is no use when your time has come."

"Vivian—"

"If there's anything we can do, anything at all, please don't hesitate to ask."

"Vivian, what are you talking about?"

"The trip to France, we're not allowed to go."

"Oh. Not even you?"

"Especially not me."

"Oh."

"She had a good life, and that's what we must focus on: a long and healthy life."

"Who had?"

"My sister says—"

"Your sister's dead?"

"No, well, I don't know, I haven't talked to her this morning. Last night she said there aren't enough bedrooms in the house, and she didn't want us to be squashed."

The lie sounds so true, it sings.

"I understand."

I don't know how she can understand something that's not true; if you understand a lie, does that make you a double liar? A whole bag of silence follows. I don't want to dilute my lie with more details, and I'm scared of catching myself out with stories that twist and ramble, so I try to cheer Penelope up.

"If my sister *is* dead, then maybe I'll inherit the house in France."

"Is she sick?"

"Not that I know of, but there are car crashes sometimes. And aeroplane accidents," I add, hopefully. "They're better because there's more chance of the whole family being wiped out."

Penelope sighs.

"But there are life jackets and whistles for every passenger."

I think for a moment.

"If the air steward had an off day, she may have forgotten to pack all the whistles. That's what we need to cling onto."

"Maybe."

"Penelope?"

"Yes?"

"We could go on our own holiday."

She draws a sharp breath.

"We could—we could go anywhere in the world!"

"Hold on, I need to get my list."

I put the phone on the floor and run to fetch my notebook. I open it on my List of Nice-Sounding Places That Exist, and run back to the phone.

"We could go to: Golgotha, Meat Camp, Ouagadougou, Humpy Creek, Bell Buckle, Mudsock, Dirty Butter Creek, Bean Station, Tightsqueeze, Spuzzum, Unicorn, Burkina Faso,

Sulphur, Pencil Bluff, Vladivostok, Bumba, Chugwater, Monkey's Eyebrow, Slicklizzard, Ulan Bator, Robbers Roost, Tulsk, Zook, Buttermilk, Limpopo, Pondicherry, Udupi, Gough, Esmeraldas, Poskov, Jammerbugten, Gdansk, Pyongyang, Hindu Kush, Ningbo, Muscat, Necker, Mermaid Reef, Spratly Islands, Guam, Mogadishu, Djibouti, Tonga, Wollongong, Inglewood, South Sandwich Islands (I don't think there's a North Sandwich Islands, but we could find a group of rocks in a lake in Northern Ireland and eat sandwiches on them to officially name them), Walla Walla, Tbilisi, Lesotho, Oberpfaffenhofen, Timbuktu or that town in Wales with the longest name: Llanfairpwllgwyngyllgogerychwyrndrobwllllantysiliogogogoch. I'm not sure if I've pronounced the last one properly."

I draw breath.

"That's a lot of place names," Penelope says.

"I've been making my list for a while."

"Sounds like all of them are abroad apart from Tulsk?"

I look back over my list.

"Yes."

"Why Tulsk?"

"It's the big heap of consonants," I say, "they make my throat catch and my skin crawl. I need to get over my fear of consonants, and Tulsk would be good practice for going to Gdansk."

Penelope laughs.

"Viv, you're a ticket."

I don't like being called a ticket or a card or any other flat object; I would prefer to be called a three-dimensional thing.

"There's another reason," I say. "Oweynagat Cave is near Tulsk, it's supposed to be a portal to the Otherworld."

"Reckon it works?"

"Reckon it might."

I've dropped my first pronoun; this is the start of things to come.

"Tulsk it is, then," she says.

"Tulsk it is," I say. "It's in the middle of Roscommon—if County Roscommon was Africa, Tulsk would be the Central African Republic—and I need to become middle."

I'm glad I've given up on the accent that squeezes vowels between every consonant; whole seasons would change before I'd get the word "Tulsk" out.

"Next week suit you?" Penelope asks.

I let a small silence fall, to pretend that I'm sifting through pages of plans in my head.

"Next week is very busy for me," I say, shaking my head so only select syllables drop into the receiver.

"The following week, then?"

"That'd be perfect," I say. "Midsummer's that week, the year's on the turn. The gates to the Underworld are supposed to open up at Oweynagat every Samhain to abduct humans, but Midsummer's a bit bright for abductions, I could probably just go in willingly myself."

"Okay. Where will we stay?"

Penelope's head is wadded with needless practicalities.

"We'll camp," I say. "We'll pitch a tent near the mouth of the cave, and we can ask other campers for some propane and butane for the bonfire. If we get to a second conversation, we can call them prope 'n' bute."

"Right," she says, "I can drive."

"Good," I say, "I don't like the smell of egg sandwiches on the train."

"Grand so, Viv, I mean VIV. I'll get back to you about arrangements later in the week."

"Bye."

Penelope hangs up and I continue to hold the phone against my ear, listening to the beep. It's like a song with only one word. Then I place the receiver back in the cradle and go upstairs to pack my suitcase. It's important I bring the right things.

READING GROUP GUIDE

1. Vivian makes a lot of lists and plays with word associations and sounds. She also searches through her notebook of lists in contemplating her own feelings and significance. What insight do we gain into Vivian from the ways she plays with language? What do we learn about her character specifically and only through this device?

2. The drawings in the book show not only how visually perceptive Vivian is, but also how abstract she can be. How literally can we interpret these images to be her mental maps and shapes?

3. Many moments in the book feel as though they honor Irish traditions and lore, such as the plaque that Vivian reads: "Near here is the reputed site of the well where St. Patrick baptized many local inhabitants in the 5th century AD." Do you feel these scenes connect to a broader

4. The way Vivian mentions certain landmarks recalls James Joyce's *Dubliners*. Scholars of Joyce have noted that his observations of Dublin differ in his stories depending on whether the travel is either passive (e.g. by bus) or active (e.g. on foot). Is the same true for *Eggshells*? Are Vivian's experiences and

observations different or more important whether she is passive or active?

5. In Greek myth, Penelope is the wife of Odysseus, and she is known for her faithfulness to him while he fights in the Trojan War and completes his long Odyssey home. Do you think the issue of faithfulness is what prompts Vivian to advertise for a friend named Penelope specifically? Do you think she feels she needs a Penelope of her own, because she is on an Odyssey of her own? If not, what are other reasons why she might have preferred this particular name?

6. Is it possible, in the world of this book, that Vivian really is a fairy? Or that there is a portal to another world? Do you think she really believes this? If so, what does that belief say about her?

A CONVERSATION WITH
CAITRIONA LALLY . . .

How did you come to write Eggshells, and how did you come up with the character of Vivian? Did you have the character in mind first, or the story, or . . . what?

I didn't set out to Write A Novel, it grew from notes and over-heard snippets. I'd been made redundant from my job during the recession, and I found myself walking the streets of Dublin a lot. I noticed that many of the city's street signs had letters missing, and I wrote these new spellings in a notebook, imagining what new meanings they signified. From that, I came up with the character of Vivian, who takes notes of these street signs and tries to find a pattern or code in the missing letter. So, the character of Vivian evolved from me in a way; that sense of aimlessness when you lose your job and the daily structure a job brings, comes through in Vivian. I started with the voice, the voice of a character who sees the world a little differently. I was interested in the idea of a misfit character who felt she didn't belong in society, who sees things a little differently. But while I was out of work, I only took notes; I didn't have the confidence to actually start writing until I found a job one year later.

Why did you decide to make Dublin, and not some other city or town, the setting for this story?

For the simple (and slightly lazy) reason that I live in Dublin and it made the research a lot easier. I'm a little bit obsessed with maps, and I looked through maps and atlases of the city for names of streets that sounded magical or otherworldly and then visited these streets, just as I had Vivian do. I've lived in Dublin most of my life, but it was only when I had the time to wander the streets, really examining the buildings and the street signs, that I began looking at the city through Vivian's eyes and imagining: What if this other layer existed underneath the real city?

There's a wonderful uncertainty about the supernatural in the story. Does Vivian really believe she's a changeling?

Her parents brought her up to believe she's a changeling and I don't think she questions their beliefs too deeply. She sees it as a logical reason for her inability to belong, to fit into society. So, it makes sense in her mind to walk the streets of Dublin looking for this portal to another world in which she eventually will belong.

Changelings and fairies are such a rich part of Irish folklore. What did you mean to get across in weaving such elements into your story?

I've always been fascinated by changelings – the idea that fairies come in the night to steal the human child and replace it with a fairy child has sometimes been used by Irish parents in the past to explain why a child was acting strangely or differently. I think a changeling is the ultimate in not belonging, and it suited the story for that purpose. I liked Vivian's relentless hope that she would find a world in which to belong. I've used some other elements of folklore in the book—the legend of the Children of Lir, holy wells— but Vivian's attempts to find these otherworldly elements in the city are always thwarted by gritty reality; instead of a holy well, she has to make do with a public toilet. I liked the idea of folklore from a traditional, rural Irish setting being transplanted onto a contemporary city and being misunderstood. As well as Celtic folklore, the worlds of European fairy tales and Greek myths are as real to Vivian as the actual "real" world is.

The story of *Eggshells* seems to be, ultimately, about battling loneliness. Do you agree with that, or what, more precisely, would you say it is about?

I do agree. I think the book is about the loneliness that comes from not belonging. I've always been drawn to misfits or people who think differently, and sometimes these people are excluded from society. I wanted to write a character that people avoid sitting beside on a bus, and not just because of her poor personal hygiene. I'm not sure that Vivian sees herself as lonely, however. I mean, she puts a notice on a tree to advertise for a friend called Penelope, but the reason for that is to ask why she doesn't rhyme with Antelope. Vivian has a resilience and a lack of self-questioning that I liked—as someone who second-guesses herself constantly, it was refreshing to write a character who persists with her whims or plans and, even when they go awry, picks herself up and gets going again. I think the reader sees Vivian's loneliness more than Vivian does.

Why did you select the name Penelope for Vivian's friend? Did you intentionally model her on the character from Greek mythology?

In a word, no. I kind of wish there was more depth to my answer here—I've been asked before if I named her for the chapter in James Joyce's *Ulysses*, and again the answer is no. I'm afraid this is just from my own head. When I was a child I read lots of books but somehow mispronounced many of the names of the characters. I came across Penelope in a book (long forgotten) and thought it was pronounced *Peeny-loap*, and so I had Vivian advertise for a friend called Penelope in order to find out why she doesn't rhyme with antelope.

The open ending of the book is one of its most wonderful aspects—it's like the end of *Casablanca*, where Humphrey Bogart turns to Claude Raines and says, "I think this is the beginning of a beautiful friendship," and they go off together into the fog. Do you think at this point in the story Vivian feels she has obtained, finally, a good friend? Has she some sense of achievement?

Again, I'm not sure if Vivian reflects deeply about these things in an abstract sense. Her idea of a successful friendship is having someone who will come to her funeral—and if she continues to try and feed Penelope carrots instead of cake to prolong her life, maybe Penelope will outlive her and fulfil this wish. Their friendship is unorthodox—it seems to be based on Vivian's ability to tune out Penelope's chattering—but I think there is genuine affection between them. Penelope is possibly more eccentric than Vivian, and Vivian has some not-altogether-charitable moments in which she feels superior to Penelope, so she's probably not going to win Friend of the Year anytime soon.

The open ending, with Vivian and Penelope going off on a new adventure together, makes the question obvious: Will you ever return to the character of Vivian?

Not right now, I'm all Vivian-ed out—it's a pretty intense head to live in for a year! But in the future, who knows. I'd need to put her in a different setting to mix it up a bit. There is something very exhilarating about writing a character like Vivian and consciously stripping away your expectations and assumptions to try to see the world afresh—and that's something I'd like to come back to.

What's your writing process like?

Currently unpredictable. When *Eggshells* was published in Ireland a couple of years ago, I described my writing process as mostly trying to write one thousand words a day and just pushing through regardless. That was true for *Eggshells*, but my process now is much more sporadic. My day job involves getting up at 4:45 a.m. and my writing time comes after work, but I'm fighting a constant battle with sleep urges. And trying to ignore piles of dirty dishes and laundry and the shopping list. Some days writing wins the battle, some days housework and real life wins out. I try to write in chunks before the critical side of my brain kicks in. That way, I end up with an unwieldy sloppy great big beast of a first draft which requires a lot of reworking and editing before it's readable.

Did you always want to be a writer? How did you get started?

It somehow never crossed my mind that I could be a writer; it seemed like something that other people did. I've always devoured books, and I wrote stories as a child and was encouraged hugely by my parents, but somewhere around adolescence the urge to write was overtaken by other urges. Then I got sidetracked by studying, traveling, and working until my early thirties. I had been running marathons and was training for an ultramarathon when I injured my knee, which put an end to my running. I needed a new obsession so I signed up for a creative writing course with Greg Baxter, who instilled a horror of lazy clichés and hackneyed phrases in his students, which helped to cut out a lot of excess verbiage in my writing. I wrote a few short stories and essays, but failed miserably in my attempts at publication, so I hit the streets and focussed on the novel.

What's next?

I'm writing that difficult second novel, which is taking a lot longer than the first novel did. The current novel has two main characters, which is refreshing after the intensity of living inside

Vivian's head. This novel is set in Hamburg, in Germany, a location I happened across when I visited a friend who lives there. I was ripe for a new setting and Hamburg was it. And there may be more trips to Hamburg required—for research purposes, of course.

A NOTE ABOUT THE AUTHOR

CAITRIONA LALLY studied English literature in Trinity College Dublin. She has had a colorful employment history, working as an abstract writer and a copywriter, in addition to working as a home helper in New York and an English teacher in Japan. She has traveled extensively around Europe, Asia, the Middle East, and South America. She was short-listed for "Newcomer of the Year" in the Irish Book Awards in 2015.